The Hitchhiker's Child

Robin Baker

HARD NUT BOOKS

Robin Baker is represented by:
The Susijn Agency
3rd Floor, 64 Gt. Titchfield Street, London, W1W 7QH, UK
www.thesusijnagency.com

Published by HARD NUT books, 2013
Email: hardnutbooks@gmail.com

Printed in the United States of America on acid-free paper.

Dedication

To maverick scientists everywhere

ALSO BY ROBIN BAKER:

FICTION

Primal
Caballito

NON-FICTION

Sperm Wars
Baby Wars
Sex in the Future
Fragile science

For more information:
http://www.robin-baker.com/books/

Chapter 1

In a dimly-lit corner of the empty car park I switched off the car lights, reclined my seat, and closed my eyes. Only twenty minutes I told myself – but I didn't manage even one. Just as I was drifting off I was jolted awake by a banging on the window, then startled by the sight of a bruised and bleeding white face only inches from my own. I froze and stared in shock and the person backed away. Now I could see. The pale figure was a woman, hands behind her back, a gag in her mouth, naked.

I peered into the dark to see if anyone else was lurking nearby but the car park seemed deserted. So I eased out of the car then advanced slowly, sensing how afraid the woman was. I tried to reassure her saying I would help if she would let me; that she had nothing to fear. Did she want me to untie the gag and her wrists? Because if she did, I would need to come close. I would need to stand behind her. She wavered, then slowly turned.

Close-up her long hair smelled of petrol. The knot of the gag was tied tightly and incorporated thick strands of her hair. At the front it was pulled hard back between her teeth. I could neither untie it nor slide it up or down without pulling out her hair. As for her wrists… My rapidly cooling fingers could do nothing to free her. She was shivering violently, her skin freezing to the touch.

'Best get in the car,' I said. But she squealed and shook her head. 'You've no choice,' I continued. 'You need warmth and I need light. I can't see what I'm doing.' Again she squealed, so I moved around to face her, hoping that she could see enough of my eyes to trust me. 'I won't hurt you, I promise. You're safe with me. I'm a doctor – of sorts. You'll be hypothermic if you stay out here.'

She appeared to calm down – or maybe accepted that she had no other option – and I helped her awkwardly into the passenger seat. Then I rummaged in the car-boot for a knife; a blanket too, which I draped over her. As soon as I cut away the oil-soaked gag, the woman spat out the taste. Her hands were tied with what looked like piano wire which had begun to cut into her flesh. As I sawed at the bonds she gave tiny cries of pain. 'Sorry,' I said at each whimper.

Once free she examined her wrists, wincing as she rubbed them. 'I need a shower,' she said.

'But…'

'I need a shower. Now! Can't you smell me? They had matches.' She burst into tears and began to rock backwards and forwards holding her head in her hands.

I placed my hand on her bare back but she shrugged me away. 'Sorry, but I need my phone?' I said gently.

'What!'

'My mobile. You're sitting on it.'

'Phone! Why?'

'The police.'

'No! Not the police. Not anybody. Promise me. My husband…'

'But…'

'No! Just a shower. That's all. Please!'

***

I loaned her my tracksuit, pulled from my weekend bag, the trouser-legs and sleeves way too long for her. With no spare footwear to offer, I found her the least dirty pair of my socks. Then with her face wiped as clean of blood as I could manage, she stayed at a distance while I booked us into the service-station motel.

'Where's your room?' she asked, standing framed in the doorway to her own.

'Next one along. I hope your shower works.'

'So do I. I will pay you back. Honestly.'

'I should hope so. Call if you need me. Or bang on the wall. Don't worry about the time.'

She began to close her door, but opened it again. 'What's your name?'

'Mark.'

'I'm Mia.'

***

Next morning, we travelled back north along the M1 to the service station where Mia had been attacked, grabbed from behind while unlocking her car, then bundled into a large white van. She told me that much at least as we drove. But when we searched the parking area her car – a red MG midget convertible – had gone, and with it her overnight case. So I bought her some clothing, the minimum she needed to be comfortable and not attract attention. Then we went to the restaurant for breakfast.

'Do you work out?' Mia said. 'You look as though you do.'

'Occasionally. When I'm in England. Not the rest of the time.'

'Really? Why's that?'

'Long story.'

'Oh... OK,' and for a while we ate in silence, Mia needing to concentrate. 'You have beautiful eyes,' she said eventually. 'Kind – and very...' She winced, and I winced with her. The weeping cuts on her lip and cheek looked raw and painful.

'Maybe best not to smile.... .... Very what?'

'I was going to say very brown.' She put her pale and delicate hand with its long and painted fingernails to the corner of her mouth to deal with a pastry flake. 'Much like the rest of you. I mean – that's either one terrific tan or... Are you English?' Suddenly she flushed. 'Oh, sorry! I didn't mean... Of course not. But isn't that a slight accent?'

I smiled. 'No need to apologise. And yes, I am English... At least, according to my passport. My mother was English you see. But I was born in Zimbabwe after my father escaped there from South Africa – and even now I spend half my time in Botswana. Maybe that's the accent. So – you're right – this colour is partly the African sun. But you're right about the other bit too. My father's father. Seems my grandmother was married to a Boer but also had a moment of racial unity – with a Zulu, so I'm told. And quite a lot seems to have surfaced in me.' A look of discomfort flickered across Mia's face. 'Does that bother you?' I asked.

'Me? No! Of course not. A Zulu... Wow!' She hesitated, staring at me as if studying my face. 'Are you sure you don't mind taking me home?'

***

'Unusual way to thumb a lift,' I said as we drove down the motorway towards London.

'Not my choice.' She glanced at me. 'What's your address? So I can send you a cheque? Pay you back all this money you've spent on me.'

'Oh, it's not so much – but I won't say no. Just rummage around in there.' I indicated the glove compartment.

'You should find a business card or two. Unless I gave them all away over the weekend.'

She found a card and studied it for a moment. 'So that's what you meant by "sort-of."'

'Afraid so. But the doctor bit worked didn't it? Isn't that when you began to trust me?'

'Not sure that it was. I think it was more that you knew the word "hypothermic".... .... By the way... Have I said 'thank you' yet?'

'Not exactly. But did I have a choice? I could hardly just leave you, could I? Anybody would have done the same?'

'Would they? I'm not so sure. But... Tell me. Honestly. Would you have been such a Samaritan if I'd been a man? Or ugly? Or even just wearing clothes?'

I didn't answer – just smiled – then broke off from conversation for a minute or so while I overtook a two-carriageway string of lorries. 'Now... What about you?' I said eventually. 'Are you ready to tell me what happened yet?'

For a few moments it seemed that she wasn't. But then: 'They didn't rape me you know. If that's what you thought.'

That was what I thought. 'So why did they strip you?'

'For the other reason. There is only one isn't there? That I know of any way.'

'Is there? What's that?'

'To humiliate somebody. Break them. Get information from them. It's the first step. And if stripping doesn't work...'

'...you tie their wrists with piano wire, pour petrol over their head and threaten to light a match, eh? My God! Who are these people? And what were they trying to get out of you? It must have been important to merit that. Did it work? Did you tell them?'

'I couldn't tell them. Because I don't know. And it's probably just as well I don't.' She pointed at a large hoarding. 'Can we stop? At this Service Station? I need the loo. Do you mind?'

She also seemed to need time on her own. So I sat at a table and let her wander the shops for a while, occasionally glimpsing her in the newsagent, flicking through magazines. She was very petite, very graceful in her movements; in her mid-twenties I would guess. I tried to imagine her as a spy, or an undercover policewoman – but couldn't. Eventually she joined me and began sipping the cappuccino I had ready for her.

'Are you married,' she asked. 'Children?' Her look was quizzical, her swollen upper-lip making her mouth lop-sided. 'My guess is no.'

'Your guess is right. Just a girlfriend or two. And what about you? I mean, I know you're married and... OK. Here goes. My guess is that you do have a child. Am I right?'

'Yes... Ha. How did you know?'

'A size-eight with stretch marks?'

She spluttered into her drink. 'Oh my God... Do they show that much?'

'It's the car light. It's weird. Highlights things like that. I noticed them while I was putting the blanket over you last night. So... Where is he? Or she? Your child?'

'He. Lex.' She fell silent, cup to her mouth but not drinking. And when I saw that her eyes were watering I didn't press, just waited. 'He's with my parents. Nottingham. I've just spent the weekend with him. Every chance I get....
.... I love him so much. It kills me every time I leave him. But...' Her eyes were still welling.

'So why leave him? Can't you...'

'I've had no choice but go back to work. So it was either a doting Grandma or a paid stranger; a large comfy house or a tiny bed-sit. Which would you...?' Her sad and lingering look made me feel I was being judged. 'Actually... Can I trust you? Lex is what all this is about.'

'Really? How?'

'You're going to think I'm crazy but... He came out dark-skinned. As dark as you.'

'Is dark-skinned a problem?'

'Oh yes. My husband, you see...'

'Ah... But I still don't... Not 'crazy' anyway. Unlucky perhaps. But you must have known the risk you were taking. You know... Having a lover who...'

She shook her head. 'That's the whole point. There never was a lover. White or black. I wouldn't dare.'

'So what are you saying? That your husband – or you – also once had a grandmother...'

'Now that really would be funny. More than you know. But... No. Not as far as I know.' She hesitated again. 'We – I – had paternity tests. Several. After the first, my husband threw us both out: me and Lex. But I couldn't just let it go. Those tests, they had to be wrong. Yet they all came back the same. My husband couldn't be Lex's father. I genuinely thought I was losing my mind.'

'So wasn't Lex yours? Had the hospital...'

'What hospital? I was at home, with my own midwife and doctor. All the care and attention money could buy. Until...' She gave a despairing laugh. 'No, the baby was mine all right.'

My own laugh was one of confusion. 'OK. Then I give up. So what is the explanation?'

'No idea. All I know is: I was never unfaithful to my husband, but the baby isn't his. It really is crazy, yes? Or at least, it would be if...' She stopped in mid-sentence.

'If... What?'

'I'm so frightened Mark. Because I know... Last night was nothing. If my husband ever does decide he knows who Lex's father is... Well... That man is dead. And me and Lex with him.'

Chapter 2

'Of course he won't kill her. Where did you say they lived?'

'I didn't. She made me drop her at Wimbledon Underground.' I was at the window gazing out at the galaxy of lights that was London at night.

'Well, wherever. She had her fun, she's been found out, now she's worried her alimony is going up in smoke. So she's come up with this stupid story. As for you, she just wanted your sympathy. And your money. You'll never see that couple of hundred quid again.'

'Mike... Do me a favour and shut up! Go and do something useful. Make us both a coffee. It's your turn.'

While he obliged I picked up the latest edition of *Animal Behaviour* and began reading.

'Anything interesting?' He handed me my cup of instant black.

'Cheetah infidelity in the Serengeti. It's good work. I heard a preview at the Glasgow conference at the weekend.'

He chuckled – 'Cheetahs or cheaters?' – then held up his hand. 'OK. Sorry! So how did it go? Your conference? How was Scotland?'

'Cold. Grey. But my conference was fine. Lots of new contacts. And my lecture went well, I think.'

'Any women?'

'Lots.'

'And?'

'And nothing.'

He grunted. 'OK, so don't tell me then. But while we're on the subject, that Psychology lecturer you screwed a few weekends ago rang. She thinks she left some earrings here.'

'Marsha?'

'Hell, no! The other one. The one with the laugh.'

'Oh God. What did you tell her?'

'That I'd tell you. Have you found them?'

'They don't exist. They're just an excuse. Anyway. How was your weekend? That stag-thing? And the wedding, I suppose... What did you subject this poor sod to?'

Mike began stirring his café au lait, mixing in his three sugars and splash of whiskey. 'The usual. But... Tell me honestly Mark. Am I getting into a rut? The lamp-post thing... I don't know – it just doesn't seem funny any more.'

'It never did.'

'Used to make me laugh. Besides, that's why they ask me. They want it to happen. But now...' He sighed. 'Even the treacle-and-feathers seems to be wearing thin.'

The phone rang and Mike answered. 'It's for you.' He threw me the receiver.

I half-expected to be asked about lost earrings, but it was a man's voice, with an accent. Maybe Scottish. 'Mark de Vries? PhD?'

'Yes. Who's that?'

'I've got your business card here. All your details.'

'That's what business cards are for. Who is this?' Outside on the street below, I heard an ambulance speed past with its sirens blaring.

'"Lecturer in Zoology" it says. "University of London." Picture of a lion. I just wanted you to know.'

'Know what? Has something happened?'

'Not yet.'

The line went dead. Under 'Received Calls' all I found was 'Private.'

***

'Sir! Doctor de Vries!' Three second-year students were bearing down on me; two earnest looking men and a disturbingly pretty woman of probably Middle-eastern or Pakistani extraction.

'Christ Almighty,' I chastised them. 'Call me Mark, please.' They looked uncomfortable.

'We just wanted to say...' said one of the men, '... how much we've enjoyed your lectures this semester.'

'And how gutted we are that they're over.'

I thanked them.

'And we were just wondering – if you've got a moment that is – if we could talk to you. Some time soon.'

'It all looks so amazing. My God... Chasing around the Kalahari after lions. Just brilliant.'

I checked the clock on the lecture-room wall. 'Look, I can't stop right now. But if you really want to talk, meet me in the 'Cockney Arms' at two. Buy me a drink and I'll spare you an hour.'

They exchanged disappointed glances. 'We can't. We've got a Physiology practical all afternoon. Part of our assessment.'

'Then I'm afraid you've left it too late. I'm away now until October. Well, apart from a flying visit or two.'

They thanked me and left the theatre, but a few moments later the woman returned. Until now, she'd said nothing. 'Please... Dr de Vries. You are in a hurry, I know, but...'

'You really will have to be quick.'

'OK. Very quick. Your laboratory project next year? The DNA one? Using your samples of lion blood? I am on the short-list and I was wondering. Have you decided who will do this project yet?'

'Sorry, I can't tell you that. Departmental rules. You'll have to wait until you get the official e-mail.'

'Really?... .... Oh, I am sorry. I should not have asked, should I? I can see that you are cross with me.'

'Not cross, no. I can't blame you for asking. But rules are rules.'

'I know. But my father... He is always telling me and my brother. When you really want something... Anyway, if you can give me just one more moment, there is something else I wish to say. Something that my father has also urged me to tell you.' Long black hair, big brown eyes, white even teeth – she really was very striking.

'What's that?'

'That, if you are interested, he is prepared to pay for me to do a PhD after I graduate. Or at least, he is prepared to do so as long as I work hard and get a First Class degree. For my father, I have to earn this money.'

'A PhD?'

'Yes. On lions. In the Kalahari. With you. If you will accept me. I have told my father: I now know that this is what I wish to do. My ambition has always been to do wildlife research, but I could never decide on what. But since your very first lecture, sitting and listening to you, everything just clicked for me. You really do make it all sound so exciting.'

'Well... I try. Look... What's your name? I should know but...'

'No, please. Do not apologise. Why should you know me? There are so many of us. My name is Sharda. Sharda Kaur.'

'Ah...' I knew the name very well. Many of my colleagues had eulogised about her – some of them even for the right reasons. She had a very good chance of getting a First. 'Sharda, eh? A Hindu goddess, no less. Right... Sod the

Rules. You can relax. You were top of my list. The first name pencilled in.'

'Really? Really? Oh my God. That is fantastic. Can I tell my father?'

'Probably best to wait until you get the e-mail.' I glanced at the clock again. 'Look... I'm sorry Sharda but...'

'Of course. And no, it is me who should be sorry – for delaying you. But thank you for telling me this thing. Getting that project means so much to me. So... I shall go and prepare for my practical then. Let you fly off and chase your lions for a few months. See you next October...'

As soon as I was back at my office computer I opened my 2010-11 project list, deleted 'Ian Mayhew' from alongside the lion DNA project and replaced it with 'Sharda Kaur'. Ian was a good student. Adaptable. He could do something else. But my Kalahari research station needed money and research students like Sharda far more than I needed principles.

***

After telling Mike I would walk, I resisted the urge to hail a taxi despite the early-evening drizzle. But unlike the other pedestrians with their umbrellas, hoods or waterproof coats, I was unprepared. All I could do was turn up my jacket collar, bow my head and walk fast, anticipating the cosy pub where I was to meet everybody. Mike had insisted on arranging a farewell party for me; tomorrow was also my thirtieth birthday.

A car drove past at kerb-crawling speed; a large car, with darkened windows. Ahead of me it pulled in at a vacant parking meter and the driver climbed out wearing a peaked hat, dark clothes and black gloves. He gave the meter a cursory glance then stood on the pavement and watched me approach. 'Mark de Vries?' he asked as I drew near.

The car's rear door opened and another man got out. 'Mr Cruickshank wants to talk with you.' And before I could say anything or resist I was bundled on to the back seat and sandwiched between two burly men. The one seated to my right was holding a dagger in black-gloved hands. The blade was glinting in the light from the streetlamps – until blinds came down over all the windows leaving us suffused in a dull green light.

'I don't know any Cruickshank.'

'Well he knows you. Now be quiet. Just enjoy the ride.' Built like a night-club bouncer his eyes were hidden behind sunglasses and his voice was gravelly. He and the others were such caricatures and the set-up so clichéd they just couldn't be real.

'This is Mike isn't it?' I said, looking from one to the other and hoping I was right. '*Rent-a-Hood*. He's told me about you.' Their expressions stayed set; I slumped back in the seat between them. 'Oh, God! Where is this party? Birthday or not, I've got a plane to catch tomorrow.' In the dim light I tried to take a closer look at the dagger to see if the blade was plastic. Maybe it was. Perhaps noticing my attention the man sheathed the knife inside his jacket. 'Whatever Mike's paying you, I'll double it. Say you missed me. Or I escaped. How about it?'

***

I judged the journey lasted about an hour – and despite my attempts to get the two men to talk they remained silent all the way. London streets gave way first to Motorway then to quiet and winding lanes. My guess was that we travelled North then West but with the blinds down I couldn't be sure of anything – except that we had travelled too far for the destination to be a surprise party, even one of Mike's. But if not a party... Four words were going round in my head: Cruickshank; Scottish; 'not yet'. And if 'Mr Cruickshank' really was the voice on my telephone, where did he get my business card? I hoped it was Glasgow.

When the car eventually crawled to a stop and the doors opened we were in a spacious garage containing several other cars, all expensive. The smell of engine oil and exhaust fumes hung in the air. Light-headed and with racing heart I was ushered into a lift which took us to the third floor. As the door slid open my last faint hope of a friendly explanation disappeared. There was no drunken gathering, no party sounds. Just a small brightly-lit room without furniture or windows. The tiled walls and floor were white and bare. A large plasma television screen was high up on one wall and a CCTV camera high up on another.

'Take off your clothes,' growled the man with the knife.

'What? Don't be stupid. No!'

'Take them off.'

'C'mon. You're joking.'

'No joke. Bollock-naked Mr Cruickshank said, so bollock-naked it is.' My arms were grabbed from behind and the man in front of me pulled the neck of my T-shirt with one hand and stuck his knife-blade down inside the front with the other. 'Take them off or I'll cut them off.'

My lips were dry. 'That knife... It's plastic, right?'

In one continuous movement he slit my shirt from neck to waist. 'Your choice,' he growled, now pulling at the waist of my jeans and again sticking his knife inside.

The door to the room opened and a woman came in. Dressed in a nurse's uniform she was carrying a sealed plastic bag which she began to open. I glanced up at the camera. It moved. 'Your choice,' the man repeated, tensing his knife-hand.

I began undressing, trying to kill the tremor in my hands as I fumbled with my belt.

'Open your mouth,' said the woman once I was naked.

'What?'

'Open your mouth,' echoed one of the men, yanking back my head by the hair and pulling down my lower jaw. The woman inserted something very like a cotton bud into my mouth and began working it against the inside of my left cheek. When she finished the three of them left, taking my clothes with them.

'Who the hell are you?' I shouted at the camera, though by now I was almost certain. 'And what do you want? Because it can't be me. You've got the wrong man.' Frantically I pressed the lift button. The doors stayed closed.

Suddenly the plasma screen lit up and a picture appeared: a magazine cover showing a pair of hands – a woman's. One hand was stroking the back of the other, showing-off long and painted finger nails. The picture faded and another magazine cover appeared, this time showing a hat photographed from above. Clear blue eyes gazed up at the camera from beneath the rim. The model's hair was blonde – and all remaining doubts disappeared. The picture changed again, but this time not to a magazine cover. Mia was standing on steps outside the large door to a very large church; a cathedral even. She was wearing a white wedding dress with a long train. In her hands was a posy of white flowers. 'I don't understand,' I said to the camera. 'What has any of this got to do with me?'

As if in answer, the picture of a building – a service station motel – appeared on the screen followed seconds later by another picture, this time of Mia and myself at a table eating croissants and jam. And when that picture faded it was replaced by the image of a newborn baby, his skin as dark as mine. Suddenly a voice boomed round the room. 'You've humiliated me Boy. Now it's pay-back time. Behave like a dog and you'll be treated like a dog.' It was a man's voice, with an accent. Probably Scottish.

The room was stiflingly hot but still a shiver ran over my back. 'You think that baby's mine? That's crazy. I've met Mia once, that's all.'

'Don't lie to me Boy. I knew she'd lead me to the father one day.'

'Lead! That meeting was a complete accident.'

'Accident! You were following her. You were going to meet her at some sleazy motel. And when you saw her get into the white van you just kept on following. Did the pair of you really think I'd believe her crazy lies?'

'Well there's one thing you'll have to believe. Those mouth swabs. They were for a DNA test, yes? OK, fine. Get the results. Then you'll see. I am not that baby's father. And hurry up about it. Because if you don't, you're going to owe me a plane ticket to Botswana.'

The picture on the plasma screen changed. In place of the baby there appeared a tombstone with a simple inscription:

Mark de Vries
14 April 1980 – 14 April 2010

Chapter 3

'**B**reakfast?' I said to the camera when I grew hungry. But none came – nor again after 'Lunch?' and 'Dinner?'

'Come on. You must have that result by now. Admit it. You made a mistake. Let me go.'

Long past the time that I judged I should be on my plane, the picture of my tombstone was replaced by two others that I'd already seen: the Motel that Mia and I used, and our breakfasting together the next day. 'I helped her. And that's all. We didn't even share a room. You should be thanking me.'

'Know what you need to learn Boy? Respect! Now get out of my sight, before I decide that even just having breakfast with my wife is a firing-squad offence.'

The door to the empty lift opened in invitation, and down in the garage the car was waiting with engine running and rear door open. I could just make out the driver through the darkened glass. 'Hey! Where are my clothes?' I shouted after I climbed in, expecting to see them on the back seat. Nobody answered, the blinds came down, and the car began moving forward. When we finally stopped we were back somewhere in London. 'Clothes!' I demanded again.

'Fifteen seconds to get out,' said the driver through an intercom. 'Or never.'

So still naked I clambered out on to the pavement. There was a cold April wind blowing down Charing Cross Road, and everybody except me was dressed for warmth as they hurried past. Some stared at me, some pretended not to notice. Some giggled, and some looked afraid.

'Excuse me,' I said to a man. 'Can I borrow your phone?'

'Fuck off, pervert.'

A few seconds later, I tried somebody else. 'Excuse me...'

'Leave me alone! I'll call the police.'

'Good. They can take me home.'

But he didn't call anybody, just walked quickly away. A woman scuttled past virtually dragging her two gawping children. I looked around for a phone booth.

'Dr de Vries? Is that you?' I spun round. 'My Goodness! What are you doing?' It was Sharda Kaur, her expression flickering between surprise, concern and amusement. In contrast, the tall man with a white turban and black beard by her side looked disapproving and irritated.

'I'll explain later. Can I borrow your coat? And could you help me get a taxi home?'

Sharda took off her calf-length bright-red coat and handed it to me. It barely reached my knees. 'You drew less attention wearing nothing,' said the man.

'This is Mazher Singh, my brother. He is reading Law.'

***

Sharda and I stepped into the lift at my apartment block while Mazher stayed with the taxi; they were on their way to the theatre. The journey had been long enough for me to explain everything that had happened and for the conversation to move on. 'Before you put on my coat at the railway station...' said Sharda, 'I noticed... You have a big scar on your shoulder. Can I ask how you got that?'

'From stupid bloody impatience. It was during my PhD in the Serengeti. I didn't wait long enough for the sedative to work after this big lion rolled over. As I knelt down he swung round and grabbed me in his mouth. Took out a big chunk of flesh. I was lucky it wasn't my head. I won't make that mistake again.'

Her eyes opened wide but she said nothing more until we stepped out of the lift on the ninth floor. 'Is there somebody in your flat? To let you in?'

'I doubt it.'

'Then how… ?'

'Digital lock.' And moments later I was keying in the number. 'Do you want to wait here?' I said. 'I'll just put on a dressing gown and you can take your coat and go.'

'And miss the chance to see inside your apartment? Oh – unless there is something you would prefer me not to see of course.'

I invited her in, then went into the bedroom to get dressed.

'Are these all your scientific papers?' she shouted, my bedroom door slightly ajar. 'How many have you written?'

'Fifty-two at the last count. And two more *In Press*.'

I peered through the crack in the door. She was flicking through one of the journals. 'Are you decent yet?' she called a few minutes later.

'Nearly. Just a moment…. …… OK.'

She appeared in the bedroom doorway and leaned against the jamb, watching as I rummaged for a T-shirt. 'It must be so fantastic to see your work in print. And to have it discussed in newspapers, magazines. I have seen articles about you. You seem quite famous.'

'Hardly famous. I have a long way to go yet.'

'Well… I cannot wait. Just the thought of doing something that nobody has done before. Discovering something new. Something really important. Maybe even a new theory. It all seems so amazing and exciting. I even lie awake at night, you know. Sometimes, just imagining.'

I smiled at her passion, and decided not to tell her about the hard work, disappointments and put-downs that were also part of the researcher's life; not to warn her about the inordinate amount of time she would need to spend begging for money just to keep her dream alive. Unless, of course, her father...

'Dr de Vries? Are you alright?'

'Oh... Yes. Sorry. Was I staring?'

'A little, yes.'

'It's just that... The things you were saying. You could have been me, ten years ago.'

'Really?' The comparison seemed to please her.

I pulled on my T-shirt, unable to see her for a few moments. 'Yes, really. I never wanted to do anything else either. Still don't.'

She watched as I pulled my hair out from the shirt-neck. 'Are you really not going to report what happened today to the police?'

'No point – and I haven't time. I've credit cards to cancel and a flight to re-arrange.'

'Oh... Have you not heard? Your flight will have been cancelled. There is a volcano erupting in Iceland. A big cloud of ash. All flights to and from the UK and Europe are grounded.'

Chapter 4

In the speeding open-topped jeep I spat out a fly, then raised my arms to let the hot dust-laden wind dry my armpits. 'It's so good to be back at last,' I yelled; if I didn't shout I couldn't be heard above the sound of the engine.

'It's good to have you back,' said Inga, her long plait of sun-bleached blonde hair whipping from side to side behind her. 'The place loses its soul without you. So how was Maun? Still infested with donkeys?'

'More than ever. But everything else... I really miss that 'Wild West-ness' we used to like so much.' Our jeep hit a pothole on the dirt track and as we lurched and bounced Inga swore at herself. I laughed – 'Maybe slow down?' – but the suggestion only made her laugh too, then nod towards the approaching thunderstorm. Every few seconds forked lightning from the towering black cloud hit the acacia-dotted grassland. Earlier, as my air-taxi descended toward the landing strip, the huge anvil of the distant storm had looked magnificent.

'Do you think we'll make it?' Inga said. 'Or should I have driven something with a roof?'

'The way you drive? We'll make it.'

As we rounded a rocky outcrop our ramshackle camp came into view. A battered large pick-up truck with half-a-dozen people in the open bed sped out of the gate only moments before Inga accelerated in. She braked hard to halt in the centre of the compound, enveloping us and everything about us in a cloud of red dust. Immediately she checked her watch – 'Damn! Sixteen! Total crap.' – then sprang out and slammed the door. 'This stupid jeep needs servicing.'

I was home.

The camp-site had been in existence for just over a decade, established not by me but by one of the first home-grown ecologists to graduate from the University of Botswana. Seretse Masire was a huge personality: a passionate traditionalist who never missed an opportunity to speak out against what he called the "desecration" of the Kalahari, the "genocide" of the Bushpeople, and the "Christian emasculation" of the African people. After winning over the Tswana in a tiny grass-hut settlement in the south-eastern Kalahari, Seretse sank a water bore-hole and erected a couple of more-permanent buildings. This was to be his base for a research programme aimed at conserving not only the local fauna and flora but also what he saw as the traditional way of life of the local people.

I first met Seretse at a conference in South Africa. He invited me to visit his camp, tempting me with an invitation to take over the large-mammal side of his research, particularly of the Kalahari lion. My visit was a success on all sides, largely – he said – because I was the only European to have visited the place who was prepared to adopt the camp's ethos rather than "prance and pontificate like a colonialist". But only months after I started to work alongside him two policemen arrived at the camp in my absence, arrested him, and drove him away. No jail ever admitted to his arrival, and no trace has been found of him since. In effect the camp site became mine to try to finance and use – and for six years now I had been working there whenever my teaching commitments in London allowed.

Inga and I began unloading the jeep, mainly crates of rum and a few boxes of cigarettes that the plane had delivered with me. Two men ambled over, both tall gangling and very black, their loose and rhythmic gait almost a dance. 'Hey, Mark. Welcome home Man.'

'Kopano... Tau...' I hugged them each in turn, remembering afresh the salty smell of their bodies. 'How are the wives? Still only the three?'

Kopano smiled, displaying a mouthful of grey crooked and chipped teeth. 'Still lazy. Still hate us. Who would want more?'

The three of us slapped each other's shoulders. 'Real booze,' I said, gesturing at the rum. 'We'll talk more this evening, yes?... ...... Oh, by the way... Who were the people in the pick-up truck that Inga nearly hit?'

Kopano spat on the sand. 'Missionaries. Second time this year.' Whether the camp Tswana had been anti-missionary before Seretse Masire had joined them I couldn't be sure. But to hear Kopano or any of them speak now was like hearing Seretse all over again, especially when it came to missionaries.

'Missionaries! Here! I'm surprised they dare. What did they want?'

'Same as before: to save us from hell. This time they bring us shorts to save us. Why are Christians so afraid of cocks?'

I laughed. 'Beats me. So what did you do with the shorts? Throw them back at them?'

Tau answered for his brother. 'Naagh. First he piss on them. Then he throw them back.'

'Kopano! Really?'

The man was beaming. 'Sure I did. Because shorts supposed to stink, ja? Bit of piss, bit of shit, lots of fart, dribble and sweat. That why men wear them, ja? So they can smell like a goat.'

'But you could have kept them to wear when you visit the other villages. Or you could have traded them for something.'

'Wear them? Naagh. When I must wear something, I like my wrap better. Shorts hurt my balls. And who would want them?'

Tswana in settlements nearer to Gaborone than our own possess a hybrid mixture of beliefs and customs. Most still turn to a traditional Shaman for healing, but otherwise their values are those dictated by the missionaries. Clothing is a mishmash of loin-cloths, animal skins, cotton sarongs or second-hand western-style clothes. Even the most minimal covering is considered acceptable as long as it hides the genitals. And much as Kopano despises himself for doing so, he always wears something – usually a sarong – when he goes visiting.

A third man joined us. Much shorter than the other two he was tan rather than black; a bushman. 'I hear you've new cubs for me Nick,' I said after we embraced.

He nodded.

'First light tomorrow?'

He nodded again. Nick's real name was something like N!xau with a tongue-click in the middle and a strange 'whoosh' at the end. But on the grounds of "either pronounce my name properly or call me something you can" we'd found a compromise. I had known him for five years.

***

Rucksack over my shoulder, I followed Inga into the dormitory hut. 'The perimeter fence still isn't finished,' I remarked.

She untied the full length patterned sarong she had worn to meet me from the plane and dropped it screwed-up onto the bed. 'We've run out of metal poles and wire netting – not to mention money. And we've been busy. Besides, according to Nick we haven't had a leopard or hyena anywhere near the camp for over a month. Haven't lost a goat for ages.' Just like her face, Inga's top half – both front and back – was tanned almost mahogany but from waist to knees she was paler. After over a decade in the African sun, only the colour of her hair and the paleness of her buttocks betrayed her Scandinavian origins. She reached for a packet of cigarettes on the bedside table, sat on the edge of the bed and a few moments later was taking her first contented draw, sucking so hard that her cheeks hollowed.

'Still not pregnant then?'

Her answer was an almost imperceptible shake of the head, then another deep draw on her cigarette. 'So much for my big family, eh? At this rate I'm going to be lucky to manage one.' A peal of thunder rocked the hut.

I took off my sweat-stained shirt and threw it on my own bed, then made a show of scrutinising her. 'You're too thin, that's the problem. You should eat more and smoke less. If it weren't for your bush I'd swear you were pre-pubertal. You've got the tits of a twelve-year old.'

'So what? I had my first period at eleven.' The tilt of her head was defiant. 'And who's to say I'm the problem. Maybe it's Fredrik.'

'Maybe it is.' I looked her in the eyes. 'So why don't the pair of you go somewhere and find out, once and for all?'

She frowned – 'Can't be done. Fredrik's phobic about all things medical, except me.' – then swung up her legs and sat on her bed cross-legged, smoking and watching through narrowed eyes as I took off the rest of my clothes. After unpacking my rucksack, I clambered on to the bed opposite hers and let the ceiling fan move air over my sweating body.

'You've lost weight,' she said. 'Less muscly.'

'London Marathon. Thanks to the volcano.'

'Barefoot again? Did you finish?'

'Best time yet.'

She took another drag, still scrutinising me. 'Your cock looks different too. Not as thick.'

'Lack of exercise.'

'Liar! How many this time? And don't say 'just the two' again.'

'Of course just the two. Zuri and I have this sort-of unwritten agreement. 'One' hints it might be serious and more than two sounds excessive. So we both always admit to two. Equal, you see. That way neither of us gets jealous.'

'What's wrong with you both saying 'none'?'

'Because neither of us would believe it.'

'So... What are you really saying? That it was more than two?'

'No, I'm saying it was just the two.' I stifled a yawn. 'Anyway. Stop chattering. I need some sleep before that husband of yours gets back and makes a nuisance of himself.'

***

'Christ, Fredrik. You stink.' His broad-shouldered silhouette was framed in the doorway but his aroma had blown way ahead of him.

'Hey, Mark. You've arrived.' He made a show of sniffing at himself. 'My God, I do. Must have been too busy watching the lions to notice where I was sitting.'

Inga threw a bottle of shower gel to him. He caught it one-handed. 'OK, I get the message. Back in ten.'

I sprang off my bed to follow him into torrential rain. Despite the hot April air the water from high up in the thunderstorm felt cold on the body, otherwise we would have showered in the downpour. Instead we went to the site's 'Wet House.' Situated about twenty yards from our dormitory, this breeze-block building was a fairly basic toilet and shower facility. The shower was communal, a single three-sided room with four wall-mounted shower-heads – one of them loose – and a single drainage channel that led directly to the outside.

At first we weren't alone. One of the three 'wives' that Kopano and Tau share was already in the shower, her ample bosom and buttocks wobbling as she tried to wash the smell of livestock from the hair of her struggling young son. In the end he just ran off, leaving his mother to flash us a resigned grin, snatch her sarong from a coat-peg and set off at a fast waddle after him.

The shower water should have been heated by a solar power unit on the roof but according to Fredrik one of the panels needed replacing which we couldn't currently afford. While Fredrik worked away on himself with the shower gel, I just stood in the spray for a while. 'Now that I'm back, why don't you and Inga take yourselves off to a fertility clinic somewhere?'

'Can't be done.'

'That's what Inga said.'

'There you are then. Did she also say it was none of your fucking business?' He held his face into the spray to rinse the gel from his bushy Viking beard and blonde hair, the only visible signs that he – like his wife – was Scandinavian.

'Of course it's my business. You're my oldest friends. I want this to happen for you. People like you two should have children. Lots of them.'

He stared at me through the spray for a few moments, his expression awkward. 'No more, Mark, OK? I'm up to here with talking about it.'

'OK. Fine. Forget it. Throw me the gel.'

'Catch. Now... To hell with babies. What about the plane? Any news?'

'Not yet – but any day. The grant application went in months ago.'

'No hints? No inside information?'

I shook my head.

Clearly disappointed, he was hunched now, wet hair flat against his head. 'Hell. We don't stand a chance do we? There's no money out there. Not for our sort of research anyway. This whole project is going down the pan and me and Inga with it. No jobs. No house. No money to speak of. Christ, the last thing we should be doing is trying to have a baby. I've told her this.'

***

Despite Inga's carefree tone the look on her face hinted at something more serious. 'Oh, by the way... You've got two e-mails. They arrived at midday – just before the satellite link packed up again.'

The desk-top computer perched on a rickety table in the far-corner of the dormitory. The PC had been state of the art when we bought it with our first Research Council grant five years earlier. Seemingly immune to the summer heat, to the Kalahari dust that clogged its fans and the tiny insects that flocked to die amongst its cards and chips, it had proved robust and reliable. In contrast, the two-way satellite system that linked us to the outside world, while also state-of-the-art when we bought it, was slow expensive and too often in need of attention.

There were eight beds in the hut in total, four of them double. Each had a ceiling fan above and a mosquito net around but otherwise was fairly stark: metal frame and legs;

wooden slats; a thin pad for a mattress; and a single cotton sheet both threadbare and grubby.

For a brief moment I was excited. 'E-mails? The plane?' But Inga shook her head. 'What then?'

'One is from some student of yours.'

'And the other?'

'From the Research Council. We're going to have a Health and Safety inspection.'

'A what!' Fredrik and I exclaimed in unison. 'And you've only just told us.'

Inga's face filled with indignation – 'I was being considerate' – then she reached for another cigarette.

I checked the Research Council e-mail first.

30 April 2010
Dear Dr de Vries
Thank you for your application for further funding for your project: Factors Affecting Fertility and Conservation in the Kalahari Lion. *Your proposal has now been subject to peer review. I have to report that two of your reviewers have expressed concern over health and safety aspects of your research. Both consider that to make a proper appraisal of your application an independent report will be necessary. To this end we wish to arrange for a Health and Safety Inspector appointed by this council to visit your field station and to assess both your living conditions and your research protocol. The cost of this exercise will be deducted from the final payment of your current research grant. Please contact this office at your earliest convenience to make the necessary arrangements.*

Yours sincerely
Ronald Greencock (Dr)

Almost in shock, I nearly left my second e-mail for later. But when I read it…

30 April 2010
Dear Mark!!!
I hope you do not mind my writing to you, but I have just noticed the attached in the London Evening Chronicle.
Best wishes
Sharda Kaur

Attachment:
Ex-Fashion Model and Baby Son Missing

Police are searching for both the estranged wife of the billionaire philanthropist, Cameron Cruickshank, OBE, and her one-year old son, Lex. Mrs Cruickshank, better known by her modelling name, Mia Bodin, was last seen entering her Wimbledon home on the evening of Tuesday, 20 April. A few hours earlier the same day in Nottingham, Lex disappeared from the garden of his grandparents, George and Muriel Bodin. Police are keen to speak to anybody who might have seen a red MG convertible in either of these areas. They also wish to eliminate from their enquiries the driver or drivers of a large white van or vans seen in the two areas around the times in question.

Chapter 5

A Black-backed jackal howled in the darkness beyond the camp. Then almost in our midst, high up in the Mopane tree, a male Spotted eagle-owl gave his musical call: two hoots. I listened for his mate, who finally answered with three. She was further away, maybe in the Baobab tree beyond the perimeter fence.

The air was thick with wood smoke. Sitting cross-legged on the ground Kopano prodded a fire with a long stick before calling for one of his 'daughters' to bring more firewood. Tonight, being a special occasion, the fireside group was large. About twenty Tswana men were sitting around talking, drinking and smoking while maybe thirty women tended fires as their children ran around playing noisy games. Stews and soups bubbled in cauldrons, a goat and illegally-shot gemsbok were spit-roasting, and bottles of rum and joints of dagga circulated freely. One of the Tswana men began to play a drum, the sound soft and the rhythm slow. Another joined him and before long my welcome-back party was under way.

Although always bare-breasted, the camp's Tswana women cover their bottom half with a sarong tied round the waist and reaching to the ankles – but not for modesty. When needed, the garment is removed and folded appropriately; in seconds a woman can have a sack, a basket, or even a baby-sling and has no concern that she is then naked. Nor – usually – is the sarong worn while dancing. It is too restricting, too quiet. In its stead is a belt adorned with beads, shells or bones that with matching anklets and bracelets rattle with every shake and stamp.

On a typical party night most of the dances and songs are traditional Tswana, some just for men, some for women, and a few for both. Anybody who feels in the mood can take part. But the last dance is mandatory for young and old; even babies, who are carried. A name is called and that person then performs alone or with others while the audience claps, stamps and chants. Anybody can call out anybody – and to refuse is not an option, at least not on first call. For some the performance is competitive as each tries to outdo the others with a show of energy, endurance, athleticism or just blatant eroticism. For the rest, it is more a question of simply taking part. This dance can last for hours.

Tonight, Fredrik and I took our turn as always, doing our best to stamp, clap, and jump like true Tswana. My repertoire is energetic but limited. So is Fredrik's, though he does have his very own party-piece which he is never allowed to forego: while in handstand position he can 'dance', a sight which always drives the Tswana women and many of the men and children into hysterics.

After my 'performance' I made to leave. 'But why?' said Kopano. 'The night still young. You can still stand.'

***

In the cool of the early morning on a track through tall grasses Nick ran ahead of me, his buttocks contracting and relaxing with the rhythm of his deceptively small steps. His stride was so smooth that he seemed to glide over the ground. Ten kilometres he said; it should take just over an hour. 'How long since we do this Mark?'

'About eight months.'

'You sure you keep up? Not die on me?'

'I'm sure.'

'Hangover not too bad?'

'What hangover?'

After a while our sweating bodies were itching from grass-seeds and dust. So when we began to cross a more open area we stopped to rub ourselves clean with the coarse grains of sand. Then for a while we jogged side-by-side. I was carrying a digging stick and a small hand axe; Nick a bow, quiver and small knife.

'How long you stay with my people this time Mark?'

'Two nights. Three maybe.'

'Good. But one time you must stay much longer. Then you learn much more. Now run faster. We need arrive before it too hot.'

***

'There! You see her? She have babies fourteen nights ago. Two – in hole in those rocks.'

I thanked him and glancing around made sure I could find the location again. One day soon Fredrik and I would drive out to tag the new cubs.

'Now... We go kill antelope, ja? Then go to my people. Be big heroes with much meat. That always worth a fuck or two. The children not eat meat now for one whole week.'

I don't enjoy killing antelope but it was part of our deal – and Nick and his family were just as dependent on such kills as were the lion cubs we had just seen. Always heading in the general direction of Nick's current camp-site, we detoured the worst patches of thorn bush and skirted the meadows of tallest grass – and as we walked we looked for antelope spoor. I had to peer intently to spot anything, but Nick needed only the most cursory of glances. Every few metres a narrow track of red or yellow dust was criss-crossed with hoof and paw prints. Suddenly Nick stopped and crouched, then turning his head he gestured at me – but I had already seen. Through a gap in the thicket was a small antelope looking in our direction. It was a Steenbok with flickering ears, brown eyes, and little straight horns; an alert and nervous creature. We were very close. It was upwind. Its head dipped to graze again.

With sign language, Nick told me what we would do, his fingers of one hand making gestures against the palm of the other. I replied the same way, then crawled away to my right before making a slight noise so that the antelope looked towards me and away from Nick. Then I froze and simply watched. After unscrewing the cap of his quiver of stiffened hide, Nick silently shook out an arrow; below its small steel tip it was sticky and dark with a poison made from certain roots and mashed beetle larvae, all mixed together with saliva.

Arrow nocked, Nick rose to a half-standing position. One swift movement lifted the bow and poised the arrow at eye level. Then leaning forward from the hips he looked down the shaft at the antelope which was still grazing, calm and unaware. Without a sound the arrow arced through the air to embed itself in the antelope's haunch. The Steenbok's head and neck jerked up and for a moment the animal froze, then it leaped into the air and began to run. We followed, gently jogging when we could see our prey, following spoor when we could not.

The poison acts slowly, depending on where the arrow embeds. Twice we saw the distant antelope sink to its haunches, only to have it find the strength and spirit to rise and run away as we approached. But the third time it just lay there, breathing heavily, its limpid brown eyes seemingly staring at Nick as he cut its throat.

'You remember how we do all this?' Nick asked me. I nodded and slit the animal's belly. Then while Nick squeezed the dung from the intestines and placed the lengths of gut on the lower branches of a small tree to dry in the sun, I freed the haunches and shoulders and carried the joints of meat to place them on the lower branches of a thorn tree.

'OK. I do rest,' said Nick, cutting out the liver and handing it to me. 'You cook hunter lunch.' I made a quick fire by rubbing two sticks together on a small pile of dry grass.

After eating then relaxing with a little dagga in a pipe of hollowed bone that we passed between us, I fetched the Steenbok hide which had been drying in the sun. A cloud of small butterflies – attracted to drink from little pools of blood in the folds – flew into the air. We cut the leather into strips and sections and fashioned two knapsacks which we sewed using a bone needle and fibres stripped from the leaves of *Sanseviera* plants growing nearby. The Steenbok meat was to be carried back to Nick's camp in sacks made from its own hide.

Nick and I rubbed ourselves down with sand to remove all the blood and dung. Then after impaling the racks of ribs on the digging stick we shouldered the hide knapsacks and began the long hot walk to Nick's camp. Flies buzzed around our faces, genitals and bloody loads.

Standing water is a luxury in the Kalahari and much of the time bushmen rely on the water stored in plants to quench their thirst. Tsamma Melons and Gemsbok Cucumbers are favourites but not always available. Other plants store water not in fruits but in underground roots and tubers and it is a question of recognising the right species from what can be seen above ground. So once or twice on our journey we hacked at the ground with the digging stick, unearthed a large round tuber, cut it open and drank the water that dripped from the white flesh.

As we walked, we occasionally nibbled on sweet moretlwa berries. Once or twice Nick climbed on to my shoulders to pick caramel-tasting acacia gum from where it had bubbled out and dried between the forked branches of the thorn trees. 'Tonight you fuck my wife, ja? So I can go behind the dune with my mistress.'

I laughed and shook my head.

'You must. Otherwise I tell Zuri you fuck all my sisters – twice.'

Chapter 6

He was short and bald and wearing a safari suit and the only person to emerge from the air-taxi from Maun. On the bottom step he paused to look around but became enveloped in the dust being thrown up by the plane's propeller. In one hand he was clutching an overnight bag, in the other a briefcase and straw sombrero. The heat haze of the Kalahari shimmered all the way to the horizon.

'Dr de Vries?'

'Please... Call me Mark.'

'I'm Dr Goldman.'

'I guessed.' When I relieved him of his bag he placed his sombrero firmly on his head and tucked its strap under his chin. 'Good trip?' I asked.

'A woman pilot! Did you know? In a place like this. I nearly refused to board.' As we walked, I was fully six inches the taller. 'Do you have a shirt Dr de Vries?'

'Probably. There's usually one in the jeep somewhere.'

'Then would you mind putting it on. At least try to make me feel that you're taking this inspection seriously – or do you actually want to get skin cancer? Only last week,' he continued as I searched for the screwed-up shirt I hoped was there, 'a quite respected young scientist began proceedings against both us and her university. Do you want to know why?'

'Is it relevant?' The shirt was under the back seat. I shook off the dust and began putting it on. It stank.

'Ten years ago, we funded her PhD on the behaviour of Red Kangaroos in the Australian outback. Now she has been diagnosed with a malignant melanoma which may well have metastasised. She claims it is our and the university's fault for encouraging her to go to Australia in the first place and for not giving her better health and safety protection while she was there. And what is more in this day and age she will quite likely win her case. That malignant mole could be set to cost us a great deal of money.'

'Well I'm not going to sue you whatever happens.'

'That's what they all say.' He peered at the jeep's dashboard. 'Where's the air-conditioning?'

'Air conditioning! You have to be joking.'

'Heat exhaustion. Dehydration. You think they're funny?'

'Of course not. But air conditioning... Come on! I thought I was doing well remembering to bring a jeep with a roof.' I saw no hint of a smile. 'I don't see what any of this has to do with our applying for money for a plane.'

'It hasn't.'

'Look... No offence Dr Goldman, but are you sure the Research Council has sent the right person for this job?'

He clasped his pale hands together on the black briefcase perched on his knees. 'Oh, believe me Dr de Vries. They've sent exactly the right person.'

***

'This is the dormitory. We've prepared a bed for you over there, near the computer. And this is Dr Inga Bergman. She's our computer wizard cum secretary. She's also our resident medic; she has an MD from the University of Tanzania.'

Smiling, Inga reached out her hand. Goldman shook it without enthusiasm. 'Yes, indeed. I am well aware of everybody's qualifications. Your husband, I believe, has an engineering degree from the same university. It seems a strange place for two Swedish nationals to meet.'

'We didn't meet there. We went there together. Escaping our parents. Escaping the cold. Seeking adventure.'

'And did you find it? Adventure enough for the pair of you to work here for next-to-nothing?'

'Judge for yourself over the next couple of days. As for the money... We don't need money while we're here.'

He looked her up and down. 'You have nothing on your feet Dr Bergman.'

Inga's dainty but leathery tanned and dust-covered feet were poking beneath a full-length sarong. 'Bare feet are healthier.'

'Not according to my manual.... ...... Nor is being as brown as you are. Tanned skin is challenged skin, as I am sure you are aware.' He looked at me. 'Nowhere in your initial application did you itemise expenditure on sun block.'

'Just an oversight.'

'Nor hats. Nor appropriate clothing. Not even laundry costs.'

'And again. I was so busy thinking 'bush plane', I completely forgot about a new wardrobe for us all.'

'Hmm.' He was looking round the dormitory. 'As I understand your situation, Dr de Vries, your research team currently consists of yourself, Dr Bergman here and her husband, and a young research student – another woman – from the University of Johannesburg.'

'Zuri, yes. She's working on lion sperm. But she's not here at the moment. You needn't worry about her skin though. She's got the best protection of all.'

'So I understand. Zambian, I believe. But it isn't her skin I'm concerned about. You appear to have only the one dormitory.'

'Is that a problem? For a few years my mother paid a lot of money for me to attend a school where I slept in a dormitory.'

'So I gather. A college in Wiltshire I believe. But I guarantee that no girls shared that dormitory with you.'

'Huh. Well... It wasn't for the lack of trying. So what are you saying? That health and safety has a moral element these days? Besides, each bed has a mosquito net. That provides as much privacy as we four need.' I looked down at him. 'Our initial grant was too small for salaries and building work. So we focussed on the important stuff.'

'And what is wrong with tents?'

'Everything. But if it's your own modesty you're concerned about, we can provide you with one for the two nights you're here.'

'I'll think about it. But for now, what I want more than anything is a shower. And please don't tell me that is communal too.'

***

Inga was already half-way through a furtive smoke by the time I returned from showing Goldman to the Wet House. 'Not sure if this is the moment, but while you were meeting him at the air-strip you received another e-mail from that student of yours.'

'Really? What does it say?'

'You'll have to read it for yourself. Something about a Jamaican rapper.'

11 June 2010
Dear Mark
Latest update (tell me if you don't want me to send any more.)
Best wishes, Sharda

Attachment:
Missing Model and Baby: mystery of the disappearing rapper

Police still searching for the ex-fashion model, Mia Bodin, and her one-year old son, Lex who disappeared on Tuesday, 20 April are now seeking to interview the Jamaican-born former rap-artist, Jomo Joubert, better known as JJ. In a statement, Detective Inspector Robert Stansted who is leading the search says that the police have learned that Mr Joubert and Ms Bodin met at a party just two days before Ms Bodin and her son disappeared. Mr Joubert was due to return to Jamaica on 3 May but it is now known that he never boarded his flight. The police have appealed for anybody who either knows the current whereabouts of Mr Joubert or who has seen or heard from him at any time since Sunday, 18 April to come forward.

***

'Good shower?'

'Except for the two very large black ladies who barged in on me. Who are all these natives roaming round the place? Employees? Because if they are, there is absolutely no mention of them anywhere in your grant application or risk assessment.'

'Employees?' I laughed. 'They live here – and we live with them. All facilities shared.'

'And what do you get in exchange? Given that I presume it is the Research Council that finances these 'facilities' you so freely share with them.'

'Get? Where do I start? The Tswana – they're the black people you've seen... Basically the women look after the camp and the catering and the men help us with the lions

– you'll see that tomorrow. In exchange, they get to use the trucks for collecting firewood and food. And just occasionally for visiting the villages to the south of here.'

'I help out medically,' added Inga. 'Run an occasional school for the children. At least try to teach them basic reading and writing.'

'Mmm. And the Bushman? I'm sure I saw...'

'Quite possibly. That's Nick. His band are escapees from one of the resettlement camps to the south. They hunt and forage the area around here – trying to dodge the Botswana authorities – and he calls in when he can to give us any news he's picked up about lions.'

'And in return?'

'Well... Nothing really, except to be an occasional member of the team. For us, it's brilliant. A complete bush intelligence network passed by word of mouth to him and then to us. Until we get a plane we couldn't do our research without them.'

'Really! So what if this bushman network – or this arrangement you have with the Tswana – breaks down?'

'A disaster. No doubt about it. We haven't the money or the manpower to manage without either of them. But why should it break down?'

'Well the Botswana authorities might actually succeed in rounding up the bushmen for a start. Or take a dislike to you for some reason.' For a moment he stared at me. 'Come on Dr de Vries. Look at what happened to the man who ran this place before you. And to your father and sister in the then Rhodesia? If you and your mother hadn't been in the UK at the time... Well... Are you saying that things like those couldn't happen again?'

Chapter 7

'Lions? Polygynandrous. Each pride has two or three adult males and four to eight lionesses, plus youngsters of various ages. The pride disperses during the dry season, then reforms when the rains return.' Twisted round in my seat I was talking to Goldman in the back of the truck – and stifling a laugh. While Goldman was tugging at the collar of his shirt, trying to mop the back of his neck with a handkerchief, a cool and naked Nick was sitting next to him with a rifle upright between his legs.

'That's a lot of lions to keep at bay while you take your blood samples,' said Goldman.

'Not today. This lioness is on her own. She left the pride a few weeks ago to give birth. And she won't rejoin until her cubs are nearly a couple of months old. Don't worry. This is totally routine for us.'

'I'm glad to hear it.'

I went back to helping Fredrik spot and avoid potholes as he drove, but even our combined vigilance wasn't always enough. 'One, two, three – lift!' I said.

'Aagh – fuck it. Nearly,' said Fredrik. 'Next time.'

'For God's sake,' shouted Goldman. 'Tow it out, don't lift it. You'll give yourselves hernias. Or slipped discs. Are you insured? Because if you're not, we're not paying for...'

'Help or keep quiet,' I told him. 'OK Fredrik. Ready? One, two, three – li-i-i-ft.'

Minutes later, distant antelope were raising their heads to watch our convoy of two trucks motoring across the landscape once more, the second truck being driven by

Kopano. Then, perhaps deciding we were no threat, the antelope lowered their heads again to graze the lush grass.

A short silence was broken by Nick speaking his first words since we left camp an hour earlier at dawn. 'In my next life, I want to be a lion.'

'For the freedom?' asked Goldman

'Hell, no. For the fucks.'

Fredrik and I burst into schoolboy laughter. 'He means this...' I explained to Goldman. 'When a lioness comes into heat she's insatiable, demanding sex every thirty minutes or so, day and night, sometimes for up to four days.'

'With just one of the males?'

'No. They all get their turn. She might even slip away for a bit on the side with the odd nomad as well. But even so... Over four days? Especially if more than one female is on heat at the same time... Just imagine... Those males in the pride... I feel exhausted just thinking about it.'

'Not me,' said Nick.

'That's not what your wife says.'

'Which wife?'

'Your current one.'

'Well not ask her. Ask my mistresses,' and the three of us laughed again. 'Right. Stop here,' Nick said quickly, tapping Fredrik on the shoulder. After clambering out of the truck the bushman pointed into the distance with his rifle. 'By that Camel-thorn tree – OK? With the big weaverbird nest.' Then he set off at a steady lope, skipping and jumping to clear obstacles that we couldn't see.

'The trucks have to take a more roundabout route,' I explained to Goldman. 'Nick is going to locate the cubs for us before we arrive.'

***

'Remember that sight Dr Goldman. Take it back to England with you. Mahogany, black, tan. Tall, medium, short. Blue sky. Raw land. Common purpose. Does that excite you as much as it does me?'

'All I see are men and desert.'

'Men? No! Man! In his primeval environment. Armed only with the instincts that have seen him survive here for millennia. Doesn't that send a shiver down your spine?'

'What sends a shiver down my spine Dr de Vries is the sight of those three – and you – all of you directly or indirectly supported by the Research Council, working in a totally inhospitable environment without even the most basic regard for health and safety. Not one of you is wearing shoes, hat, shirt or sun-block. And as for the two natives... Well, I prefer not to think about the accidents they could have. And did you and Mr Bergman really feel the need to be quite so exhibitionist when you danced last night? Or so vigorous? You were accidents waiting to happen. Couldn't you at least try to show these natives how civilised people behave?'

'When in Rome, Dr Goldman. And let me tell you... They can't stand aloofness. You were very lucky that they didn't make you dance as well. Which they would have done if I hadn't told them you had a weak heart.'

'Ah... Right... Yes... Well... Thank you then.' He cleared his throat. 'But even so... At least spare me your fanciful "Armed only with the instincts..." What about the guns? Which, by the way, I am very pleased to see.'

'Philistine!' I laughed, and for the first time thought I saw a flicker of a smile on his chubby bespectacled face.

In the shade of the tree's blue-green foliage the three men settled amongst large boulders, the colours of their skins merging with the colour and shadows of the rocks. I drove the truck slowly forward until it was in shade and just a few yards from the men. 'Make yourself comfortable Dr Goldman. We could be here a while.'

'Can't I get out? Stretch my legs?'

'OK. But don't wander off. Your death wouldn't look good on my safety record.'

***

A Cape Vulture slowly circled it's way high across the sky, pausing above a distant herd of antelope. A few were stotting, leaping high into the air on stiffened legs. 'That's probably the lioness hunting,' I whispered to Goldman.

An hour passed. 'How can you possibly work day after day in this heat?'

'Heat? It's early June. Nearly winter. You should be here in October. These aren't even Spanish-summer temperatures.' But then I took pity. His eyes were bloodshot from the dust and glare and his safari suit was now soaked with sweat. A swirl of wind carried the smell of stress from his underarms. In one hand he held his straw sombrero, using it as a fan. In the other was an empty water bottle. I took it from him. 'Wait here. There's more water in the cooler in Kopano's truck.' I ran there and back.

'Are you sure there are cubs here?'

'Shhh. They probably won't show themselves until the mother returns.'

Time passed. 'What's all the noise coming from that tree over there,' whispered Goldman.

'Birds, telling each other there's a predator about.' I listened for a few seconds. 'A snake Nick?'

He nodded. 'Big one. Maybe Black Mamba.'

Goldman immediately looked nervous; agitated.

More time passed, then Nick raised his hand and pointed. 'Something coming. The antelope all looking in one direction. They nervous, but they not the targets. And look... There... Plovers in the air.' Without a word, Fredrik shouldered his tranquilliser gun.

I turned to Goldman. 'If I say so, get straight in the truck. Back seat, and leave the doors open. It's our bolt-hole if anything goes wrong.'

Through the grass on the far side of the clearing the lioness appeared and approached the boulders where her cubs were in hiding. Fredrik's shot found its mark, the bright pink head of the dart bobbing around just behind the lioness's right shoulder. Twenty yards from us, she stopped and sank to her haunches. Just squatting there she stared straight ahead not even responding to the two cubs that rushed out to greet her. Eventually she gently rolled to her side and lay there, her chest rising and falling with laboured breathing while her cubs suckled. It was Nick and Kopano's turn to shoulder guns, steadying their barrels on the rocks. And two shots later each cub also had a dart in its haunch; a dart with a green head.

'We have to work quickly,' I told Goldman as, by a cub's side, I put my medical bag on the ground and clicked it open. 'We don't like youngsters to be sedated for long.'

Fredrik and I took a cub each and set about taking a sample of blood from a leg vein. 'Our DNA database is now so large,' I continued as I worked, 'that we have a 90 percent chance of identifying the father of each of these cubs.' I withdrew the needle and dabbed the tiny puncture with disinfected cotton wool. 'And antibodies in the blood allow us to build up a profile of the diseases this community has to cope with.' Then I took another broader hypodermic and pushed it just under the skin at the back of the neck. 'This is the first time with this cub, so I'm putting in an identity chip, like for pet dogs and cats. You see? About the size of a grain of rice. But...' I picked up a digital camera, '... we also need to identify individuals at a distance so we photograph the face. Then we can use biometrics like on modern passports. For lions though the main identifier is the whisker spot pattern. That's as individual for them as a fingerprint is for humans. Our computer can identify a lion from any reasonable photograph of the face, even from a telephoto. Just imagine being able to do that from a plane...'

Finishing with the cub, I ran to the mother and made sure she was fully sedated. Then I beckoned to Goldman to join me. 'Have you ever been this close to a lion? Come on, pat her. Stroke her.'

'Is it safe?'

'Of course. Do it. Maybe the only chance you'll get in your entire life. Velvet soft – yes? Feel her ears, too. Isn't she beautiful? And smell her. That's the Kalahari. Just think where she's been. Imagine everything she's done. Yes? Now... Feel her flanks. Here. No, feel them properly. Squeeze! All that power. Determination. Courage. Isn't she magnificent? Doesn't she make you want to know absolutely everything about her? To understand her life in every last detail?' I was getting no reaction. 'Because unless somebody gains that knowledge believe me... When the time comes – when the Kalahari becomes a bloody diamond mine – we won't stand a cat-in-hell's chance of saving her kind from extinction.'

Goldman glanced from the lioness to me and back again. 'Right, but... Are you sure she's not going to wake up?'

'Not until I give her a wake-up shot.' I sighed in resignation. 'OK, once a philistine, eh? Then at least look at this. Our latest project. We began development a couple of years ago, and this lioness was one of the first to be fitted.

She's not only got an ID chip, she's also got... See this slight swelling on her shoulder? It's a tracking device, just under the skin. The microchip records her GPS position, like in a sat-nav but in this case only once an hour. Then, with this reader...' I took something very like a mobile phone from my bag. '... we can download the data and immediately have a record of all her movements around the Kalahari since we last tranquillised her – which was about a year ago.'

At last, he looked impressed. 'But how long does the battery last?'

'We don't know yet. We think about five years. We hope more.'

Then he frowned. 'Isn't the implant uncomfortable for her? Won't it irritate her?'

I turned my back on him, and bent a little so that he could see my shoulder. 'Run your hand along there. Feel that tiny lump just under my skin? In a fit of guilt I once vowed to experience personally everything we do to the lions. So two years ago I had the exact same device fitted in myself. Fredrik did it.'

'And?'

'No, it's fine. Honestly. No problem at all.'

He shook his head. 'I didn't see any mention of that particular piece of tomfoolery on your Health and Safety record.'

I groaned. 'Ah... No... Bit of an oversight again. Sorry.'

***

Goldman was staring straight ahead with his hand over his mouth. He and I were sitting in the jeep at the landing strip waiting for his air-taxi to arrive. 'Nomads are young males,' I was saying. 'The lion equivalent of teenage yobs. They spend years just wandering round the Kalahari in gangs of two or three, looking for a pride where the males are growing old or weak. Then they kill them, or chase them out, so that they can have the females for themselves. And during their wandering years they're almost impossible to track down even with all the bushmen eyes we have helping us. A plane would make all the difference.'

'Really,' he muttered from behind his hand, swallowing hard, until a few seconds later he sprang out of the jeep and rushed to the rear. I listened to him retching, emptying his stomach. It was a while before he crawled back into his seat.

'Better?'

'Maybe.' He looked at me. 'It's obvious why you need a plane, Dr de Vries. It's also obvious that it would bring a whole new load of risks. I'm not even going to think about it.'

I sighed and looked into the distance, waiting to spot the air-taxi that was going to end the charade of his visit. 'You haven't even asked about Zuri,' I said. 'Her work is important stuff. Male fertility. In lions. Don't you want to know?'

'Not really. Not now.'

I began beating a rhythm with my hands on the steering wheel – until he gave me a pained look that told me to desist. 'She needs to collect semen samples from as many different males as she can. A plane would… Ah, never mind. But surely you want to know how she does it?'

'At this precise moment, no.' Goldman jumped out again. While he was retching the plane appeared in the distance. I watched it descend, its wings rocking slightly from side to side in the cross-wind. Goldman appeared at the jeep door and looked at me, his pale round face furrowed with pain and anger.

'It will be the Tswana hooch,' I said. 'You did drink rather a lot for a novice.'

'It's not the bloody hooch. It's bloody food-poisoning – and you know it. I'm straight to the Centre for Tropical Diseases when I get home. To find out what you and your Tswana friends have given me. The hygiene during the preparation and cooking of that meat was non-existent. It's a wonder any of you are still alive.'

'OK. I get the picture. So no plane then?'

'Oh, for God's sake Dr de Vries. This was never about the plane. This was about pulling your funding completely. Starting now.'

'What! But you can't. What have we done to deserve that?'

'You're spent up anyway – and after paying for me...' He glowered for a few moments, then his expression softened a little. 'Look... Dr de Vries... Mark... I shouldn't be telling you this but... Don't beat yourself up too much about my visit. You wouldn't have got your plane or your new grant from the Research Council anyway, even if your Health and Safety protocol was exemplary. Money is tight and the decision to ditch you was made – quite suddenly – well over a month ago. I was told in no uncertain terms before I came here that my report was just a means to an end. Though, I have to say, you have made it rather easy for me.'

I focussed on the aircraft just landing, my stomach churning with disappointment. 'But why? The plane, I can understand. That's a lot of money. But to pull our funding completely? I thought the work we're doing here...'

'It has nothing to do with your work. Everybody thinks your studies are amazing – including me. But I think you're going to find...' He hesitated. 'You're going to find that somebody high-up has decided they can make better use of your set-up here than you can – and that seems to be the end of the matter.'

***

'Medicinal,' said Inga, handing me a large glass of rum as I stalked into the dormitory, slamming the door behind me. Hers and Fredrik's glasses were already half-empty. 'We thought you'd appreciate some good stuff instead of hooch tonight. The news is bad we assume?'

I took the glass and downed half of the rum in a single gulp. Then, between expletives, I told them the news.

Fredrik exploded. 'What! What better use? What high-up? What fucking bastard is that?'

'Goldman wouldn't say. But sure as hell... When I go back for all those damn examiners' meetings in a couple of weeks I'm going to make bloody certain I find out.' I drank the rest of my rum, then held it out to Inga for a refill, but something about her expression made me hesitate. 'What?' I asked.

'No. Nothing.'

'Oh, for fuck's sake,' said Fredrik. 'You may as well tell him. Get all the bad news out of the way, then we can all get rat-assed.'

'Tell me what? What bad news?'

Inga took a deep breath. 'OK. It's this. You've had another e-mail from your student. The police have found Mia and her son. Fished her red MG out of some Scottish loch. They're both dead. Drowned... I'm sorry Mark. I mean... I know you didn't know her really but...'

'God...' I began. 'Are the police sure it's them?'

'The bodies were badly decomposed but... Her dental record. DNA. They're sure. But that's not all.'

'Not all?'

'The rapper was in the car too. In the driver's seat. Empty bottle of whiskey, etcetera. And guess what?'

My racing mind was filling with images: a confused frightened and beautiful woman; a newborn baby, his skin as dark as mine; and three blackened stinking lumps of flesh, one of them tiny, being dragged from even blacker water. 'What?'

'Turns out... From the DNA... The rapper was the baby's father. Seems Mia lied to you. She did know who it was after all.'

Chapter 8

In the distance the air-taxi was just taking off, heading back to Gaborone. 'So you're pleased to see me then,' said Zuri as we separated from a long kiss, her full black lips parting to show her white teeth. We'd corresponded since we last met; seen each other on video phone; spoken often. But for five long months we hadn't touched, smelled or tasted each other. 'But... Not here. Not this time. Later. Is that OK? There's something we really need to talk about.'

'Some 'thing' or some 'body'?' I put her luggage in the bed of the pick-up. She kicked off her sandals so I threw those in too.

'Some 'thing' of course. Why? Have you... ?'

I laughed. 'Me? No. Nothing's changed. Just two again.'

She began taking off her Western clothes and throwing them to me, one-by-one. When she finished I handed over the sarong I'd brought for her. She tied the garment round her waist then raised her arms to the side. 'There. Now I'm me. Now I'm home. I'm not sure which I hate most, cities or underwear.' I made to start the engine as she got in the truck, but she stopped me. 'No! Don't drive yet. Let's talk first. This thing – it's awful.' My stomach lurched and Zuri must have read my face. 'Oh! Sorry. No, not that either. Just listen. This last trip back to Jo'burg... To get my lab work done...' She hesitated.

'Go on.'

'Well... The semen I took back with me. It wasn't all lion.'

'So what then? Leopard? Nothing awful about that.'

'Not leopard, no. Some of Fredrik's.'

The surprise made me laugh again. 'He didn't tell me. When did you collect that?'

'I didn't. Inga did. From herself, about half-an-hour after they'd had sex. Fredrik doesn't know. But... That's not the point. And it's not funny either. Remember that research in the nineties? The stuff that comes out contains about thirty percent of the sperm that went in? Sometimes a lot more, but never none?'

I understood immediately what she was saying. 'Oh my God...'

'Exactly! I swear Fredrik's not producing. Everything else is in there: all the right fluids, white blood cells and so on. But not a single sperm. What am I going to do? I can't tell them something as terrible as that. Can you?'

***

Zuri Chidumayo and I first met when I chaired a lunchtime seminar on lion conservation at Johannesburg University. It was early in 2007 and Zuri was a final-year undergraduate. We spent the afternoon at the alcoholic reception that followed talking about my work and her ambitions, the evening at her favourite restaurant talking about more personal things, and the night in my hotel room hardly talking at all. Unusually for both of us – or so we later learned about each other – we kept in contact, and when the moment came she asked her department to appoint me as field supervisor for her PhD.

Born in Zambia, Zuri is the eldest daughter of a man who made a small fortune from copper and cattle en route to becoming a second-tier Zambian politician. He also became a complete stranger to her. When Zuri was only 12 her mother died of breast cancer, her father almost immediately remarried, and Zuri was sent to an all-girl's boarding school in Southern England. Almost from the moment she boarded the plane, her father showed minimal interest in her life or career. Then on her eighteenth birthday he explained to her why: she wasn't his daughter, not according to her mother on her deathbed. Since that birthday 'father' and 'daughter' have never met; Zuri is now twenty-five. In a sense she and I are both orphans: my last surviving family member, my mother, died when I was eighteen.

Despite Zuri spending almost all of her teenage years in England, her affections never left the African wilderness that she so loved as a young child. Even Johannesburg isn't home enough for her, and her display of liberation whenever she returns to my camp in the Kalahari is always intense and on occasion amusing. Tonight at her welcome party I could see that even before midnight she had drunk far too much hooch for a first night back. Otherwise when the drums and the chanting grew faster she would have begun to twitch her hips, judder her buttocks, and bounce her breasts along with the best of the younger Tswana women. But as her line of dancers began its build-up to a naked frenzy Zuri lost first her rhythm and then her balance. I broke from my line of stamping, cock-bobbing, balls-bouncing men and ran over to her.

***

'No, don't go,' she slurred as I lay her down on our bed. And before I could disentangle myself from her arms, she pulled me down, wrapped her long strong legs around my waist and proceeded to have sex with me, apparently in her sleep. And by the time we finished, I was ready for drunken sleep myself. But then the dormitory lights went out. Such a blackout on camp could mean only one thing: the large solar-charged batteries in our archaic electricity system had failed yet again and something had to be done. An unbroken electricity supply was important to us: we kept blood and semen samples in a deep freeze.

I lay in Zuri's arms for a few minutes hoping that the even more archaic back-up generator would kick-in. Or, if that also failed, I hoped that Fredrik – not yet in bed – would deal with it. Then I heard the sound of an argument outside, a man and a woman.

After easing myself out of Zuri's now-limp embrace, I made my way to the door. But as I drew near it flew open, silhouetting an unmistakable figure against the moonlight. 'Perfect timing,' I said. 'The generator needs a kick up the backside.'

'Fuck the generator. Fuck Inga. Fuck Zuri – and fuck you.'

I groaned – 'What is it this time?' – though I could guess.

'None of your fucking business.'

***

After nudging the generator into action I searched for Inga and found her well beyond the camp perimeter, staring across the moonlit desert. She was crying. I put an arm around her bare bony shoulders and stared with her in silence for a while. The hot air of the early-winter's day was cooling fast. 'Shall I get you a shawl?'

She shook her head then nestled under my arm, pressing her tiny breasts against my side. 'What I did... Was it really that bad?'

At Zuri's request I had been present when Zuri told Inga what she had seen – or rather not seen – in Fredrik's semen. Zuri tried to soften the news by saying that the sample wasn't a good one, that it must have overheated at some point, that really it proved nothing. But together we also urged Inga to admit to Fredrik what she had done and to use the results, such as they were, to pressure him into conquering his phobias, going to a fertility clinic and undergoing proper tests. And it seemed that was exactly what Inga had tried to do.

'I don't know which annoyed him most: that I went behind his back, that Zuri helped me, or that he might actually have a problem. He's always been so convinced it was me.'

I kissed her salty smoky hair, then rested my cheek on top of her head for a moment. 'Just go and get it sorted Inga. Who knows what proper tests will find. You can't rely on what Zuri saw.'

She eased away from me. 'It's not just his doctor phobias. It's hope versus certainty. Which would you choose? I know Fredrik.' Hand-in-hand we walked back to the camp, her sarong rustling at each step.

'At least come into the dormitory and make up with him,' I said. 'I don't want to leave for England tomorrow with you two at loggerheads. Try to calm him down. Be nice to him. Give him a hug.'

Inga wiped her eyes and nose with the back of her hand, then wiped that on her sarong. 'That's exactly what started it. We were under the Mopane trees. After I told him about it all, I gave him a cuddle. And that was fine but... I don't know why, I suddenly felt so randy that I... But he pushed me away. He's never done that before. Said it was pointless. Pointless! Can you imagine how much that hurt?'

In the dormitory we fumbled and stumbled our ways to the beds of our respective partners. After negotiating the mosquito net I slipped alongside Zuri, still asleep, and tuned in to the sounds in the room: whispered voices, angry at first, then quieter, calmer. Eventually, I heard the suck and smack of kissing, and finally the unrelenting rhythm and noise of sex. I smiled to myself. Normality had been restored.

By my side Zuri stirred and mumbled, 'Not again Mark. I'm trying to work,' then promptly fell asleep once more.

***

'I wish you weren't going,' Zuri sighed. It was less than twenty-four hours since I'd driven her from the landing strip; now she was driving me back there to say *au revoir.* 'We've hardly had chance to talk about anything. I wanted to go through my latest analyses with you. I'm not sure I believe them.'

'Why?'

'You'd have to see for yourself. I've probably made some stupid mistake with the stats.'

'I doubt it. So come on, tell me. What don't you believe? I'll check the stats for you when I come back.'

'Well… It's about which of the lions in the pride fathers most cubs.'

'But you settled that ages ago: the male with the biggest balls, as per theory. Don't tell me that's changed.'

'No, no. Course not. Biggest balls and most sperm per ejaculate. But now there's something else. Something really weird.'

'Weird? Like what?'

'OK – but don't laugh. It's those backward-pointing fleshy spines on the lion's prick.'

'Really? Huh, that is weird. So which way? Positive or negative?'

'Positive. The more barbs and the longer they are, the greater a male's share of the cubs in the pride. How the hell can we make sense of that?'

***

With no sign of the air-taxi at the landing strip we settled down to wait. 'Is that Nick?' Zuri asked, nodding towards a distant band of Bushpeople.

'Can't tell.'

'I think it is.... .... Which reminds me.' She slapped my leg. '"Only two" you told me yesterday. "Just a couple of oversexed psychology lecturers".'

'But it's true.'

'Really? So what's all this about Nick's sisters a few weeks ago? All of them, he said. Twice.'

I laughed. 'The bastard! You believed him? I'm flattered.'

'Well... Actually... No, I didn't.' It was her turn to laugh. 'Even you couldn't manage that. How many sisters has he got anyway?'

'Too many for me,' and we slipped into silence for a while. 'Look... Zuri... I know you don't want to talk about it – but about the funding...'

She groaned. 'No-o-o. Not just as you're leaving Mark, please. We've talked and talked. All of us. There's nothing left to say, and it's terrible. If this camp folds...'

'But that is what I want to say. It won't fold. I won't let it.'

'But without money, how can you prevent it?'

'I don't know yet. But I'll find a way. I promise.'

'But how? It doesn't even bear thinking about. All those years it's taken you – us – to tag and measure all those

61

lions. I can't start-over somewhere else, I just can't. I haven't time.'

It was always there, always in the background, always on her mind. 'Zuri... You don't know that.'

'Of course I know it.'

'No you don't. Look... This isn't how I wanted this conversation to go. I wanted to reassure you. Leave on an optimistic note.'

Zuri reached for my hand. 'I know you did. And I appreciate it.' The air-taxi came into view. 'But time Mark. It's going too fast for me. I need this place to keep running. I can't start-over.'

'And neither can I. Look... Let me get to London. Try to find out who's behind all this; who we're up against. I know I've only got three weeks, and most of that time I'll be drowning in examiners' meetings, but one way or another...'

'Talking of drowning... Don't forget that inquest. That'll take at least a day.'

'No it won't. That dead-keen student of mine and her brother have offered to go for me.'

***

'Three espressos please,' I shouted. Early evening and we were meeting in a shaded side street at what passed for a pavement cafe. 'You two spend a lot of time together for brother and sister.'

Mazher gave me an easy smile – 'Not through choice. Really I hate her' – then laughed when Sharda slapped his arm. 'It is the orders of our father. He bought us an apartment to share here in London so that I can keep an eye on her. I am supposed to vet any man that she sees, discourage him by saying that she is already engaged to be married, and describe to him all the terrible things that will happen to him if he even thinks about touching her. Then I have to report back to our father in Lahore – and if he considers any man a risk, I am never to let him see Sharda alone, if at all.'

'You're here today. Does that mean he considers me to be a risk?'

'A man who runs naked into the London underground? What do you think?'

'You told your father about that?'

They both burst out laughing. 'Stop it Mazher,' Sharda scolded. 'No, of course he did not tell him that. And he is joking about the other things too. Well… Except about the apartment. That bit is true. Our father did buy it for us, and we do share.'

Mazher was still chuckling. 'In truth, Mark… Can I call you 'Mark'? I do not need to keep an eye on her. All she does is work. Nearly as hard as me. She is very desperate to prove to our father that she deserves to do a PhD. And now, she tells me, she wishes that PhD to be on lions, in the Kalahari, with you as her supervisor. And I must say, she makes it sound very interesting and exciting.'

I failed to control either my thoughts or my expression, and Sharda picked up on it almost immediately. 'Mark? Why the frown? Please tell me there is no problem with my plans?'

What could I say? That there was now no chance? That my research – my whole Kalahari project – was about to die from lack of funding? That unless we found a rich sponsor – their father perhaps – Sharda would have to look elsewhere? I thought fast. 'Problem? No, of course not. I was just wondering whether to break a rule, that's all. Your results aren't published yet – but I was going to tell you both that so far your marks have been excellent Sharda. That if you can keep that up for another year…'

'Oh... She will. You have our word,' said Mazher.

Sharda looked relieved and exchanged a smile with her brother.

Mazher leaned forward to rest his arms on the table, his expression changing. 'Anyway... To business. The real reason I am here tonight is that I am most interested in this case of the drownings.'

'Any particular reason?'

'I will tell you. But first I very much want to hear your views. To see if you have the same thoughts as myself. What did you expect the verdict to be?'

Our espressos arrived and for a moment we busied ourselves with sugar or chocolate mints. 'My expectation? Death through misadventure. I don't see what else it could be, given the circumstances. I mean... Don't get me wrong. I would dearly love to be able to implicate Cruickshank in some way but... Was the driver drunk?'

Mazher answered. 'No real evidence. Just the empty whiskey bottle. But that is the police assumption. So... You have no further thoughts.'

I shrugged. 'Not really. Do you?'

'Yes, I do. Several. For example. It is a long way from Buckinghamshire to Scotland, would you not agree? Yet there was not a single sighting of a red MG on the days or nights in question – not by the public, not by motorway cameras, not by anything. Then there is the mystery of the large white vans, quite big enough to contain this midget car. Were there really the two? Or only the one? CCTV cameras captured them both in Nottingham and Wimbledon. And yes, they had different registration numbers. But neither number was registered to a large van. It seems that both sets of number plates had been removed from abandoned cars.'

'Mmm. Interesting.' I took a few sips of very hot coffee. 'Still... None of that proves the verdict is wrong does it?'

'No, but...' The pair of them were sitting opposite me, both grinning, both showing teeth so white and perfect that it was difficult to believe they weren't the result of cosmetic dentistry.

Sharda, who so far had let her brother do the talking, put her hand on his arm to stop him. Her nails were painted with black and white zebra stripes. 'Mazher! Please. Let me tell Mark the best thing.'

I grinned. 'There's a best thing?'

'Well... See what you think.' As she leaned across the table towards me her sleek jet-black hair slipped off her shoulders and fell forward to hide the front of her white shirt. 'The Detective Inspector was describing how they used dental records and DNA to identify the bodies.'

'So?'

'So... He said something about the rapper. Just a comment, but Mazher and I, we picked up on it immediately. It seems that, between the teeth of JJ on one side of his mouth...' She gave a quiet laugh of excitement. '... they found a few fibres of cotton wool.' She sat back as if in triumph. 'Now. What do you make of that?'

Chapter 9

'My name is de Vries. I have an appointment with Detective Inspector Robert Stansted at two o'clock.'

'Two o'clock, you say.' The desk sergeant looked down a list. 'Ah yes. Take a seat, Doctor. He's still out, but he should be back soon.'

"Soon" proved to be an hour and when DI Stansted did eventually return "out" had meant a curry house, with beer, followed by coffee – unless my sense of smell was fooling me. 'So... What can I do for you Dr de Vries?' he asked after showing me into a bare interview room then gesturing for me to sit opposite him at a table. 'Because the Mia Cruickshank case is closed. Did you know?' His hair was greying and his face lined; he looked near to retiring age and already bored with his afternoon.

'Well... Maybe you should open it again,' and after telling him who I was I described both my meeting with Mia and my being kidnapped by Cruickshank's men. All the time I was talking he seemed to be finding it difficult to keep a straight face.

'So... Let me get this straight. On the basis of those few fibres we found in JJ's gob, you're expecting us to believe that he was kidnapped like you say you were, except that when his DNA proved to be a match he, Mia and the baby were 'executed' for their 'crime' against Cameron Cruickshank, OBE.'

'Something like that, yes.'

He laughed and shook his head. 'You do know who Cameron Cruickshank is, don't you?'

'Can't say that I do. But does it matter who he is?'

'For Christ's sake. Which planet were you born on Sunshine? Of course it bloody matters. He's a magistrate. Ex-army. Owns half of Buckinghamshire. His cousin is married to the Chief Superintendent. He's in line for a knighthood.' He studied me for a moment or two. 'Look... Dr de Vries... Stick to what you're good at. OK? Go chase lions. Leave the sniffing out of murderers to the professionals.'

'Happy to. Any idea where I can find one?' I held up my hands. 'OK. Cheap joke. But... Does that mean you are going to look into this? Or not?'

'Nothing to look into.' He stood up. 'Now... Thanks for coming in. The desk sergeant will show you out.'

I stayed seated, placing a piece of paper on the table

'What's that?'

'A print-out of my GPS position at hourly intervals on the days I told you about. Check it out. That property I was taken to in Buckinghamshire...? I guarantee that belongs to Cruickshank.'

'GPS! How the hell...?' He narrowed his eyes. 'Wait a minute. You said they stripped you. Left you with nothing.'

'Makes no difference. Check out that location.'

***

Sharda and I sank back into the plush interior. This time I took note: it was a Rolls Royce, probably vintage. 'Thanks for coming with me,' I said to her. 'I decided I might need a witness. Sorry it was such short notice.'

'Not a problem. And how could I say no? But why me?'

'Who else? You're the only person who knows what this is about.'

'I suppose I am – apart from Mazher.' Then she leaned towards me and whispered, 'Is this really the same car they kidnapped you in before?'

I nodded and said in a loud voice, 'Says a lot about the man's confidence and arrogance, don't you think?' The driver on the other side of the glass window glanced at me in his mirror.

Sharda studied me. 'Flip-flops, shorts, and a T-shirt saying "Lions do it every 30 minutes". I understand your motives – but are you sure you have not gone too far?'

'We'll see. But if three days after I go to the police, Cruickshank feels moved to invite me and "a friend" to his house to attend his fiftieth birthday garden fête. And to offer to chauffeur us there as well. To me that says he badly wants to see me. He won't care that I'm not wearing a tux.'

'Well, I hope you are right. I am quite excited about seeing this man and his house. I would be disappointed if we were not allowed in after all.'

'Don't worry, he'll let us in. Besides, anything I lack sartorially... I must say you look stunning. Oh, is that allowed? Or wouldn't your father approve?'

She gave a beaming smile. 'Oh, yes. That is definitely allowed.' Then she paused for a moment. 'Look, Mark, can I say something? I know what Mazher said after the inquest, but most of that really was just him trying to be funny. This is Mazher. My father is actually very liberal in his interpretation of all things Sikh.'

'Liberal? In what way?'

'Do you really want to know?.... ………….. Well, for example... He asks only three things of me: that I never cut my hair; that I stay a virgin until I marry; and that the man I do eventually marry is a Sikh. One day my father and I – and maybe others in his family – will sit down and draw up a short list, then he will approach those men and their families. But everything else he is very happy to leave to me. So I confess to you: I do not pray, I do only meditate occasionally, and I wear only the clothes that make me feel good. And today that happens to be my favourite sari. I am very happy that you like it.'

The Rolls-Royce was virtually gliding along the M1, the driver keeping precisely to the speed limit.

'You and Mazher... You only ever talk about your father, as if he rules the household. Now I don't know much about Sikhism, but the one thing I thought I knew was that you uphold sexual equality in all things. Even your deity has no gender, has it?'

She nodded and gave an appreciative smile. 'All true, but sadly my mother is dead. I was only two and really I do not remember her. But Sikhs believe that when a man and woman marry their souls unite. So even though my mother is dead my father has always been both of my parents. He is a very kind and generous man. Mazher and I, we love him very much.'

'You say 'Sikhs believe.' Is that what you believe too? That married souls unite?'

'As a Sikh, of course.'

'And as Sharda?'

'Ah, as Sharda.' Briefly, she looked out of the window at the passing scenery. 'As Sharda, I believe it is a very pretty thought.'

We fell silent for a while, and when the lack of conversation began to feel awkward I asked her to tell me more about her childhood in Lahore. I had visited the city once and couldn't imagine what it would be like to grow up there. Was their house large? Detached? An apartment – what?

'Big, yes. And in its own grounds, on the outskirts. But my childhood? It was nothing, just what childhoods are.' And although I pressed her a little, she told me nothing of consequence.

The driver signalled left and we began to leave the motorway to join the A41 towards Aylesbury. 'Now I am very nervous,' Sharda whispered.

***

The car skirted a large lawn with a huge marquee and many assembled guests then slowed to a halt inside a large underground garage. As we and the driver got out of the car the garage door closed behind us. The place looked just as I remembered.

'The invitation said "Black-Tie,"' said the driver.

'I don't care what it said. Does Cruickshank want me here or not?'

'Only if you're properly dressed.'

'Then I think this is stalemate. Maybe you should tell him.'

He got back into the driving seat and spoke a few words to somebody on a phone or radio. 'Games room,' he said, gesturing towards the elevator. 'First floor. You can discuss it there.' As the lift began to ascend Sharda looked so nervous I took hold of her hand and gave a gentle squeeze.

The room was very different from the one on the third floor on my previous visit. Carpeted and with the lighting subdued it contained many armchairs and paintings. There were also assorted tables for chess, cards, a roulette wheel – and a full-sized snooker table, with the balls already in position. We were alone. 'Look! Mark...' Laid out on one of the chairs was a black tuxedo along with a white dress-shirt, black bow tie, and even a pair of socks and black shoes.

The room's large arched double-wooden doors opened and a cigar-smoking middle-aged man entered. With him was an elegant blonde woman in her 40s. The man didn't remove the cigar to speak, just manoeuvred it into the corner of his thin-lipped mouth. 'Miss Kaur... Dr de Vries is about to change his clothes. Go with Sarah. She'll look after you until he is decent.' His brogue was Scottish, and although he was speaking to Sharda his piercing blue eyes never wavered from me.

Nothing more was said until the two women left the room, Sharda looking concerned as she glanced back at me on her way out. I turned to Cruickshank. 'If you want to talk to me then go ahead – but I'm not changing my clothes.'

'Yes you are.' His hair was brown and closely cropped, greying above the ears. His face was craggy and clean-shaven with a strong square jaw.

I gave a quiet laugh. 'No, I'm not. This meeting is for you, not me.'

'For me? Don't flatter yourself Boy.' Taking the cigar out of his mouth he placed it carefully on an ashtray, then selected a snooker cue for himself.

'Yes, for you. You heard that I went to the police to urge them to re-open Mia's case, so you asked me here to persuade me to back off. And I accepted your invitation because I'm intrigued to see whether you plan to use bribery or threat. I told the police I was coming by the way.'

'I'm sure they were fascinated.' He placed the white cue ball on the table. 'And for your information your invitation was printed long before you even thought of going to the police.'

'I don't believe you.'

'Please yourself. Now, get changed so that I can talk to you.'

'Talk to me, or I'll go. Your loss.'

'Get changed Boy. That's an order. This is my home. You will conform.'

I strode towards the double doors. As I passed Cruickshank he calmly cued-off, the white ball glancing from the triangular pack of reds and returning to the far end of the table to nestle tightly behind the yellow. Only three red balls had moved; almost the perfect break.

The doors were locked. For a moment I stood there, then turned to the room. 'You can hold me here, but you can't make me wear those clothes.'

'One thing the army taught me Boy...'

'Stop calling me "Boy".'

'One thing the army taught me Boy is how to break people. Step one is to strip them. Make them feel vulnerable. Threaten them with public humiliation.'

'Nudity doesn't scare me. I thought you learned that last time.'

'Ah, but this time you've brought a friend. I'm sure nudity scares her.' He laughed as if pleased with himself. 'I knew you would bring a young woman. And very fuckable she is too. The only thing heathen women are good for. But just one pull on this bell-rope here and your pretty Sikh companion will get the humiliation of her young life. Now... Put on those clothes.'

Chapter 10

Cruickshank selected a new cigar and chopped off the end. 'Help yourself,' he said – but I declined, then waited while he worked on lighting his own. He sat opposite me in a large leather armchair. 'Now Boy... Listen to me, and listen good. I hear your research funding has been pulled; the project that matters to you most in this world is about to end. Something to do with Health and Safety I believe.' I said nothing, just fixed on his eyes as they laughed at me under his bushy dark eyebrows. He took a long draw. 'Well, you can relax. I'm going to bail you out. You want a plane to search for lions? I'm going to buy you that plane. You want money for more and better vehicles? You've got it. Salaries for your two friends? Fine. Hi-tech dart-guns, better computer, solar-powered electricity that actually works, tracking devices...? You've got them all.'

I studied him, searching for sense. 'So... It is bribery after all. I'm surprised. I'd have laid money on threats. But either way Cruickshank, you've just confessed to murder.'

'Mr Cruickshank to you.'

'Ha! Murder, Cruickshank. Dress it up how you like, your offer's just hush money. Now, give me one good reason why I shouldn't go back to the police and add what happened here to my story?'

'Oh, I can do better than one. End of your research? End of your career? Maybe even end of your life? Are those reasons enough?' He chuckled. 'You've no idea have you Boy? Totally out of your depth. Do you fish? Ever dangled a minnow in a pond full of very large Pike? DI Stansted is here, out on the lawn. So is his Chief Superintendent. Mia's case is closed, and I promise you it will stay closed whatever evidence you produce. Though that GPS record...' He pointed at me. 'Impressive. I enjoyed that. But you'd best understand: I'm immune. I don't need to bribe you to stay silent. Or to threaten you. This is a genuine offer.'

'It can't be genuine. What can possibly be in it for you?'

'I'm a philanthropist. Known for it. Admired for it. And I like lions. They're strong. Fearless. They have a good image.' He sucked on his cigar. 'Then there's you. Coloured pagan though you are, I like your spunk. You handle yourself well. And I've heard good things about your research. Together, we can guide the world towards understanding and conserving the Kalahari lion. The cost becomes trivial.'

'Bullshit! You? Care about the Kalahari lion?' I studied him for an age, still trying to make sense of his offer. Then everything clicked into place. 'It's your knighthood, isn't it? That's what this is about. It was you all along. You arranged for my research funding to be pulled. What did you do? Pull strings? Call in favours?'

'No fooling you, is there Boy?' His huge smile revealed nicotine-stained teeth.

'Is that really all you need? Just one more act of philanthropy? Oh, and me not white... Does that help too? Need something as evidence you're not a racist, do you?' There was a drinks cabinet in the room. Without asking, I walked over and helped myself to a large whiskey. 'You did kill Mia, didn't you?'

'According to the police I was in Chicago when the accident happened.'

'OK. Then you arranged the "accident." Didn't have the stomach to do it yourself. I can believe that.'

He joined me at the cabinet and poured himself a Brandy, standing near enough for me to smell the cigar smoke on his breath and clothes. 'Mia was a whore Boy. She broke her wedding vows with that talentless nigger and God saw to it that they paid full price for their sins. There's nothing more to say.'

I stared him straight in the eyes. 'You had them killed, I know you did.'

All he did was shake his head. 'Spare me your posturing. Mia or no Mia, you need my money. You're desperate for it. So are those colleagues of yours back in Botswana. What are they called? Inga? Fredrik? Zuri?'

I took a swig of my whiskey. 'How the hell do you manage to know so much about me?'

Self-satisfaction oozed from him. 'You don't really think I'd make an offer like this without checking every last detail about you and your operation do you?' He laughed at me. 'Anyway, tomorrow, you'll receive an e-mail from my secretary – Dominic – making you a formal offer and spelling out the details. And when you've accepted – which you will…'

'Oh, I will. No fear of that. Like you say, we need it. I'll take everything you offer and still ask for more. This knighthood of yours won't come cheaply.'

'You see! Spunk! Splendid!' He still seemed to be laughing at me. 'Right… Dominic will arrange everything with immediate effect. Let him know what sort of plane you want and you can be flying it by the end of August. There'll be no messing about with start dates and end dates.'

'Until you get your knighthood eh? What happens then?'

'Relax! My support will last until there is nothing more we can do for each other. And that could be a lot longer than the average Research Council grant – and be a lot more generous. Now, you've had more than your share of my time. Go back to your heathen plaything and take advantage of the hospitality on offer.'

Happy to oblige, I began moving towards the door.

'By the way,' he continued, finishing his Brandy. 'I'm pleased to see you fucking your own kind now. Knowing your place Boy, that's the key.'

***

I weaved my way across the lawn, passing anonymous men monotonous in their tuxedos and a sparkling array of women in elegant expensive-looking clothes. As I reached Sharda the man who'd been talking to her made his excuses and left. I grabbed a glass of champagne from the tray of a passing waitress. Sharda and I were the only non-white people in view.

'Would he have done that? Really? Oh my God! That is one of my nightmares. I would have died of embarrassment,' and 'Why did you not tell me that you had lost your funding? I would have asked my father to support you,' were Sharda's responses to my story of the meeting with Cruickshank. But when I suggested that accepting her father's money might smack of corruption if she didn't qualify for a PhD on merit she was unimpressed. 'More corrupt than taking money from a man you believe to be a murderer? Besides… I shall qualify on merit – because I shall work very hard to make sure that I do.' Then it was her turn to describe her afternoon, and she immediately seemed amused. 'Sarah offered me a job.'

'A job?'

'Yes. Look!' She handed me a business card: *The Elite Escort Agency – for the discerning and very rich.*

'That's hilarious.'

'I know – but Sarah thought that I would jump at the chance. It seems that most of her girls are students struggling to manage on their money. Of course – we soon encountered a problem.'

'Virginity?'

'Actually... We never mentioned sex. Maybe *The Elite* really is just an escort agency.'

'Oh sure. So... If not virginity – what?'

'Oh, something much more serious. It is this. I am sure you have noticed.' She placed the palm of her free hand flat on top of her head. 'Sarah did not know that as a Sikh woman I cannot shave off this hair under my arms. And when I told her that I would not wish to remove it anyway, she rather lost interest in me.' She lowered her arm again and took another sip of her non-alcoholic cocktail. 'Had you noticed?'

'Of course.'

'And?'

'And nothing. Maybe it's the biologist in me, but I actually prefer my women as nature intended.'

'Really? Ah, but why am I not surprised? And can I say? Your preference may be biological but it is also very Sikh.' She cocked her head slightly as if to study me. 'Do you know what I think Mark?'

'What?'

'That in a previous life you really were a Sikh.' She smiled. 'I like this thought.'

I grabbed another passing glass of champagne and for a few moments looked around in silence. Then Sharda touched my arm to regain my attention. 'Mark... This afternoon... I learned something from Sarah that I think you will find interesting. It is about Mia and JJ... It seems that

Sarah is the person who introduced them to each other. Do you remember the newspaper report?'

'You mean – she thought she introduced them.'

'Well, this is the interesting thing. According to Sarah she had known them both – you know, separately – for two years or more. Sarah organised the wedding for Cruickshank – this is how she knew Mia. And she knew JJ because the rapper used girls from *The Elite* sometimes. Yet not once during the time she knew them both did either Mia or JJ give any hint that they were acquainted. And when she did finally introduce them, she said they really did behave as if they were meeting for the first time. Yet Mia had given birth to his son nearly a year earlier.' Sharda again touched my arm, this time as a warning. 'Do not look, but it is Sarah. She is coming over to us.'

'Very smart Dr de Vries. A big improvement. And may I say that you and Sharda look wonderful together. Anyway… I'm sorry to interrupt but there's a gentleman over there who would like to talk to you, once you have a moment. He says that you and he know each other.'

I looked in the direction she was pointing. 'I don't see anybody I know.'

'He's probably gone into the marquee.'

'Did he give you a name? Is it DI Stansted?'

'Bob? You know him? But no, it wasn't him. This is Leonard.'

'Leonard? I don't think I know a Leonard.'

'Oh! Really? Though I can understand that. Don't tell him I said so – but he is a very easy man to forget. He works for one of the research councils. Goldman I think his name is.'

***

Around the camp fire we were all – Europeans and Africans alike – wearing shawls of animal-hide for warmth. It was mid-July and the temperature was dropping towards a maybe frozen dawn. At least the food was hot and the hooch fiery, matching Fredrik's mood. 'What do you mean, you haven't accepted yet? A plane? Money? An actual salary for me and Inga? No strings? What's to think about?'

I had only just arrived in the camp but a few days before leaving the UK I forwarded the e-mail with details of Cruickshank's offer. I wanted everybody to have chance to think the matter through before we discussed it. 'He's a murderer Fredrik. I thought you – or somebody – might object to us taking his money. I know it's my name on that contract but I wanted everybody to have their say before I commit us to anything.'

'You don't know he's a murderer.'

'Yes I do. He's a murderer, he's a racist, and he's using us.'

'He's also offering us everything we ever wanted.'

'But is he? You know the saying 'if something seems too good to be true…' Who's to say this offer is all it seems? Maybe he's playing some game with us.'

'What game? Anyway, who cares? I can't see anything in the contract that we can possibly object to. Christ, Mark… Sod everybody having a say. You should have bitten his hand off there and then. If your pissing about has lost us this offer, I think I'll fucking kill you.'

Fredrik wasn't the only person to voice enthusiasm for Cruickshank's offer and dismay at my tardiness. Zuri had met me at the landing strip and spent the entire drive back to camp in a state of high excitement. 'It solves everything Mark. I can admit it now: I was so depressed while you were away. Just the thought of starting from scratch somewhere else… I couldn't do it. I'd decided – I really had – if we couldn't stay here after I'd finished my PhD... I was going to give up on research. Get a job, any job. Not put off having my baby any longer. But now... It's so brilliant. Just think what we can do here with funding like that.'

I looked to the far side of the fire. 'Inga... What about you?' She blinked up at me as if I had just woken her. 'What do you think we should do?'

Trembling slightly, she put a hand to her lips as if about to draw on a cigarette, except there was nothing between her fingers. And when she spoke, she didn't answer my question. 'Did the pilot give you a package for me? I phoned her yesterday. Please don't say she forgot.'

'A package? Oh, sure. It's in my bag. In the dormitory. What is it?' Inga didn't answer, just stood and wrapping her shawl tightly round her shoulders stepped over a few logs and legs on her way from the fire. 'Hey! Inga? You didn't answer my question. What do you think we should do?'

'Do?'

'About the offer.'

'Oh, the offer.' She stood still for a moment gazing into the flames, then looked at me. 'We can't afford principles Mark. You've got to accept, and see where it takes us. If we don't like what happens after that, we can always opt out. But until then...' And in mid-sentence, she began walking towards the dormitory.

I watched her for a while, then turned back to the group. 'Kopano? Tau? What do you think?'

Kopano answered. 'We talk about this, my brother and me. About what life would be like here without you four. No more jeep rides into the desert. No more fun shooting lions. Needing to collect firewood and hunt antelope on foot again. No more rum, always hooch. No more sexy Zuri to watch dancing, just wives and daughters. What life is that for a man?'

Annakiya, the 'wife' nearest to him and also the largest, picked up a piece of firewood and hit him ferociously on his shawl-covered back. Two of his or Tau's or somebody's young children also joined in. With good humour, Kopano defended himself from them all. 'You see,' he said at last. 'You must accept this bad man's money Mark. Save us from our wives and children.'

'No! To save us from husbands,' responded Annakiya in mock anger. 'If you not here, these lazy men be under our feet all day long. And worse, we women no longer have you two to look at...' She gestured at Fredrik and myself. 'When you men dance, you so...' She exchanged a few words with Zuri in Bantu, then laughed, clapping her hands and rocking her ample body backward and forward. 'Yes, yes, you so "hot." Ha, I love this word. One day you must marry our daughters. Give us hot grandsons like you'selves, not like these ugly men here.' She pushed Kopano away from her. All the Tswana began laughing and shouting.

I laughed with them. 'OK, then. It's unanimous. Let's bleed this evil bastard for all the money we can. Then when we don't need him any more, I'll do my damnedest to get him arrested and sent to jail. I'll e-mail my acceptance tomorrow.'

Fifteen minutes passed in toasts and mounting jubilation. 'Can I fly the plane?' asked a drunken Kopano at one point. But when Fredrik and two of the young Tswana men sent the first drum beats reverberating across the desert, Zuri by my side began to stand. 'I'm going to look for Inga. She doesn't seem herself. I think she might still be in the dormitory. Come with me?'

Even before we reached the open door we could hear choked crying from inside; Inga was sitting on the edge of her bed, head in hands. Zuri scurried to sit by her side, place an arm round her shawled shoulders, and ask the matter. Inga straightened up and I glimpsed something white in her hand; a digital thermometer I thought. With her eyes streaming she looked up at me – she was smiling. 'I knew I felt different,' she said, choking on a tearful laugh. 'I just knew it. Mark... Zuri... Can you believe it? I'm pregnant! Look!' She showed us the test-stick. 'Three weeks gone, it says. Where's Fredrik?'

Chapter 11

A cold hand touched my bare back. I twitched violently.

'Mark... Honey... Are you OK? You were making terrible noises.'

I opened my eyes and stared in the darkness. 'Zuri.' Then I exhaled in relief. 'Nightmare. Sorry.'

She kissed my ear, snuggled against my back, and together we pulled the double sleeping bag that we share on cold winter nights up under our chins.

***

'I was watching Inga having totally manic sex with all the Tswana men.'

'Is that a nightmare?'

'Then suddenly the camp was full of soldiers carrying machine guns. Somebody was playing the bagpipes. They gunned down all the Tswana – men, women and children. Just massacred them as they ran around screaming, blood everywhere. Then they turned on you, raping you. I tried to stop them, but the next thing I knew, I was alone, being chased by Cruickshank. He was in combat uniform, big heavy boots, carrying a machete. I had nothing, totally naked, just running from one hiding place to another. Then this cold hand touched my back...'

In no rush to start the day, Zuri and I were still in our sleeping bag, wrapped loosely in each others' arms, her head resting on my shoulder. I kissed her corkscrew black hair.

She sighed a little. 'Try not to let the man get to you too much.' But then twisting to whisper in my ear, she became hesitant, even nervy. 'Actually... The start of your dream. About Inga...'

I also whispered. 'The Tswana men? It was only a dream.' I gave her shoulders a squeeze.

'But if the baby can't be Fredrik's...'

'I know what you're thinking but... OK, so he's not producing the zillions he should. But as long as he's producing a few – too few for you to find down your microscope... One is all it takes.'

She sighed again. 'I know. And I know I should forget it – but now let me tell you my dream.'

'Dream? You too?'

'A bit different from yours. More interesting than scary.' She shifted position so as to watch me as she spoke. 'In mine, Inga asked you to give her the baby that Fredrik can't. And guess what?'

'Zuri...' but before I could say more she put her hand over my mouth and smiled.

'It's OK. It was only a dream. I know it never happened.'

'Good. Because I'd have told you – right?'

'Right. And besides... Three weeks ago when Inga conceived... The day I arrived... You didn't have chance. Did you? Between getting back from your two weeks' lecturing in Gaborone and leaving for England... You were only here a few hours. And all that time you and I were together. Every time I surfaced from my drunken stupor you were there.' She wrinkled her broad nose and grinned. 'Usually inside me, if I remember rightly.'

I hesitated, weighing up options, sifting through shades of honesty. 'A slight exaggeration. But all more or less true.'

Suddenly Fredrik's voice boomed across the room. 'Hey! You two. Quit the whispering. It's doing my head in.'

***

Two hands grabbed my shoulders, spun me round and pushed me back into a corner. I banged my temple against a shower-head. 'What the hell...?' I spluttered. For a few moments I could only blink as shampoo filled my eyes, but when my sight cleared I saw Fredrik standing in front of me, a hand on each wall penning me in the corner.

He spoke with a steely calmness, raising his voice just enough to be heard over the noise of the water. 'Sound plays tricks Mark. At a party or a restaurant... Sometimes you can hardly hear the person next to you, yet people on the other side of the room...? Clear as you like.'

'What are you talking about?'

'This morning. You and Zuri whispering. I heard every word.'

I spat a mixture of water and shampoo from my mouth on to the floor. 'Shit!'

'Precisely. Now... What the hell was all that about?'

'Not here.' I reached to turn off the shower that was still spraying us both, but he knocked my hand away.

'Leave it. It'll wash away the mess if I decide to beat the crap out of you. Now what the fuck was all that stuff about you and Inga. Is Zuri right? Did you screw her?'

'Of course she's not "right." She was describing a dream.'

'Fucking nightmare more like.'

'But it's not as if Zuri believes it. Didn't you hear her?'

'Oh, I heard her all right. I also heard why she didn't believe it. She thinks you didn't have chance.'

'But he didn't have chance.' Neither of us had seen or heard anything until Zuri spoke; she and Inga had come into the cubicle for their morning shower. 'He was with me all the time.'

Fredrik turned on her. 'How the fuck would you know Zuri? You were so pissed that night the roof could have fallen in and you wouldn't have noticed. Mark went out. I saw him. He was gone half-an-hour. More.'

'I had to fix the generator. Remember Fredrik? You couldn't be assed.'

Open-mouthed, Zuri stared at me. 'Mark...? Why didn't you tell me?'

'Why do you think he didn't tell you? Because after fixing the generator he went out into the desert to 'comfort' my wife. And don't try to deny it – either of you. Annakiya saw you.' He glared at me. 'You heard Inga and me arguing, didn't you? Probably thought it was the perfect moment to offer your services to her again after all these years.'

'Utter crap.' I turned off the shower, then in the new silence raised my hands to gesture at everybody to calm down. 'Look... What did Anna say she saw? Because it sure as hell wasn't Inga and me having sex.'

'I didn't say it was. But she did see the pair of you coming in from the desert holding hands on the night that she... ,' he jabbed his finger towards Inga, '...probably conceived.'

'She! Right, that's it. Have you quite finished? Moron! Just listen to yourself Fredrik. Why not ask me eh? Instead of shooting your mouth off and making a fool of yourself.' Inga paused for breath. 'This baby is yours Fredrik. Because it can't be anybody else's. More fool me but you're the only person I've had sex with since Mark and I split up ten years ago. Sure, Mark came to find me that night three weeks ago. And I'm glad he did. I needed a friend. Remember why? No? What a surprise. Now I haven't the faintest idea why you and I managed to make a baby that night, and I don't care. All that matters is that we did – and don't you dare question it again, ever.'

Chapter 12

'Lower Mark. There's a male, nine o'clock. By that small waterhole........... And two more under the nearest Acacia tree.' Although only in the seat by my side Fredrik was talking to me through his headset so that I could hear him above the sound of the engine and howling air. 'They look like nomads to me. No females around.'

'Fantastic. How the hell did we manage before we had this plane?'

We had opted for a four-seater Maule light aircraft. 'A beauty isn't she?' said the guy who delivered her to us at Orapa Airport. 'Best bush-plane around in my humble opinion. Large wheels. Tundra tyres. Land and take off in 50 to 70 metres. You'll be able to go anywhere you like. You are two very lucky people.' Both Fredrik and I already had Private Pilot Licenses that allowed us to fly such a plane and ever since the hour's instruction on the aircraft at Orapa we had argued daily over which of us should have the pleasure. Today, I'd won.

I lined up the plane then tried to fly a trajectory that would give Fredrik the best chance of a full-frontal photograph of the first male's face. 'Shit! The bugger turned his head. Try again. One more circle. Lower if you can........... That's it. That's it. Hold that........... Damn and fuck it! The bloody zoom has stuck again.' He let out a growl of exasperation. 'This is crazy. You're going to have to ask Dominic for a new lens. And get some better binoculars while you're at it.'

'Right... I wonder if he's ever going to say no to anything.'

***

I pulled and turned the steering column while pushing gently on the right rudder pedal with my bare foot. The plane climbed, circled and eventually we began heading back towards home. Fredrik downloaded all the day's photographs and GPS locations on to our new lap-top computer, then settled back to enjoy the journey as best he could. Outside the plane the temperature of the September air was over thirty degrees and despite the open air-vents Fredrik was sweating profusely, as was I. He took off his headset for a while, until I gestured that I wanted to talk to him. 'Inga's looking good, don't you think? Putting on a bit of weight at last.'

He grunted. 'That's because she's stopped puking her guts up every time she eats or smells anything. I swear the only thing she could keep down at first was alcohol.'

'At least she's quit smoking.'

'And a right pain in the backside that's made her too? Anyway – I don't want to talk about her. Or it. This pregnancy is our business, not yours.' There was a long pause. 'Watch those three vultures, ten o'clock level.'

I scanned the direction. 'OK, got them. You watch them too.' I looked at him, his sapphire blue eyes crowned with bushy golden eyebrows, almost all I could see between his earphones and microphone. 'Can we still not talk as friends about this?'

'We just have.' He started jigging his right leg. 'Look, Mark. You and Zuri can run your lives how the fuck you want. If you don't want to be a real couple, then don't. But I'm a possessive bastard. OK? Anybody messes with my wife – and that includes you, maybe especially you, I might just... Well let's say I'm with Cruickshank over this. Now I know you deny it, and Inga denies it. And I know Zuri says you'd have told her because of this honesty crap the pair of you get off on. But the thought's still there, stuck in my head, and I can't get rid of it. OK? So if you know what's good for you, change the subject.' He fell silent for a while, making a show of keeping an eye on the vultures until they were behind us. 'Three o'clock. Looks like the first storm cloud of summer.'

'Who the hell cares. Are you going to stay this touchy for the next six months?'

'I don't need to. You'll be back in London in a couple of weeks and apart from your usual few days at Christmas we won't see you until Easter and by then with any luck the baby will be born. Then we'll all know everything, won't we. Hey what the hell are you doing?'

'Landing.'

'Are you blind? There's a Giraffe on the landing strip. Go round.'

'It'll move.'

'And what if it doesn't? Go round.'

'It'll move.'

'It won't.'

'It will.'

***

Zuri was sitting at a table in the dormitory with Inga peering over her shoulder. Both looked up as I came through the door – and both laughed. 'Mark... Perfect timing,' spluttered Zuri. 'We need sperm.'

'What!'

'I need to finish testing this machine. So far it's brilliant. Exactly like the set-up I saw at the IVF clinic in Jo'burg. I never dreamed in a million years I'd have one all to myself.'

'So what are you looking at then?'

'One of my lion samples. From last month.'

Inga joined in. 'I've never seen lion sperm before. I can't get over how much like human sperm they are.'

Zuri was all-but drooling over the machine. She kept touching it, flicking off specks of dust. 'Come and look: microscope, monitor, computer, camera. It gives me every measure I need for a sample. And all in a matter of minutes instead of hours.'

'But if you've got sperm, why do you need more?'

'Idiot! Because all the sperm in my lion samples are dead, aren't they? In formaldehyde – remember? So although I've got the machine working for numbers, concentration, and so on, I can't test the movement and speed-monitoring systems. I need some live sperm to look at. Which is why…' She offered me a glass cup. 'I'll give you a hand if you like.'

***

There they were on the monitor: a multitude of wriggling inter-writhing animalcules looking like a cross between tadpoles and migrating young eels. Adjusting settings, pressing buttons, checking print-outs, Zuri was making no comment. 'So…?' I eventually had to ask. 'How many? About average? Or…'

'Just a minute. Let me check… Right. OK. See how quick that was?'

'Yes, but… How many?'

'How many? Oh, how many. Mmm… 102 million in each millilitre.'

'That's OK, yes?'

'Mark, you know full well that's OK. It's more than OK. What do you want? Compliments? Don't be so transparent.' Zuri looked from one to other of us. 'This is so brilliant. So easy, so quick. Look… Already: Motility – 72 percent. Normal sperm – 75 percent. And lots more besides. I so love this machine.'

The sense of excitement was still hanging in the air when a shadow fell across the open doorway. 'Hey! At last. I wondered where you all were. God, it's hot.' Fredrik was padding across the concrete floor towards us. 'Have you got it working? Let's see? What are you looking at?'

'Oh, just some lion sperm.' Zuri turned off the monitor.

'Why did you do that?'

'Crap preparation. Let me find a better one for you to look at.'

More or less pushing us out of the way, Fredrik turned the monitor back on and gave an impressed laugh. 'My God, look at that. That's not crap, that's brilliant!' He looked at each of us. 'And they are just like human sperm, aren't they?' He watched the screen for a few moments, then slowly frowned. 'Wait a minute. These are alive. Zuri... How's that?' Slowly straightening up to his full height, he turned to glower at me. 'Are these yours?'

He didn't wait for an answer, just swung round to Zuri. 'Right! What do I wank into? I want to see mine. Now! For myself.'

***

The door slammed so hard that the whole dormitory seemed to shake. Inga went over to the mosquito net that Fredrik had torn from around their bed on his way past. After collecting it from the floor, she screwed it into a ball, then threw it on the pillow before slumping on to the bed-edge. 'Just a million. Or a hundred, even. Anything but zero. Zero! That can't be possible.'

I sat by her side. 'Look... Inga... I know what you told Fredrik about never questioning again – but it's just Zuri and me here now. If there's anything you want to tell us... Maybe one of the Tswana lads? We'd understand. Honestly we would.'

Anger sprang into her eyes, then faded. She shook her head. 'I know how it looks. But I promise you both on my life. This baby is Fredrik's. It has to be. I just don't understand why that machine... It's crazy. Totally crazy.'

The door opened and the slim black figure of Kopano walked in, glancing back to the outside. 'What wrong with Fredrik? He just get into jeep with crate of rum. Then drive into desert like all spirits of underworld after him.'

Chapter 13

At dawn the next day Zuri and I set off to drive north on a familiar route. We had six hours of very bumpy driving ahead of us and there were storm clouds on the horizon. Our target was the trio of nomads that Fredrik and I had seen from the air the day before.

'What's that,' said Zuri nearly two hours into our journey. 'Under that cluster of trees.'

'Not sure.' But as we drew nearer it became obvious. In the dark shade was a jeep with a man by its side; Fredrik, carrying a gun.

'What if we hadn't come today?' I said through the open window after pulling up alongside. 'Or taken a different route?'

'But you did – and you didn't – so that's OK. Must be fate.'

'Or if we'd decided to fly instead of drive?'

'You wouldn't. Not for this job. You need to get close. You need a bolt-hole. I knew you'd drive. Anyway, let me in. I'm coming with you.'

'No you're not. You're going back to Inga. She's worried about you.'

'Sod Inga. Until she tells me the truth I'd rather chase lions. Besides, the jeep's broken down. It's not going anywhere until I get back with some parts.'

'Then at least phone her. Let her know you're safe.'

'I'll let you two do that.'

***

The three lions leaped to their feet, looked around, looked at our truck, looked at the blue-headed darts in their sides, then one-by one squatted on their haunches and eventually rolled over. We waited twenty minutes for the anaesthetic to take full effect then took the truck as near to them as we could before walking the last few yards with caution. Each male was 200 kilograms of awesome power. 'I'll give them a shot of ketamine to keep them under,' said Zuri, knowing that we needed around thirty minutes with each animal. 'Do we know them? Did we tag them as cubs?'

I checked. 'Yep, we know them. They've all got IDs.'

With Fredrik standing guard, an array of guns by his side, Zuri and I began work on the first lion. With his furry golden scrotum nestling neatly in the palm of her hand Zuri measured the length and width of each testis with callipers. As she read off the measurements I typed them into a data recorder. 'OK, now the penis.' Squeezing the base of the prepuce Zuri pushed out the tip then pulled out the whole slender pink-red organ to its full extent along the length of a ruler. I took a photograph, then another, this time a close-up of the tip to show the barbs.

'Condom going on,' I said sliding a stiff plastic tube on to the lion's organ.

Zuri lubricated a thirty-centimetre-long, three-centimetre-wide, electrode with jelly then gently and carefully pushed the rod through the animal's anus and a short distance into its rectum. With the battery connected and everything ready she turned the switch on the stimulator to give a series of tiny electric 'tickles' to the lion's prostate gland. Eventually as if by magic about 4 millilitres of semen squirted into the 'condom'.

Zuri glanced at the sample approvingly then grinned at me. 'Remember that vow you once made Mark? That you wouldn't do anything to a lion that you weren't prepared to have done to yourself. I'm still waiting.'

I laughed. 'I was hoping you'd forgotten.'

'There's something else you haven't experienced yet,' shouted Fredrik from his look-out position. When I glanced up I found a tranquilliser gun pointing at me. The trigger clicked.

'For Christ's sake Fredrik. You know better than that.'

'It's not loaded.'

'Well it should be. And pointed somewhere else. What if there's a fourth lion around?'

With a satisfied smile on his face, he lowered the gun and loaded a blue-headed dart. 'Did we ever find out how long it would take a man to die if he got shot with one of these?'

I studied his face. 'He dies. That's all we need to know.'

***

With an hour of daylight left as we headed back towards camp we spotted a suitable place to spend the night. 'That sand-flat. No problem lighting a fire there.' We were in a dried-up river-bed and there was an abundance of firewood: flotsam carried downriver during some past wet-season had been left high-and-dry on the banks as the water level fell away to nothing.

Hardly had the three of us started to collect firewood than the shower clouds that had been threatening all day finally reached us, just light drops of rain at first then a sudden deluge. And with the temperature still above thirty degrees and our bodies covered with sweat, dust, lion hair and dander we stripped off, put our clothes in the truck, then stood out in the open to let the fresh cool water wash us clean.

Lost in the bliss and swish of heavy rain I only just registered an engine starting. Fredrik reversed the truck to us. 'When we flew over here yesterday, I noticed a big patch of Tsamma Melons. About ten minutes away. Here's a wager for you: I'll be back with three melons before you get the fire burning. If I win, I get the tent and you two sleep in the truck.' And in a moment he was driving away.

I ran after him waving my arms and shouting for him to stop, but even though the boulders littering the gravel-bed slowed the 4x4 a little I couldn't catch it. Giving up, I returned to Zuri.

'Why chase after him?'

'He's cheated. He's driven off with the matches.'

'More than matches. He's got the food that Annakiya packed for us. And the water. And the guns...'

A sudden thought made me look around. 'The tent too.'

'Our clothes. The phones...'

I stared in the direction Fredrik had disappeared then looked at Zuri. She was frowning too.

***

It was difficult to find tinder-dry grass and twigs after the shower, so it was nearly dark before my frantic rubbing and blowing produced the first tiny flame. 'He's not coming back tonight, is he?' said Zuri, looking in vain for approaching headlights. She had just returned from her final foray to collect something – anything – for us to eat and ease our thirst. 'And look what I found, just up there. Melons. And cucumbers. He didn't need to go driving off.'

Stacking ever larger pieces of wood on to the growing fire, I glanced at the fruit she'd collected. 'No protein?'

In the distance a lion roared and another seemed to answer.

***

We had no need to find protein; protein found us. Once the fire was burning, the flames attracted locusts which we caught and cooked. We had eaten many such insects before, the Tswana women regularly serving them as appetisers, usually boiled. But here we baked them wrapped in leaves and after stripping them of their spiny long legs and hard outer wings ate them whole. To me they taste like shrimp but to Zuri their flavour is more vegetable. One by one, interspersed with water melon and cucumber to quench our thirst, the large insects gradually sated us as we sat cross-legged by the fire.

The clouds had cleared and the moonless sky was a shiny black, studded with the incandescent stars of the desert. There was a brilliant planet too: Jupiter we decided. And every few minutes, a shooting star. The clean fresh smell of the damp landscape alternated with the acridity of smoke. And from all directions came the night sounds of the Kalahari: eerie, ominous and magnificent. An unusual number of lions were roaring, some distant, some closer. Something epic was happening. Hyenas called intermittently, hunting dogs yelped and desert owls screeched, all against the humming background noise of insects.

Zuri was staring into the flames as if transfixed. 'So... You think it's the truck.'

'Got to be. It's broken down. Or maybe just stuck. He'll be back after first light – if he can.'

'And if he can't?'

'Then we'll have to go and look for him.' I stood and began to walk away from the fire.

'Where are you going?'

'For a slash.'

'Wait. I'll come with you.'

We went together to the edge of the circle of light and squatting or standing looked out into the darkness while we relieved ourselves side-by-side. Returning to the fire I threw on a branch. Sparks flew upwards. Next I began rummaging among the stash of firewood, looking for a piece suitable as a club or a spear; I couldn't find one. When I straightened up Zuri was standing behind me, brushing sand off her buttocks, her expression inscrutable. 'Are you OK?' I asked. She nodded. 'Not cold?' She shook her head. 'Afraid?' Again she shook her head. 'What then?'

She placed her hands on my chest, ran them up to my shoulders, then down my arms to my hands to twine her fingers with mine. Her breasts lightly touched my rib cage. She was staring up into my eyes. 'Look around Mark. Look up! Breathe! Smell! Listen to all those animals out there. Don't you just love it?'

'You know I do.' Letting go of her hands, I cupped her buttocks and eased her against me. 'But we could die here tonight.' I said. 'You know that, don't you? What protection do we have apart from the fire?'

'Exactly! We should be scared. Terrified even. But we're not, are we? Admit it! Being here, like this. Together. It's such a buzz, I'm tingling with it. Just like you are.' I bent to kiss her, but she put her hand on my mouth and shook her head. 'No, none of that. Not here. It doesn't feel right. Let's save all that for the bedroom.'

'So what would feel right?'

'I'm not sure. Something animal. Something raw. Let's find out.'

***

Flanked to the east by an apricot sky we set off along the river bed to look for Fredrik. Every so often gravel and rocks gave way to damp sand and we were able to spot the imprint of tyres. After an hour the trail led to a stand of Tsamma melons so large that it would certainly be visible from the air. Fredrik's truck had parked nearby but there were no footprints to suggest he made any attempt to pick melons. No hint either that he eventually turned round to drive back to us. On the contrary, further on we found more tyre-tracks. But then the river bed became shallower, lined only with gravel – and when we next found sand there were no further tracks. We had a choice: to double back and try to find where Fredrik had left the river bed; or... 'If nobody finds us Mark... How long would it take us to walk back to the camp?'

'Somebody will find us. Even if Fredrik doesn't, Inga and Kopano will drive out here. They know where we came.'

'But... Just supposing. How long?'

'Not sure. We can't travel during the heat of the day, not at this time of year. Nor at night. And we'll need time each day to find food and water. Over a hundred miles? Only three to four hours a day? That's ten days, maybe more. Just a guess.'

'Is that all? Then let's head home. Teach me how to survive here, like this. How to navigate. Let's do it.'

Without her sarong to carry any food we collected as we travelled, Zuri wove a crude basket from grass. I fashioned two wooden spears – one thick for defensive stabbing and to double as a digging stick and one slender for throwing – but I still felt vulnerable. 'We need a bow.'

'What will you use for string?'

'Sinew; shredded tendon from an antelope.'

'But how will you kill the antelope?'

'Precisely! We need a bow. Or look out for vultures, maybe we can find an antelope already dead.'

We walked on, Zuri at times almost skipping. 'Ten days. No pill. I could get pregnant.'

'Many more nights like last night and you will.'

She laughed. 'I will, won't I. A year earlier than planned. But that's OK. It means that he...'

'Or she.'

'No way. It means that he will be nineteen, not eighteen. And I'll be even more likely to see him through.'

'Zuri...'

'No. It's OK. Happening here, like this. That's perfect.'

'But... What about your lottery? You'll know who the father is.'

'Not necessarily. Maybe we'll meet some San. Does Nick have any brothers?'

When it became too hot we settled in the shade of trees, re-hydrating ourselves on melon or fleshy roots and eating the morsels of fruit, leaves and insects we had collected on our journey. We did our best – but failed – to spear lizards and birds; we needed that bow. Then Zuri found a plover's nest. After sucking out the eggs, we settled down to sleep – only to be woken by the sound of an approaching truck. It was Fredrik.

Zuri swore under her breath.

'What's wrong?'

'I wanted us to do this.'

***

Fredrik said nothing as we opened the truck door.

'By dark, you said. What happened?'

'I don't want to talk about it. OK?'

'Why? Were you actually trying to kill us?'

'How? By leaving you in the desert? Give me some credit. You're virtually a bushman. It was a rush of blood, that's all. A gesture. Except... It gave me time to think about things, and I've made a decision. Until that bloody baby's born I'm going to do my damnedest to believe Inga rather than that stupid machine of yours Zuri. Then... Well, we'll see. But we're on the verge of doing some great work here and if I'm not careful I'm going to ruin it all. Now either keep quiet or talk about something else. How was your night?'

Chapter 14

Just after dawn on the day I was due to leave for England, two pick-up trucks and five massive lorries full of building materials drove into the camp in convoy. The man in charge was Scottish and told me he was once a Sergeant in the regiment of which Cruickshank was Colonel. The rest of his 'gang from Ghanzi' were Tswana. 'It's a real challenge,' he said looking around at the compound. 'Can't wait to get started. You won't recognise this place once we've finished.'

It happened faster than that. Just a few hours later as Zuri drove me out of the compound en route to the air-taxi the gang had already erected a hoarding at the entrance proclaiming the site to be the *Cameron Cruickshank Lion Research Centre*. 'I never agreed to the place being called that. Take it down.'

'Can't. Sorry. Colonel's orders. I've to e-mail the photographs to his secretary by the end of the day. He's waiting to use them for something.'

***

Sitting in my office on my first day back at university I looked around at the four off-white walls, the overhead neon strip light, the small window and crooked blind and felt an overwhelming sense of alienation. It was late afternoon and already dark outside. After snatching up the telephone, I pressed the call button. 'Mark de Vries here. Can I speak to Mr Cruickshank's secretary please?' And for the first time in a dozen attempts I got through to him. 'Dominic?'

'Dr de Vries. What can I do for you?'

'You could try answering my e-mails and returning my calls for a start. And you can arrange a meeting between me and Cruickshank. I have complaints to make.'

'Not possible I'm afraid. Mr Cruickshank is out of the country until the New Year.'

'Out of the country. Where?'

'Hardly your business Dr de Vries? What complaints?'

'Fredrik tells me that two men have turned up at the camp today claiming to be pilots and mechanics. Why? Fredrik is perfectly capable of flying and maintaining that plane.'

'I'm sure he is. But think of the hours the plane eats up on basic maintenance, re-fuelling flights, taxi services, picking up provisions, and so on. Our two men can do all of those things, thereby freeing your man to spend his time chasing lions and overseeing the building work. Surely that is a much better use of his time?'

'But those men are a complete waste of money.'

'Money is not your concern. But while we're on the subject we need to open bank accounts in your name in Zimbabwe, Botswana and Switzerland. There are some forms in the post for you to complete and sign. Please return them ASAP with photocopies of your passport and all the other documents I've listed.'

'Is there any point my asking why?'

'Not really. Now... Is there anything else I can do for you?'

***

My office door opened and my spirits leaped. 'Hey, Sharda. Come on in. Shut the door.' But although she returned my smile hers lacked conviction. 'So how are you? How's

Mazher? And where have you been hiding? I've been trying to contact you. You should have started your project by now.'

'I know. I am sorry. I was in Lahore until Friday.' She glanced at the door. 'Mark... I have a lot to tell you. Can we go somewhere please?'

'If you want. Where?'

'Somewhere that walls have no ears. And doors cannot suddenly open.'

It was a long time before we could talk: the laboratory to which my office was annexed was full of people working; in the lift we were never alone; and on the steps and street outside the building there were people I preferred to avoid. I hailed a taxi and told the cabbie to drive round the block. 'Now... Why the mystery?' I said to her.

'I must leave the university. London too.'

'What! Why?'

'Mazher is dead, and I am very frightened.'

I gave the driver new directions.

'Where are we going?' Sharda asked.

'Somewhere we can be alone.'

***

Back at my flat I reached into the fridge and pulled out a half-empty bottle of red wine left over from the night before. 'Do you never drink alcohol?'

Sharda shook her head. 'As a Sikh, no.' She poured herself a glass of tap-water and together we went into the lounge. 'Where is the man you live with?'

'Mike? He got married and moved to France. I've just advertised for a replacement. No takers yet though.'

As I sat in one of the armchairs Sharda – without asking – took off her sandals, placed them neatly on the carpet, then sat cross-legged on the sofa opposite me. She pulled her long plait over her shoulder so that it hung down her front.

'So... That's terrible about Mazher. What happened? An accident of some sort?'

'Not an accident, no.' She stared into her glass, slowly swilling around the water. 'Thirty-two stab wounds Mark. In a street near Leicester Square. And with the last stab they pinned a note to his chest. It said: "For 7/7 and 9/11". You know... The London underground? The twin towers?... .... Just imagine his last moments.'

'I can't even begin.' I studied her face, looking for tears. 'Sharda... I'm so sorry. I don't know what to say. Have they caught the people who killed him?'

'No. Not yet. Maybe never.'

'Why not?'

'Because the police... They think that the death of Mazher was a mistake. In America, many Sikhs have been attacked since 9/11. And some killed. People see the turban and think the clothing means Islam. Here too, in England, this mistake has been made.'

'And surely that is what happened to Mazher? Why else would somebody kill him then leave that note?'

'I don't know. But...' She reached into her handbag and took out a folded sheet of paper. 'Last night this note was in the mailbox to my apartment.'

I put down my glass of wine and unfolded the sheet:

Mazher's death was no mistake.
Your father with his weak heart in Lahore is next.
Or you.
Unless...

***

I found an aubergine, mushrooms, potatoes... 'Are you OK with brown lentils? And cheese?'

'Lentils? Fine. But the cheese... Is it vegetarian?'

'Ah! Damn! Can I lie and say yes?' which at last made her smile. Then with everything cooking we went back into the lounge. 'Can I see that note again?' I re-read the words. 'But why pick on Mazher? Or your father and you? Was Mazher involved in something perhaps? Something political? Ideological?'

'Of course not. He had no time – and he could not do anything like that without my knowing. We were always together, usually working.'

'Then why him?' I looked at the note again. 'Actually... Does your father have a weak heart?'

'This is what frightens me. Nobody in England should know this. I have never told anybody, and neither would Mazher. My father wanted nobody to know. So... Maybe this killer has friends in the Punjab. Maybe even in the hospital. People in Lahore, they know my father.'

'Because he is rich?'

'For sure.'

'Rich enough to have enemies?'

'Maybe. I do not know.'

I heard the sound of a pan boiling over – 'Shit!' – and springing from my chair I ran to rescue the lentils. 'You really should take this note to the police,' I said later.

She shook her head. 'It is too big a risk. Surely this person might kill my father if I do this. Or kill me. He knows where I live.'

'So what are you going to do?'

'I do not know.'

'Does your father know about these threats?'

'No, and he must not.'

'Because of his heart.'

She nodded.

I looked at the note again. 'This was actually in your mailbox? So you definitely have to leave your apartment – and quickly – and tell nobody your new address. Is there somebody you can trust?'

'How can I tell? Mazher and I know some people in London of course, mainly other Sikhs – but nobody well enough to trust absolutely. Mark… I do not think I can stay in London. It is too dangerous.'

'I know how it must seem, how you must feel, but… You can't leave – not London, not the university, not now. You're doing so well. You have such plans. It would be such a waste. There has to be some other way.'

'And I do not want to leave. Of course not. All summer I have been dreaming of working hard for my degree and then doing a PhD in the Kalahari with you. And my father… He is praying for the day he can write 'Dr' before my name. I know all this. But…'

'But what?'

'I am frightened Mark. For the life of my father, and for my own. Here in London I feel I am being watched, all the time. Sitting here, with you, this is the first time I have felt safe since I received this note. What can I do?' She took the note from me. 'Then there is this word "unless".'

Chapter 15

Briefcase in hand, I locked my office door and weaved my way between the benches in the laboratory. 'Last again?' I said to Sharda. She smiled. 'How the hell do you manage to keep your lab-coat so white?' She smiled again. 'Shall I wait? How long will you be?'

She shook her head. 'It is Sikh Soc tonight. A woman is coming to lecture on 'arranged marriage in the twenty-first century' and I would like to go. I shall catch the tube home.'

'Are you sure?'

'Sure. I shall have company for much of the journey. Other Sikh women.'

'In that case I'll go to the Staff Bar for a while. Phone if you need me.'

'OK.... .... Actually, no. If you can wait just a moment? I shall walk to the lift with you. I have a question.'

I perched on a stool and waited while she put tubes and chemicals into refrigerators, collected together her lab-notes, wiped the work-top clean, washed her hands and hung up her lab-coat. 'So... What's this question?' I asked as we walked along the deserted corridor.

'The records we have of where each lion travels... Can these be wrong?'

'I hope not. Why?'

'Because this last DNA profile I made this afternoon... It must be impossible.' A woman appeared and exchanged a few sentences with Sharda in Punjabi. 'This person, she is going to Sikh Soc too. She would like me to go with her.'

'OK. That's good. But at least tell me why the DNA profile is impossible?'

'It would take too long. Maybe later. Bye.'

***

The monitor screen showed Zuri clearly, but her words were well ahead of the movement of her lips. 'And is this Sharda pretty?' she asked.

'Very.'

'And sexy?'

'That too – but not in the same way as you. Go and put on a shawl or something.'

Zuri gave an out-of-sync laugh. 'You're joking. This dormitory's like a sauna. It's been sweltering here today. But I'll switch off the web-cam if you can't cope.'

'Don't you dare. I'll cope. So how are things there? How's Inga's bump?'

'Exactly the same as last time we spoke. So don't change the subject. Why didn't you tell me about your arrangement with Sharda earlier? What happened to our 'honest and open' deal?'

'Nothing's happened to it. I didn't tell you because there's nothing to tell – and I didn't want to worry you. Besides... I thought the arrangement would only be temporary. Until the police caught whoever killed her brother. But they're taking so long...'

'How long exactly?' Zuri frowned. 'How long has she been living with you?'

'She's not living with me. She's my tenant, just like Mike was.'

'Mmm. I think you're splitting hairs a bit there Mark. So how long?'

'Not sure. A couple of months, give or take.'

'Two months eh.' Zuri frowned again. 'When you said you didn't want to worry me – what about? That you'll get caught up in the threats to her? Or that you and her will start sleeping together?'

'The threats of course. Why would you worry about the other? You never have before.'

'Because your bed-mates have always been anonymous before. Part of your other life. Just like my bed-mates have been to you. But Sharda... She's supposed to be coming here, isn't she? To do a PhD? How would that work?'

'Not a problem. She's the marrying kind – and only to another Sikh at that. This virginity business actually means something to her. Even if she were secretly lusting after me, she wouldn't do anything about it. I doubt she'd even know where to start. Between you and me, I think she's led a fairly cloistered and cosseted life.'

'Cloistered and cosseted? And you expect her to cope with doing a PhD here?' She waved away flies that were buzzing round her face.

'I know what you're saying. She's a really good student, works really hard, but... Cope in the Kalahari? With us? I don't know. That does worry me.'

'Then isn't the kindest thing to tell her? Now – rather than later? Oh... Just a moment...' Zuri turned away from the camera and spoke to somebody. 'Sorry Mark. I've got to go. One of the builders wants to ask me something about laboratory fitments before it gets dark. You should see the place. It's really coming on. They've done a great job. It might even be finished by the time you visit at Christmas.' Her big smile seemed to fill the screen. 'So... Speak soon, yes? I'm going to be out of camp for a few days with Fredrik – North Dune – but I'll let you know when I'm back.'

We said our goodbyes and I ended the video call. Then for a few moments I simply sat where I was and mulled over the conversation – until startled by a noise behind me. I swung round on my chair. 'Sharda…'

She was on the way from her bedroom to the kitchen and for a moment I thought she wasn't going to speak to me – but she did. 'Sikh Soc was cancelled. The lecturer's car broke down on the M25. I am guessing you did not know I was here.'

***

For the next two days and evenings I hardly saw Sharda. Any conversations we had were brief and on her part monosyllabic. Against my advice she travelled alone to and from the university, avoided my laboratory by day and mainly stayed locked in her bedroom at night.

On the third evening I went to read in the lounge, a bottle of wine by my side. But I couldn't concentrate and couldn't settle. I had to knock on Sharda's door.

'Yes?'

'Can I come in?'

'If you must.' She was sitting on the bed, reading something on her lap-top. 'Well? What do you wish to say? Because you can see… I am very busy.' It was the first time I had seen her in a dressing gown; in fact the first time I had seen her less than completely dressed. 'I have two essays to do by the weekend – and much to read in preparation.'

'At least take a break and eat something. You're going to fade away at this rate.'

'I have no time. So… What is it you want?'

I hesitated. 'I was hoping you'd tell me about this impossible DNA at last. It sounds important. Something I should know about. But… If you're busy.'

She didn't look up from her screen. 'Yes, this DNA is important. Very important. But I dare not tell you the details now in case you decide my work in the laboratory is bad. Maybe use it as more evidence that I am no good to work with you in the Kalahari. You already think I am too 'cosseted'. Too 'cloistered'. Maybe you will also think I am too careless.'

'Sharda... This is stupid. Look... I am truly sorry you heard me say those things to Zuri.'

'You are sorry? Huh. I am sorry. Sorry to know the things that you have been thinking about me. Now shall I tell you what I think?' She made eye-contact for the first time. 'I think that you only offered me a PhD all those months ago because at the time you needed the money from my father. I also think that once Cameron Cruickshank started funding your research so generously you began to regret the offer you made to me and have already decided to withdraw it. You just have not found the courage to tell me yet.'

Thrown by the atom of truth in her accusation, I delayed too long to contradict her.

'Of course, there is another possibility,' she continued.

'Which is... ?'

'That all of your apparent kindnesses and now this sudden threat to take away what you know is so important to me are no more than a plan to get me to have sex with you. If so then let me tell you... You are wasting your time. At least that much of what you told Zuri was true.' She turned her attention back to her laptop. 'Now leave please. I wish to dress and then I wish to work. It is even more imperative now that I get a First Class Degree. Then maybe some other person will offer me a PhD. Somebody who wants me because I am a good student – not because I am 'pretty' and 'sexy' and my father has money.'

***

It was Friday night and I had just begun cooking when Sharda came into the kitchen. It was the first time she had approached me since overhearing my conversation with Zuri. She told me to hold out my hand

'Why?'

'Just do this for me please.'

When I obliged, she held her fist above my palm.

'What is it?'

She didn't answer, just dropped something. A large hairy spider fell on to my fingers, jumped on to the floor, then raced through the door to the lounge. It was a *Tegenaria* – the giant house spider – the largest and fastest species found in England and the size of a child's hand. 'He has been in my bedroom for days,' she said. 'Looking for females I think. He and I are good friends.'

She left the kitchen but I followed her. 'Sharda...'

'Yes?'

'What was all that about?'

Her sigh was angry. 'Tell me Mark... Have you ever been to the Punjab? And I do not mean Lahore, I mean the true Punjab.'

I shook my head.

'As I thought.' She tossed her head and pushed her hair back over one shoulder so that she could eye me. 'Listen... You told Zuri I have been 'cosseted' and – yes – in recent years this is true, I admit it. Since I became a woman, my life has been easy. Plenty of money. Plenty of comfort. But let me tell you... My family, it has not always been rich.

I have not always lived in a big house in Lahore like you think.'

'So where? Tell me! I really would like to know. Whenever I've asked you about your childhood you've just been evasive.'

'I know. And I am sorry. But... .....' She began fiddling with her hair. 'OK, I have made a big decision. My father would be angry with me for it but I am going to tell you. When I was a small child my father was just a poor farmer, growing mainly rice. The fields were very hot in summer. And dangerous too. Not just snakes and spiders, but leopards as well. I saw many when I was young. Then there was the hunger, the diseases... Many children died, even some of my friends.'

'Sharda... Why...'

'No, please. Let me finish. I know how I must appear to you on the outside – but I promise you Mark, on the inside there is still a tough little girl from the rice fields. And this little girl, she has no fear of the Kalahari. She can cope with anything this desert can throw at her. Believe me, I am far more frightened here, right now, in London than I ever would be in your research station.' She made to turn and leave but stopped. 'No. One more thing. What was that other word you used to Zuri? Cloistered? You are so wrong over this too. Just because I am a virgin... Just because I do not use sex to manipulate you like another girl might... It does not mean... Look... When I was a child my bath was the river and my toilet the fields. Not only that, but at night I had to share a bed with my cousins and Mazher, even sometimes in the same room as my uncle and his wife. This is not being cloistered I think. There is nothing people do in the name of nature that I have not witnessed. Nothing you can say, or do, or show me that would shock or even surprise me.'

'Sharda... Why the hell didn't you tell me all of this earlier?'

'For the same reason that I should not be telling you now. My father, he is a very proud man. He ordered Mazher and me not to tell the rich people in England that he was once a poor farmer. That his children once had to live this way. And when my father gives an order, I obey him – but through love, not fear.'

'So why disobey him now?'

'Oh, you know the reason I think.'

'I'm not sure that I do.'

She paused at her bedroom door with her hand resting on the handle. 'Oh yes. For sure. You know the reason. I just hope that my disobedience has been effective, because there is no other means I am prepared to use to influence you.'

***

Sharda had dressed-up for the meal: a vivid red sari embroidered with gold filigree; and a great deal of jewellery. But 'for comfort' she had nothing on her feet. She didn't seem to care that I was as scruffy as ever. We were after all only sitting at our kitchen table and sharing the vegetable curry I had cooked earlier.

'When I was ten my father and his many brothers formed a company to supply ingredients to the curry houses of the West. There was rice, of course, but also spices and vegetables and – oh, everything you can think of. Many Punjabi families made their fortune this way and happily mine was one of them. So when I was fifteen, my family moved to Lahore and my father paid for me and Mazher to go to a big expensive school. Not just to study, but to learn how to behave in England. Etiquette, you know. I am a very lucky girl to have such a father. Very lucky to have been given such an education.'

'No other brothers or sisters then? Just you and Mazher?'

Her chewing slowed, becoming hesitant. Then she put down her fork and took a sip of water. 'Mark... I wish to tell you something. Something else my father...' She took another sip of water. 'There was a sister. Roopjot. Much older than me and Mazher. She died.'

'Oh. I'm sorry. What happened?'

'Well... Actually... I have been wishing to tell you this story for a long time. You remember Mia? How she told you that she never had sex with anybody but her husband, yet her baby came out coloured? Something very similar happened to my sister. At least, so people tell me – I was only two at the time. In the case of my sister, the baby – a girl – was born nearly white. You can imagine the problems this created for my family, but the doctor was very kind. He told people that the colour of the baby meant nothing, that it was probably just a simple mutation. Not albino exactly, but something like that. Is this possible?'

I shrugged.

'Ah well. But my brother-in-law, he refused to accept that the child was his, even though my sister swore to him on her life that she never had sex with another man. She begged him not to shame her. But my brother-in-law, he would not listen. He told people that my sister was a prostitute. He was, and still is, a very unpleasant man.'

'Was there a paternity test?'

'1992? The Punjab?'

'I guess not.'

'Maybe if such a test had existed then all the terrible things...' She stopped in mid-sentence.

'What things?'

Well... ...... OK. But you must promise... My father must never know that I told you this thing.'

'Of course. I promise.'

'My sister – she was only eighteen. She took the baby to a railway bridge and together... Well... They fell in front of a train. And only one month later my mother also...' She fixed my eyes with hers. 'You understand Mark – there are some things that my family can never admit to the world.'

***

'Lion sperm... Can they fly?' Now bright-eyed and mischievous, Sharda was lounging elegantly on the settee and nibbling a shortbread biscuit with her coffee. Opposite her I was sprawled in a chair, bottle of wine on the floor with just the dregs to be finished.

'God, I hope not. Why?'

Before answering, she picked crumbs one at a time from her sari and ate them. 'Because if they cannot fly, something is very wrong with the data you are collecting in the Kalahari.'

'Go on.'

'The blood of the cub that I profiled earlier in the week... The DNA matched with that of the mother on your database, no problem. And I can also find the DNA of the father on your database. No problem there, either.'

'So... What is the problem?'

'This lion and lioness... If we believe the records you have of their movements... They never met. They never even came close, not by many kilometres. Yet they produced this cub. I am very confused.'

I was just daring myself to ask if she really had double-checked everything when a mobile phone began to ring. Sharda sprang off the settee and ran to her bedroom, but when she reappeared a few minutes later she was moving slowly with a bewildered look on her face. 'What's the matter?' I asked. 'Who was it?'

'The police. They have caught the murderers of my brother. Two young men. They caught them breaking into a house in Bloomsbury. Their DNA matches that under the fingernails of Mazher.'

'But that's good, isn't it? You can feel safe again. Why the face?'

'Because – according to the policeman on the phone – these two young men are from a gang of "white yobs". "Crack-heads." But that makes no sense Mark. I mean – yes, of course... Such men could kill Mazher in the street. The wrong look with the eye and these men can kill anybody I think. But to threaten my father in Lahore? Or me? That note I received – it cannot be written by these same people. Can it?'

Chapter 16

The monstrous Baobab tree a hundred metres from the camp had never flowered as late as December before. But on the morning I arrived from England the occasional pendulous bloom was still parachuting to the ground beneath. The white sand around my feet, sparkling with quartzite, was littered with the flowers' fleshy browning remains, tainting the air with their rotting smell. It was midday and save for the occasional soft 'plop' as another bloom hit the ground Inga and I were surrounded by silence. We were sitting on rocks in the tree's shade and Inga was holding open her sarong so that I could watch her belly move.

'There! See? Is that incredible or what? I really thought this was never going to happen to me.'

'I know. But as it has, don't you think you should start looking after yourself a bit more. I hear you're still drinking loads – and you've started smoking again.'

'Difficult to deny,' she said, taking a draw on the cigarette in her hand. 'But don't you start on me as well. I get enough flack from Zuri.'

'At least go to an ante-natal clinic somewhere. Get Fredrik to fly you to Gaborone.'

'Fredrik? No chance – and there's no need anyway. What Annakiya and I between us don't know about having babies isn't worth knowing.'

She stood to rearrange and retie her sarong while I looked around at the surrounding wilderness, all open woodland with small glades and clearings, everywhere shimmering with heat.

'So Fredrik's still not showing any interest in the baby then?'

'Interest? No. He's stopped banging on about not being the father but... I don't know... He's not exactly the excited and supportive father-to-be I was hoping for.'

'Well... Don't fret. I'm sure he'll change once it's born.'

About fifty metres away the brown waist-high grass in the nearest clearing began to sway in the breeze and we both watched as if mesmerised. From time to time, Inga took further contented drags on her cigarette. 'So what do we make of this mysterious conception then?' she eventually said before adding with a laugh: 'I mean this lioness, not me.'

'No idea. At first I thought Sharda had just mis-catalogued something but...'

Fredrik had checked and re-checked all the records but if there was a mistake anywhere it wasn't obvious. According to our data, the mother of this enigmatic cub had never been nearer to the father than twenty kilometres. And even that approach was only brief on a night that the female left her pride to – or so we guessed – visit nomads before quickly returning to her own males.

'Well... I think Sharda's right,' said Inga with a grin.

'In what way?'

'Lion sperm can fly.' We both smiled. 'Actually, I half-thought you'd bring her with you. Check out whether she really can cope with this place.'

'I was going to, but she's had to go back to Lahore this holiday. Her father's had another heart scare. Maybe at Easter.'

Inga threw down the butt end of her cigarette, covered it with sand, and trod it deep with her bare foot. We set off back for the compound.

'How are you getting on with the two pilots?' I asked.

'Oh, they're OK. Just never around: Zimbabwe – here – Maun – Ghanzi – Windhoek – here – Zimbabwe. The plane's backwards and forwards like a pendulum and hardly ever here for lion work. God knows what they're doing. Fredrik's really pissed off about it all.'

***

'I need to talk to you about Fredrik,' said Zuri. We were in bed early to be alone but through habit she was still whispering, her words scarcely audible above the whirring of the ceiling fan. Swirls of air were making the mosquito net quiver in the faint moonlight and beyond our muslin cocoon the dormitory was all dark shadows and silver highlights.

'What about him?'

'Every week or so he asks me to run another sample of his through the machine.'

'And?' We were lying side-by-side on top of the bed, our slippery skin radiating heat.

'Zero, every time.'

'I've said it before, but it only takes one.'

'That's what I keep telling him, but he's gone very strange about it all. You know? As if he doesn't care any more.'

'His way of handling it I suppose. The sooner that baby's born the better. Put a stop to all this.'

She turned on to her side and placed her hand on my stomach. 'But there's something else. Mark... I couldn't decide whether to tell you or not – but he's started coming on to me. Nothing major until that trip to North Dune we made together. You know, just looks, touches, innuendos, that sort of thing.'

'And at North Dune?'

'He started going on about how you and Inga have made fools of him and me. That the baby's got to be yours; you and Inga are just laughing at us; we should give you a taste of your own medicine.'

'And did you?'

She patted my midriff. 'Mark... You and Inga...'

'For Christ's sake Zuri. How many more times? We all agreed, didn't we? The only way the four of us could work together...'

The dormitory door opened and Fredrik staggered in.

***

An unfamiliar jeep painted in government-issue blue drove into the camp and pulled up in the centre of the compound. Two burly Tswana men got out and surveyed the scene. After spotting Nick and myself under the four young Mopane trees near the dormitory they swaggered over. Apart from black boots and silver pistols, holstered at the waist, they were dressed in shades of blue. 'Rangers or police?' I asked Nick quietly.

'Police. Those the two that took away Seretse.'

'You! Where the new owner?' one of the men asked me, his eyes bulging and bloodshot. He took off his peaked dark-blue cap to wipe sweat from his brow with the back of his hand.

'Owner?'

'The name by the gate.'

'He's abroad.'

'Then who in charge?'

'What can I do for you?'

'Name?

'De Vries. Doctor de Vries.'

'Doctor? That supposed to impress me? Well it don't.'
All the time, the two visitors were looking around at the
camp, apparently taking in everything and everybody.

'You asked my name and I gave it to you. Why are
you here?'

'We want to see the two pilots who work here.'

'They're in Belgium.'

'Shit.' The pair exchanged a few words in Setswana,
then the quiet one ambled off towards the grass huts beyond
the building work.

'Where's he going?'

'Look round.'

'And what if we object?'

'Then that mean you got something to hide. You got
something to hide?'

'No! What are you looking for?'

'Many things, including bushmen – like him. What he
doing here?'

'He works here. He's our tracker. And he can speak
for himself.'

'Enough to lie to us, ja, Masarwa? Which resettlement
camp you from?

'I'm a Ganakwe. Don't call me Masarwa.'

'I call you shit if I want. Ganakwe, eh? So you lived
in the Central Kalahari area. I ask you again. Which
resettlement camp?'

'New Xade.'

'And when you going back?'

'Never.'

'What's this about?' I interrupted. 'There's nothing
illegal about Nick being here.'

'Depends what he doing. All the time Ganakwe
sneaking away from resettlement camps and going back to

their old way of life. Now that illegal. We hear there some bands around here. Keep crossing to Game Reserve and poaching.'

'Poaching! How can we poach on our own land?'

'Not your land any more Masarwa. Why you naked?'

'I'm a bushman.'

'Where's your xai? Your loincloth?'

'I know what a xai is, and I don't wear one. I'm a true bushman, like in our cave paintings. Missionaries force the xai on us.'

'Huh. One for tradition, ja? Enough to want the old life back? Where your wife? Your children?'

'I don't have any.'

'Not surprised. Shit like you.'

The other policeman sauntered back from his walk round the camp, and again the two men exchanged a few words in Setswana before addressing me. 'There a lot going on here. A shit load of money being spent.'

'We're a successful research centre.'

'Successful, ja? Then you need protection. Lucky for you we stopped by. Me and my brother here, we give shit-hot protection. Place in Namibia just like this get attacked by robbers while ago. Take everything.'

'Nothing like that could happen here. There are too many people around.'

He laughed. 'That just what the boss man before you said, just before he disappeared.' He gave Nick a disdainful look before addressing me again. 'We going. But don't think we forget you. We come back when the two pilots here. Explain our terms of business to them.'

***

'Bad news,' I announced to those in the office.

'What now?'

'An e-mail from Cruickshank's secretary. I've been invited to a New Year's banquet. Cruickshank's taken over the top floor of some posh London hotel for the night.'

'What's bad about that?'

'What do you think? It probably means he's got his knighthood.'

Chapter 17

Just a taxi this time, not a Rolls Royce, but at least the journey was still at Cruickshank's expense. 'London is so dark and without colour after Lahore,' said Sharda, gazing through the window at the sodden streets. 'And for you too I think, after Africa.'

I nodded. 'How was your flight? I didn't hear you come in.'

'Tiring. And I am still very tired. Already it is the new year in Lahore. And I am worried. My father looked very sad and ill when I left.'

'So why did you leave? Why not stay with your father a few more days?'

'My father insisted. "A daughter of mine invited to such an event? It is such an honour. You must go, Sharda. Of course you must go."' There was a puzzled look on her face. 'But why did I receive the invitation Mark? I mean me, personally, not as your friend? Do you know? And why did the invitation say I must wear my sari again?'

***

We were separated from the beginning. When we checked in at the hotel that Cruickshank had taken over for the night we found that our rooms were floors apart. And our seats for the banquet were also as far apart as they could be. Sharda was next to Dominic on Cruickshank's large top table. I was at the opposite end of the dining hall seated next to Sarah, the woman who ran the *Elite Escort Agency* – and she was far from happy. 'Look at the bitch. She's Mia all over again.'

'Who is she?'

'Who is she? She's a money-grabbing bimbo. A social-climbing wannabe-a-Lady slut, that's who she is. The Caribbean at Easter – Cameron's going to announce it tonight. You should see the size of the diamond in that ring. Well he needn't think I'm going to organise this one for him. He didn't even tell me until an hour ago. Look at the pair of them. She's nearly thirty years younger than him.'

'No, I mean: who is she?'

A quiet laugh escaped Sarah's bright red lips, producing bubbles in the sherry she was sipping. 'Who? Oh my God... You must be the only man in England.' Her pale blue eyes struggled to focus as she peered at me. 'But I'd forgotten. Not exactly a fashionista are you Dr de Vries? Nor a soap addict I wager.'

'You wager right. And it's Mark, please.'

'And may I say – Mark – you're looking very tasty tonight. Properly dressed I'm pleased to see. No shorts and flip-flops nonsense.'

'What's the difference,' I asked, nodding in Cruickshank's direction, 'between my shorts, and his kilt?'

Sarah slid her hand under the table and patted my thigh. 'The difference, my dear Doctor Mark, is that your shorts do not proclaim to the world your membership of Clan Stewart of Atholl. They do not say that you can trace your ancestry back to the fourteenth century and the notorious Earl of Buchan.' She patted my thigh again. 'Who, just in case your Scottish history is a bit thin, is nicknamed 'The Wolf of Badenoch.' Remember that name. Cameron models himself on that man.' She drained her glass. 'Besides which your shorts were both baggy and grubby and not at all sexy.' She leaned towards me as if to share a confidence. 'Though I must say I did think that you had very sexy feet.' And with her face close to mine and her eyes open wide she whispered, 'I like feet, even if they're dirty. In fact, just between you and me, especially if they're dirty.'

The fish course came and went, and so did the entrée. All around me I could hear the monotonous drone of self-righteous and self-congratulatory conversation. From time to time I tried to catch Sharda's distant attention and when I succeeded we exchanged a smile.

'Why was Sharda condemned to the top table?' I asked Sarah during a lull in her flirting with the journalist to her left.

'Ah, your pretty Sikh student. Do you really not know? Watch Cameron. See how often he sneaks a glance at her. She left quite an impression last time he saw her.... ...... Are you shocked? Don't be. Wolf of Badenoch. Look him up.' And she returned to flirting with her journalist.

***

We were half-way through the meat-course before I regained Sarah's attention. 'Tell me,' I said, 'I'm intrigued. Where does a woman who runs something like the *Elite Escort Agency* fit into a set-up like Cruickshank's?'

A waiter topped-up Sarah's wine-glass and she picked it up immediately. 'Power,' she slurred, her head swaying slightly as she tried to focus on me while finding her mouth with her glass. 'Look around Roger...'

'Mark,' I corrected her.

She thought for a second then giggled. 'Oops, sorry. He's Roger.' Wine slopped on to her roasted boneless pigeon as she used her glass to gesture towards the journalist.

'"Power"? How?'

'Look, learn and admire. I'll wager there's not a man in this room who isn't in some way in Cameron's pocket, as indeed are you, my very roguishly handsome Mark de Vries with the sexy feet.' Her hand went under the table on to my thigh again. 'And in many cases it's because at some time or other they've been just a teensy-weensy bit naughty with one – or even several – of my girls. Their constituents, or wives, or even their mistresses, would definitely not approve. Knowledge, you see. Power. I'm a very important person to Cameron. My presence at these little social occasions of his is always a subtle reminder to them all of how much he knows about them.'

'I'm sure it is – and you are.' I filled a fork with pigeon meat plus a generous helping of quince jelly. 'And what about Cameron? Has he ever been "naughty" with one or several of your girls?'

'Oh, ho. And wouldn't you just like to know the ins and outs of that, eh?' – at which she squeezed my quads so hard I winced.

'But if he has… Doesn't that also give you just a little power?'

'Power? Over the Wolf?' Her face clouded then soured as she removed her hand from my leg. 'The Scottish Lochs, Dr de Vries, are very cold and very deep.' And with that, she turned away to talk to Roger again.

***

The food was excellent and from first aperitif to last brandy so were the drinks. But there was a price to be paid: having to endure the pompous announcements of knighthood and engagement; the sycophantic speeches of congratulation; the bad jokes; the toadying toasts. 'You must be the only sober person here,' I said to Sharda once we were released from our torture and allowed to circulate. 'How was the vegetarian menu?'

'Very good, though too bland for my taste. Not enough spices. But at least it was truly vegetarian. Most hotels and restaurants in England do not seem to understand this concept.' She looked around as if checking who might hear. 'Mark… Do you mind? I think I shall go to my room. I am very tired and I cannot talk to these people. All the time I have this urge to be very rude to them.'

A man walked up to us. 'Dr de Vries? Miss Kaur? Sir Cameron would like you to be in this photograph.' And he led us to a corner of the room that had been set up as an informal studio.

'Still trying to establish non-racist credentials?' I said to Cruickshank as Sharda stood one side of him and I stood the other. 'Or is this where you break it to us that now you've got your knighthood your support for our research is finished?'

'Not tonight Boy. I've got more important things on my mind.' And he refused to talk to us further until the photographic session was over. 'Now… I have something to show you Miss Kaur. Come with me.'

'I am sorry Sir Cameron, but do you mind if I do not. My day has been very tiring. I just wish to go to my room.'

'The thing I have to show you is in your room. A gift. Now come with me.'

I moved to go with them. 'Is your name Miss Kaur Boy?' he growled, and more or less closed the double-doors from the dining hall in my face. When I re-opened them to follow anyway, two of Cruickshank's burly henchmen stepped forward and barred my way.

***

Twenty minutes later Cruickshank returned to the dining area alone and beaming went straight to his fiancée. And when

Sharda still failed to appear after what seemed an age I went to check that she was safely in her room. The door was locked but I could hear sounds from inside. I knocked and called to her and when that produced no reply I knocked and called louder until I was hammering and shouting.

Eventually the door was opened. Lit from the corridor Sharda was hunched in her dressing gown, down-turned face smeared with tears and mascara. The room beyond was almost in darkness, illuminated only by the glow of London filtering through the curtains. As I stepped in I reached for the light switch but Sharda stopped my hand and closed the door behind me. By the time my eyes adjusted enough to pick out her dark form she was sitting on the bed, her arms folded across her stomach. She was rocking back and forth and sobbing.

'Cruickshank?' I asked, but she didn't need to answer. 'Right,' I said turning on my heels and heading back to the door. 'This time the bastard's going to pay.'

'No!' she screamed at me.

'What do you mean, "No"?'

She struggled to speak. 'You do not understand.' She was staring up at me, her face in shadow, featureless and black, her breathing convulsive. 'That note... It was from him. What choice did he give me Mark? Because for sure... My virginity is never worth the life of my father.'

'Oh my God. Sharda...'

'That is not all. He told me to start taking the contraceptive pill. The sort that stops my periods. Tonight is not the end of it. This is the meaning of the word "unless".'

Chapter 18

Fredrik's image flickered then returned. 'Wolf of where?'

'Badenoch.'

'Where the fuck is Badenoch?'

'Far north of Scotland. Desolate place, though the deer seem to like it. According to my encyclopaedia the Wolf bit comes from the guy's "notorious cruelty and rapacity." Seems the nickname was posthumous – nobody dared say it when he was alive.'

'And Cruickshank reckons he's descended from him?'

'So I was told. But through one of the Wolf's mistresses. The guy had seven children that he admitted to, but not a single one with his wife.'

On the monitor, Fredrik shrugged. 'It was the fourteenth century. Scotland or Sweden... Didn't every man with money have a mistress or ten in those days?'

'Maybe they did. But they didn't all destroy a city as well. Seems the Wolf thought it would be fun to burn down half of Elgin – Cathedral included.'

'And you reckon Cruickshank's modelling himself on this guy.'

'Who knows, but at the moment he's sure as hell destroying Sharda. Once a week he sends her a text ordering her to some hotel room or other.'

'And what does he do? Just screw her? I mean... Does he beat her up as well? Is he a perv?'

'No, just the sex. So far, anyway. All she has to do is be lying there naked when he arrives, get in whatever position he wants that day – though it's usually doggy-style; he calls her his dog-bitch – and let him just do it. Then he leaves.'

'Bastard! Surely there's something you can do to stop him?'

'Nothing legal – or that Sharda will risk. Sounds crazy but he's got us totally stitched. He's told her that if anybody does anything he doesn't like – you know, like killing him or trying to have him arrested – his men have a list of orders and hefty incentives to carry them out whatever. And the more angry he is, the worse the recriminations. And I have to tell you... We're on that list Fredrik.'

'Whoa... Wait a minute. We? I thought it was her father he was threatening to kill if she didn't behave.'

'It is. First her father, then her: large white van; note pinned to her chest just like her brother; that sort of thing. He's scared her shitless. But after her father and her, it's us, depending on what he thinks is appropriate: cut our funding; give the camp-site the Elgin treatment; kill one or all of us.'

'And how the hell would he do all that from there?'

'Don't ask me... But if he can send in a gang of builders, he can send in a demolition gang. Believe me, I've had nightmares. And what about those two pilots? They work for him. Could they be assassin material?' Fredrik looked stunned as I continued. 'He's got us all exactly where he wants us. And it's Sharda who's paying for it. She's going through hell, and it's partly for us.'

'Christ, try and make me feel guilty why don't you? I don't even know this woman. I mean is it so bad? All she's doing is having sex once a week. Is that so awful? She can manage that until he gets fed up with her can't she?'

'It's rape, Fredrik, you heartless bastard. He may not be hitting her but he's abusing her, humiliating her, harming her mentally. She's practically suicidal. She's started saying that for the first time in her life she can understand how her sister and mother must have felt before they killed themselves. You remember? I told you about them. But Cruickshank's actually told Sharda... If she gets out of their 'arrangement' by topping herself, the very next day her father gets tortured and killed. And soon after that it's our turn.'

***

It was six-thirty in the evening and I should have been in a Board meeting at the university, sleeping through *Any Other Business*. But always determined to be in the apartment when Sharda returned from an afternoon with Cruickshank I had made my excuses.

Kneeling by the bath I adjusted the mixer tap and swirled around the water until the temperature was about right and the suds thick and scented. Then I went to fetch Sharda from our bedroom. She was sitting on the edge of her bed looking pained and drawn but at least no longer crying. 'Bath's ready.'

She hauled herself up and pulled her robe tight around her.

'Your usual?' I asked.

'How else will I sleep.'

In the kitchen the clothes she had worn that afternoon were spilling out from the waste bin where she had thrown them, never to be worn again. I pushed them in properly, out of sight, then collected a jug of ice and a bottle of Jack Daniels. Stretched out in the bathwater, her body hidden by foam, Sharda reached up for her drink and immediately took a large swig. Condensation formed on the outside of the cold glass.

'Try not to think about it,' I said. 'You're still you.'

'No. You are wrong. This person is not Sharda. She cannot even call herself a Sikh. The real Sharda is dead. Murdered.'

'Will it help if I say that today's... I mean, I know how important it was to you but... It will all grow again? And at least it won't show? Nobody will know?'

'But I will know – and you will see.'

Today's abuse was the latest in a deliberate campaign by Cruickshank to strip Sharda of her Sikh-ness; in his taunts her 'sickness'. Not only had he taken away her virginity at the New Year and her body hair today but he had also ended her teetotalism. She was too tense he said on their third meeting. She needed to relax more. But although the first time he had to virtually force drink down her, once alcohol had passed her lips... Once she could no longer pride herself on being truly teetotal... Once she discovered that alcohol really did help her to cope... She not only began drinking from the mini-bar in the hotel room before he arrived but also continued to drink when she returned home. It helped her to forget, she said, and helped her to sleep. But I could see all too well that it wasn't helping her state of mind. 'Shall I cook us something?' I offered, but I knew what she would say.

After another gulp of her drink she rested her head back on the rim of the bath and with her hair trailing in the water looked up at me. 'No, don't leave me, please. Talk to me, like you always do. Keep the demons from my head. It really helps.'

I perched on the bathroom stool and took a sip of my own drink. 'OK. So... What? Did he hurt you when he shaved you? What sort of razor did he use?'

'The sort that women use. Very pink. But he did not shave me. He gave me the choice – and I chose to shave myself while he watched. But now I wonder: would I have felt less guilty if... ?'

'Guilty! You were being forced. Either way, you had no choice.'

'But I could have resisted more, not just beg and cry.' She took another gulp of her drink. 'That hair was of such meaning to me, to the person I was, yet I gave it up without even a fight.'

'Sharda... You couldn't fight. And it will grow again. You mustn't feel guilty.'

Again she drank, her glass already nearly empty. 'But I always feel guilty. He rapes me, he humiliates me – and then I feel guilty, as if somehow... But you know this. And today... In the taxi on the way home... If I had not known that you would be here for me...' She emptied her glass and handed it to me to pour her a second drink. 'Please Mark...' she continued after I obliged. 'Tell me that one day I shall be free of this man. I like to hear this, even if it is not true.'

I did my best. 'You will be free of him Sharda, I promise. One day. Maybe you already are.' It was possible: Cruickshank was leaving for the Caribbean at the weekend in preparation for his Easter marriage and long honeymoon.

The bathwater rippled as she shook her head. 'A good try. But I know you do not really believe it. The first Wolf was married, but he had mistresses...'

'Yes, but to give him children. Cruickshank made you go on the pill. That means he's not modelling himself that exactly.'

'And do you know why he made me go on the pill? Because this Wolf thinks that a Sikh woman is not fit to produce a child for him. She is fit only for sex, only to be used.'

I wasn't doing very well at keeping the "demons" from her head. 'At least cling on to the Kalahari. Your PhD. You'll be free of him there. Three years at least.'

'But he must know this. So many people give him information. I think he is playing with me. Letting me build up my hopes. Then one day, when it will hurt me the most, he will tell me that I cannot go.' She finished her second whiskey, emptied the ice-dregs into her bathwater, and held out the glass for me to fill from the bottle. 'No ice this time,' she said.

Did she realise? I wondered as I filled her glass. Surely she must. Cruickshank's demolition of her life was already stretching further than body hair, teetotalism and virginity. Since the New Year her degree marks had plummeted; many of my departmental colleagues had noticed and passed comment. Even if Cruickshank intended to let her take up a PhD in the Kalahari, she was no longer guaranteed the First that her father insisted upon to support her.

A spiritless expression that I knew well suddenly settled like a mask on her face. 'Sharda... Stop it! Now!'

'Why Mark? Why stop? This humiliation... I cannot stand it much more, I really can't. Not even for my father. If this man returns... If he stops me from going to the Kalahari...' In one long gulp she finished her third glass.

***

I lifted her from the settee, carried her to her bed and made her comfortable. Then I crossed our bedroom and got into my own bed. But I slept only lightly, forever alert for sounds of her being sick in her sleep, even of choking as had happened once before.

At about four in the morning she staggered zombie-like in near-darkness to our en-suite bathroom. Still I listened, waiting for the flushing toilet, the rustling packet of pain-killers, the gushing tap, then the clicking light-pull and the creaking door as she returned to bed – except she didn't. After waiting as long as I dared I pushed open the bathroom door; all locks and bolts removed. She was standing hunched and sobbing over the sink, her long black hair falling forward, the brown skin of her back, buttocks and legs looking almost orange in the fluorescent light. She must have seen me in the mirror because she didn't flinch when I placed my hands on her shoulders. I turned her round, wiped away her tears and led her back to bed – mine, not hers – where she cried herself to sleep on my chest.

When I woke, stirred by the March sun shining through the window, Sharda was still asleep but no longer in my arms. Lying on her back with her head turned away from me, her hair splayed over the pillow, duvet pushed down to her waist, she looked momentarily at peace. I did my best not to wake her as I left the room.

After the kettle boiled and the microwave whirred, I carried a tray of two black coffees, orange juices and croissants to the bedroom then climbed back into bed. Sharda stirred, opened her eyes, stretched and groaned, then managed a weak smile. 'Thank you,' she murmured.

'It's the least I can do. Now try and eat something. You're wasting away. Your ribs are beginning to show. Your hip bones too.'

'Maybe after the coffee.'

I propped myself on an elbow and freed a strand of her hair that had stuck to the corner of her mouth. 'You know... Next time you drink yourself comatose it would make my life a lot easier – and I'd get a lot more sleep – if I could put you in this bed in the first place. You always end up here anyway.'

'No. We cannot do that. Sorry.'

'Why not?'

'Because that would be sleeping together.'

'And this way isn't?'

'No, this way is not. This is different. Well... It is to me. Besides – as you said last night – maybe, just maybe, I shall never see that man again.'

I smiled. 'And maybe you won't. OK. Have it your own way. So... How is this morning's hangover?'

She groaned again. 'Very evil.'

I got out of bed once more. 'I'll get you a pain-killer.' But as I was returning from the bathroom a phone rang in the lounge. It was Sharda's mobile. 'Leave it. At least have some breakfast first,' but she ignored me and when she returned to the doorway, phone to ear, she had a worried look on her face. 'Who is it?' I asked.

Standing there she held up her hand to silence me and after a pause began speaking into the phone in Punjabi. Then she let out a wail and sank to her knees on the floor.

Chapter 19

When we first planned our journeys the schedule seemed comfortable – but on the day itself Sharda's *Emirates* flight from Lahore was delayed three hours at Dubai. I was just growing concerned when she virtually sprinted into the Departures Lounge at Frankfurt Airport. Soon after – the plane had to wait for us – we were breathlessly strapping ourselves into seats 26A and B for our *Air Namibia* flight to Windhoek. Sharda had already been in the air thirteen hours that day, and now another ten hours stretched ahead of her.

'So... Yes or no?' I asked, seeing the drinks' trolley begin it's slow journey down the aisle towards us.

'Ohhhh... . Mark... I do not know.' She stared at the trolley as if it were a monster. 'I have not had a drink now for ten days. I cannot return to being a virgin...' – the man in 26C gave her a furtive glance – '... but I can return to not cutting my hair and not drinking alcohol.'

'And will you?'

'Not cutting my hair – for sure. But alcohol? Ohhhh... I do not know. I shall decide in about ten minutes.'

I leaned against her, shoulder-to-shoulder, so that I could speak without 26C overhearing. 'And how is the hair?'

She pushed against me in return. 'Growing nicely. I thank you for asking.'

'You're welcome.' It was good to see her so cheerful. 'So... How was your visit? Your family?' I asked.

'Truly awful. I mean... Not so much the cremation itself. The cremation was how cremations are. I was very sad – as you know – not to see my father alive one more time but... It is OK. I am at peace with this now. But my wider family? I cannot begin to tell you how happy I am to escape from them all. To be with you again. All the time, all those people... They were so very stressful. I have decided. Now that my father is no longer in Lahore, I am never returning.'

'Really? Do you want to talk about it?'

She let out a long sigh. 'Not until I have a glass of wine in my hand.'

***

The trolley still hadn't reached us. 'So what did you decide? Was your father's death natural after all?'

'A heart attack in his sleep? It has to be natural, yes?'

She searched my face, her dark eyes imploring me to say that I also believed his death to be natural, to help her believe that surrendering to the Wolf truly had protected her father long enough for him to escape the man's threats for ever.

I hesitated, wanting to be kind but wrestling with doubts. It seemed such a coincidence, Sharda's father dying on the very day that Cruickshank raped her for perhaps the last time; all too easy to believe that tiring of her body the bastard had found a different way to show his domination of her. I didn't doubt that he was cruel enough – I had only to think of the fate of Mia and her son. But did I really believe that all he had to do, in effect, was click his fingers in London for a sick and sleeping man to be killed far away in Lahore? Was he really that powerful?

'Of course natural. What else? So is this why you're at peace over his death now?'

'In part – but also because of some other thing that you, being you, will not understand. The Sikh belief is that my father will be reborn.'

'And is that your belief too?'

'As a Sikh, of course. With the hope also that this time the spirit of my father will have the blessing of a body with a stronger heart and – when the time comes – much greater fortune with his children.'

I smiled at a memory. 'As a Sikh, yes. But what about as Sharda?'

'Ah... As Sharda...' Her face was still gaunt and her beauty still muted from her three months of suffering. But in returning my smile her eyes shone and her teeth showed as white as ever. 'As Sharda – I believe that this is a very pretty thought.'

***

'Anything from the bar? Madam? Sir?'

We bought four quarter-bottles of Chardonnay, but Sharda's first sip was tentative. 'You asked me about Lahore and why it was so awful. It is mainly this: my family are placing me under great pressure to marry my brother-in-law.' Her glances at me seemed nervous. 'They insist it was the dying wish of my father, but they cannot give me evidence to support this and I really do not believe them. The real reason will be selfish, about money. They are trying to stop me from receiving my inheritance – but nobody is admitting this.'

'Your brother-in-law? But you hate him.'

'And under Sikh custom I have the right to refuse him. But the pressure, it is still there. My family tell me that it is my duty to marry this man, to right the wrongs of my sister, and that I must do it soon, while he is still young.'

'Young? How old is he?'

'He has just reached forty. I have been told to return to Lahore as soon as I have my degree.'

'And will you?'

'I have already told you: no, never.' Her second sip of wine was much longer. 'Mark... I have something else to tell you. While I was in Lahore, while my father was burning, I made a big decision. But, in truth, it was not just mine to make. It affects you as well. And your friends.'

'Go on.'

'The Wolf... He is never raping me again. He will need to kill me first. White van... Deep water... Knife... I do not care. I promised myself... Never again. I thought you should know.'

***

We fell asleep apart, but when we woke to the smell of food Sharda's head was resting on my shoulder. 'Vegetarian Madam?' Once we were eating, Sharda said that she had questions for me.

'What sort of questions?'

'Like... When I was a child, sharing a bed and a bedroom, I – all of us – used to hear my Uncle and Aunt... Well, I am sure you know what I mean. But of course, I was too young then to understand what they were doing.'

'That's not a question.'

'No, I know. But... Would you mind very much if I slept in a tent, not in the dormitory, while I am at the camp?'

'If that's what you prefer. But why? In particular?'

'Oh. No reason. Not in particular.' She went quiet for a while as she wrestled to open a sachet of pepper.

'Only the one?' I asked eventually.

'One?'

'Question.'

'Ah. No. There is another. About Zuri... I know that you and she have an agreement but... Does she know that you and I have shared a bed? That we have seen each other naked? That sometimes I sleep in your arms? I mean... I do not wish to say the wrong thing.'

***

As we stood in the arrivals hall at Windhoek Airport we were immersed in a babble of Bantu, Afrikaans, German and more as people from a whole range of racial and national mixtures greeted each other. But nobody seemed to be there to greet us.

'Dr de Vries? Miss Kaur?' We spun round to be confronted by two men dressed in grubby khaki shirts and long trousers. Both were unshaven – as in being too drunk to bother that day rather than as a fashion statement – and the taller was wearing a dirty green trilby hat. 'I'm Indy,' he said, 'and this is Jake. We've brought the plane for you.'

'Where's Fredrik?'

'Having a baby. Is this your luggage? Shall we go?'

***

Sharda seemed transfixed by the black crucifix of the plane's shadow sliding across the land, first the bushveld of Namibia and – after a pre-arranged immigration at Ghanzi Airport – the grassland and desert of Botswana. At one point she grabbed my arm and pointed to a herd of elephants ambling along a dried-up river bed.

Once we were on the ground and being driven from the landing strip in the jeep she could hardly contain herself. 'I was not expecting so much to be green, even early in April.' Clusters of Mopane trees cast dappled shade on the dusty yellow ground and alternated with lush sunlit meadows. Sharda beamed at me and pointed out a Secretary bird stalking through the long grass. Ten minutes later we were on red sand, driving into the compound to park in the shade of the camp's own Mopane trees. 'The leaves of these trees,' she said. 'They are shaped just like butterflies. Oh...' As she was looking up into a tree-crown she spotted a small black face grinning down at her. Each Mopane tree had two or three Tswana children clambering around in its branches. 'What are they doing?' she asked.

'Collecting caterpillars. Mopane moth. They're a delicacy. Full of protein. We'll be having them roasted tonight... Well, not you I suppose... I hope. Inga's done her best to explain to Annakiya what vegetarian means but...' We all climbed out of the jeep.

Indy picked up our cases. 'The others were in Anna's hut when we left. Things'd only just started so maybe they're still there. Go have a look-see if you like. Jake and me'll take your luggage into your dormitory for you.'

A lot had changed since Christmas. The new laboratory building was finished, so too was the hotel-style double-chalet for visitors which currently it seemed was Jake and Indy's quarters. 'Are you sure I should come with you?' said Sharda as we walked towards the grass huts at the far end of the camp. 'I am a total stranger. Nobody knows me.'

'Of course you should. There's no standing on ceremony here.'

Fredrik appeared in the distance, first stooping out of Annakiya's hut, then striding towards us. Close behind him came Zuri wearing her red and white sarong.

'I can hear a baby crying,' said Sharda.

I paused a second. 'So can I. Hey, Fredrik...' I held out my arms to embrace him. 'Congratulations. Boy or girl?'

He ran the last few steps and before I could even begin to register what was happening he drew back his fist and landed a sledgehammer blow to the side of my head.

Chapter 20

All I could see was a blurred face. Even after blinking several times I couldn't focus. 'God, my head. Where am I?'

'Where do you think? In the bloody dormitory.' It was Inga. 'Must we really have this conversation again Mark? This is the fifth time.' As she held open first one of my eyes then the other to shine in a torch she said: 'You're lucky I'm still here. If I'd any money and anywhere to go I'd have been out of this madhouse this morning.' The light made the pain in my head even worse, so I pushed her hand away. 'You'll live,' she said. 'Though you don't deserve to. It's still just concussion.'

'Concussion?'

'And that's the fifth time I've told you that too. Do you really not remember?'

I closed my eyes and tried to piece together what had happened. 'I heard a baby... Then Fredrik hit me. He did, didn't he? Why?'

'He did hit you, yes – can you blame him? – and you banged your head when you fell. So you remember what happened before you passed out, eh? But not since. Probably just as well. You've had some pretty nasty things said to you over the past day or so. Including by me.'

I opened my eyes enough to squint at her. 'Day or so?' Then I closed them again, suddenly aware of a loud ringing in my ears. 'I've been out a day or so?'

'Well, sort of. You keep waking up, asking the same stupid questions, then going back to sleep and forgetting everything that's been said. Mind you, I have given you a few hefty doses of paracetamol. I was going to give you ibuprofen but then I remembered it can make concussed brains bleed. A close shave, eh? That's what happens when you make me angry and upset.'

I struggled to process what she'd said and may even have dozed for a moment because I returned to alertness with a twitch. 'A day or so! That's crazy. And why did Fredrik hit me like that? Where is everybody anyway?'

'Where do you think? Zuri and Fredrik left as soon as Sharda completed the test. Shame you can't remember what they said to you before they left. It was all very colourful. Can you remember what I said? That was even better.'

'I'm dreaming. I must be. This is some sort of nightmare. What test? And where is Sharda?'

'With Annakiya and the baby, which is where I should be. But – being a doctor comes first I suppose. I'm obliged to make you better before I decide whether to kill you or not. I tell you... As soon as I think you're up to it, you've got a lot of explaining to do to a lot of people. Well, mainly to me.'

I tried to focus on her again but the room began to spin. 'Inga... I think...' As I sat up, she grabbed a bowl and placed it under my chin. Two or three retches later, she gave me some tissue to wipe my mouth, then a glass of water to sip. 'Thanks,' I said, slowly lying back on the bed.

***

It was daylight – and the face gazing down at me was no longer blurred. 'Good morning Mark. And how is your head feeling today?' It was Sharda.

'Better – I think. Maybe no worse than a hangover now.'

'Good!' came a voice from across the dormitory. 'Then maybe I can start shouting at you at last.' Inga was sitting cross-legged on her bed breastfeeding a very tiny, very naked and subtly dark-skinned baby.

Sharda followed my gaze. 'Your son is very beautiful.'

'And very noisy, very hungry and forever wetting himself,' added Inga.

Suddenly in a hurry I struggled out of bed and staggered to the WC in the far corner of the dormitory. 'Absolutely bursting,' I said as I crawled back on to my bed. 'Is that really the first time in two days?'

Sharda laughed and shook her head: 'Not the first time, no. Have you really forgotten my helping you use the bottle?' And when I groaned and said I thought it was a dream she patted my shoulder and added: 'No, no dream.'

Inga crossed the room and perched on the edge of my bed – 'Come on, sit up' – and after detaching the baby from her nipple she handed him to me. 'This seems to be yours. Time you bonded, don't you think?'

Cheek against my chest, the baby immediately started rooting for the nipple he'd just lost and when he didn't find it began to cry. I handed him back. 'Look Inga, I don't want to spoil the moment but he can't be mine, he just can't.'

'But he is your baby,' said Sharda. 'I did the DNA test myself exactly as for the lions at university. This new laboratory of yours is fantastic, by the way. I cannot wait to work here.'

'No. No. It's not possible. You must have made a mistake somehow Sharda.'

Sharda shook her head. 'Fredrik and Zuri watched me do it. They checked every step. This baby is yours Mark, not the baby of Fredrik. There is no doubt.'

'And... Bastard!...' growled Inga, latching the baby back on to her nipple to stop him crying, '... what I want to know is when and how? I assume I was comatose – because I honestly do not remember a single thing about it.'

I was not ready for this; my head was throbbing again. 'Well, all I can say is... If I really did fuck you Inga, I must have been comatose too, because sure as hell I don't remember anything about it either.'

She stared at me as if weighing my words. 'No, you've got to be lying. I can just about believe that I could have sex without remembering. But you... It's not possible – is it?'

Sharda took hold of my hand. 'Mark... Please... Tell Inga how it happened. You should have seen her after the baby was born. She was so upset. So confused. And Fredrik... He was saying so many horrible things to her. She needs to know the truth.'

I tried to clear my head. 'Look, both of you. Hell! What can I say? So... OK... If the evidence is right here in front of us then – I suppose – Inga and I must have had sex. But I promise – on my life – I have absolutely no idea when or how. If I knew, I'd tell you. I'm not lying. Inga... Help me out here. The night you always assumed you conceived... It can't have been then, can it? Not if I'm the father. Think! We met in the desert. We held hands. We walked back. I got into bed with Zuri and you got into bed with Fredrik. I mean... Sure... Zuri was comatose – but we weren't. Nowhere near. Anything that happened that night we'd remember wouldn't we? So if not then... When?'

Inga was still staring at me, clearly still trying to decide whether I was lying. 'I don't know. I've been going crazy these last two days waiting for you to tell me. But if you really can't... How about before that night. Remember? It was the afternoon that Goldman told us your funding was being pulled. The same afternoon Sharda mailed you that Mia and her son had been fished out of the Loch. Zuri was still in Jo'burg. Do you remember?'

'You mean later on that evening? When you, me and Fredrik got completely rat-assed? You crashed out on one of the beds but Fredrik and I never made it off the floor – except he woke up the next morning wedged behind the toilet?'

'That's the one. It's the only night anywhere near the right time that we got in that sort of state. That I can think of, anyway. What about you?'

'I hadn't even remembered that one. But... Now you remind me... No. It can't be. I mean... I can't believe I was capable of even getting up off the floor, never mind... Are you saying that somebody had sex with you that night?'

'The evidence was right there the next morning. But when I asked Fredrik he admitted it, so I never gave it another thought. He said I'd hardly stirred. A sleeping woman turns him on you know. Makes him a right pain sometimes. But – what do you think? – might you have screwed me as well?'

Sharda interrupted. 'Can I say what I am thinking? Do you mind? This night you are both talking about – well – it seems nearly possible. So I think you should both decide that this is when it happened – and then you should give it absolutely no more thought.'

The throb in my head was getting worse. 'The only problem is – according to the pregnancy test – that night was too early? What... One? Two weeks too early? Maybe more. I can't remember.'

A sharp deep pain made me clutch my head and almost whimper.

***

The buildings were blushing in the setting sun when I made my way slowly out of the dormitory. Inga and Sharda were sitting under the distant Baobab tree, so I trudged over the still-warm sand to join them.

'He needs a name,' said Inga without asking how I was. 'A boy was always going to be Nils after Fredrik's grandfather but now... Anyway, Sharda has just suggested we give him a Zulu name instead. Do you know any?'

'Not really – though... According to family lore, my grandfather was called Imbube – which, as it happens, means "the lion." How about that?'

Inga held the baby at arm's length in front of her. He kicked his legs as if he approved. 'Imbube...' She pondered. 'Maybe... I'll think about it.'

I sat on a rock opposite. 'Fredrik won't like it.'

'Fredrik wants nothing to do with him – or me. At least, that's what he said when he left.' Her expression was serious, almost panicked. 'Mark... If Fredrik doesn't come back... You will help, won't you? Me, I mean. If necessary. You know: emotionally; financially. I don't mean as a partner – God, how would that look to Fredrik? I just don't want to feel I'm totally alone in this.'

'Do you really need to ask?'

Sharda reached out for the baby, then cradled him. She was wearing a sarong; the first time as far as I could recall. But unlike Inga who – unless we had European visitors – always wore hers tied round the waist like the Tswana women, Sharda was wearing hers tied under the arms, which really confused the baby when he started rooting. I couldn't even begin to disentangle the knot of emotions I was experiencing in the company of these two women and my unexpected son. But there was one thing that I had to unravel.

'Look... Inga... What happened when Fredrik and Zuri left here yesterday. Fredrik storming off I can understand, but not Zuri. I can't believe she would just leave like that. Not without hearing what I had to say. Not before knowing I was OK.'

'But she didn't. She had a long conversation with you. I was there – in one hell of a state I might add but at least I was there, trying to make sure Fredrik didn't kill you and that you didn't just die on us anyway. Sharda was there too. I'm afraid I told everybody you were fine – because I thought you were. I didn't realise then how much you were going to deteriorate.'

'When was this conversation?'

'While we were waiting for the test results to develop.' She took a deep breath. 'You've got to understand Mark. The baby was a real shock to us all. I mean, the moment he came out it was fairly obvious you were the father. He wasn't dark enough to be one of the Tswana's – and he certainly wasn't light enough to be Fredrik's. And you know Fredrik. Sod waiting for a paternity test as far as he was concerned – he just wanted to kill the pair of us there and then. He refused to speak to me – just swore and shouted – and... Well... You know what he did to you.'

'And Zuri?'

'Well, she was upset – of course she was. With both of us – but mainly you. But to give her credit... Unlike Fredrik she was at least prepared to give you chance to admit what you'd done. To say when and how. To apologise to us all for lying. And if you had... Maybe... Anyway, what's the point? You didn't. And the more you denied it and got angry with her for not believing you, the more upset and angry she got. I must say... By the end, you and she were saying some pretty shitty things to each other. So when the paternity test proved that as far as she was concerned you'd not only lied but kept on lying – she just hooked up with Fredrik and left. She didn't want to talk to you again.'

'Also...' said Sharda. 'I am sorry Mark, but Zuri thinks that you lied about me too. She asked me and... I did tell her. All we have ever done is share a bed. But... I do not think she believed me.'

I turned back to Inga. 'Did Zuri say what she was planning to do?'

'Stay in Jo'burg to write up her PhD thesis, then see if she can transfer her post-doc to either the Serengeti or that lion research centre in Namibia. As for Fredrik... God knows what he's going to do. Look... I tell you Mark... This is such a bloody mess. It's a good job I'm prepared to believe you: that this isn't all a result of you raping me while I was out of my head – because rape is what it would be. Otherwise, at this moment, I would be a very bitter and angry woman. I'm not too far away from it as it is.'

'No... This is crazy. None of this should be happening.' I stood. 'I need to speak to Zuri. She's being stupid. She can't start over somewhere else. Not just because of this. I'll phone her. No. I'll fly to Jo'burg. Face to face. Explain everything.'

Inga shook her head. 'Mark... Bad idea. You can't even explain things to yourself. Look... First, Zuri won't want to talk to you. Not yet, anyway. Secondly, there's a good chance Fredrik will be with her. Thirdly, you should rest for a few more days before you do anything too stressful. And thirdly...'

'Fourthly.'

'What?'

'Fourthly. This is the fourth...'

'Mark... Who the hell is counting. Under absolutely no circumstances should you fly a plane for at least two more weeks.'

'Two more weeks! Sharda and I have to be back in London before then.'

'Then get Indy to fly you to Jo'burg – but not until I say you're well enough to cope. OK?'

I started to walk away, but Inga called after me.

'What?' I snapped.

'Back to bed Mark. Promise?'

'Yeah, yeah,' and staggering a little I went in search of Indy.

Chapter 21

A major dried-up river bed snaked like a pale scar across the landscape. 'Is that the Shashe or Thuli?' I asked into my headset from the back seat. I felt more than capable, but Indy and Jake were flying the plane.

'Shashe.'

'So we're over Zimbabwe now?'

No answer.

I had waited a week before finally dismissing Inga's warnings. A week in which Zuri ignored all my calls and messages. And even now I was not heading straight to Johannesburg. Indy had claimed the plane's tyres needed replacing. Also – as he had growled through gritted teeth – my "unscheduled" four hundred mile flight had messed up his fuel calculations.

Tuli International Airport is tiny with a dirt runway and no scheduled flights. We taxied straight to the maintenance area and while my two pilots dealt with the plane I found a shady spot to sit with a book. When the plane reappeared I climbed back on board – but just as we began to taxi to the runway to await clearance a pick-up truck approached and blocked our path.

The truck contained four Zimbabwean policemen: two in the open bed carrying automatic rifles; and two in the front who at least in profile looked like sumo wrestlers. The one who struggled out had a holstered pistol at his massive waist and a star on his blue peaked hat. He spat on the ground as we climbed down from our plane, then demanded to see our passports. Despite his build his voice was high and soft. We handed over the documents, only to have them passed immediately to the other sumo, the driver, still inside the truck.

'Where's the normal guy?' asked Jake, looking concerned. 'He knows us. We don't usually have to bother with documents.' Inside the truck, the driver was reading from our passports into the radio.

'Well you have to bother today.'

'So where is he?'

'Away ill. I'm his replacement.'

'What's wrong with him? He seemed fine last week.'

'An accident.'

'What sort of accident?'

'He grew too rich, too quickly, then tried to resist arrest.' Star-hat turned to glower at me, as if the incident were somehow my fault. 'Nobody trusts a rich policeman. Now... Visas.'

Indy intervened. 'We don't need visas. We're only ever here for an hour or so, and today we're flying on to Jo'burg. I filed a flight plan.'

'I know you did. That's why we're here.' The driver leaned out and said a few words in Bantu. Despite the heavy accent, I recognised my name. Star-hat turned to me. 'Dr de Vries... In the bakkie.'

'Why? Where to?'

'Just get in.' He unbuttoned his holster and rested his hand on the grip of his pistol. 'No! The back of the bakkie.'

The journey lasted about thirty minutes and ended at a collection of barrack-style huts near the eastern bank of the Shashe, not far from a bridge that was one of the authorised crossing points between Botswana and Zimbabwe. With the two rifle-touting individuals either side of me and Star-hat waddling in front I was taken to a hut and pushed inside.

'They haven't learned the gentle touch,' said Star-hat. 'Too used to handling drunks, refugees, smugglers and murderers. But then, who's to say that you're not in that list somewhere.' The man was an enigma, his tough sumo image a total mismatch to his soft voice and educated speech. He sat at a computer directly under a ceiling fan and told me to sit opposite. Then he unholstered his handgun and placed it on the table, the barrel pointing towards me.

'How long is this going to take?' I asked. 'I've got to be at a meeting in Johannesburg in a few hours.'

'Not my problem.'

'Do you have any drinking water?'

'Not for you. Now keep quiet. I need to concentrate.'

After that he didn't speak for a long time, just jabbed one-fingered at his computer keyboard, occasionally swearing in Bantu. Eventually he took off his hat and lay it on the table by the side of his gun. He sat back, hands clasped over his chest, with a smug look on his face. 'We have a file on you Dr de Vries, and I have an order to interrogate you. Fill in a few details. Judge exactly how big an enemy to our beloved country you might be.'

'Me! An enemy? That's crazy. What sort of file?'

'Opened after a tip-off from the Botswana police. They visited your 'research centre' I believe. Evidently you suddenly have a lot of money to spend.'

'I was awarded a large grant. Nearly a year ago now.'

'Really!' He studied his screen and prodded another couple of keys. 'You have a dollar bank account in Zimbabwe I see.'

'For plane maintenance. Fuel. Visits like today.'

'And Botswana.'

'Of course.'

'And a black hole in Switzerland.' The whites of his bulging eyes were streaked with red. Saliva had collected in the corners of his mouth. 'Now why do I smell something illegal going on?'

'I don't know. Maybe something under your nose?'

His nostrils flared. 'Don't joke Dr de Vries. I might not find you funny.' He rested his hand on the table, by the side of his gun. 'Or maybe you mean it? Maybe there is something illegal going on "under my nose." Maybe I should stop being so gentle with you.'

'No. Sorry. Look… I'm just a zoologist. I don't really know anything about the money side of all this. I just spend it. I have people in London who deal with all the transactions.'

'Mmm.' He sat back and for a few moments just stared at me. 'Tell me… Where do you stand on Zimbabwean politics?'

'Politics! I don't. Why should I?'

'Why should you? Somebody who was born here? Somebody whose father and sister were killed by the squabbling factions from which our present government emerged? Somebody from a family who lost all their land when it was redistributed?'

'All a long time ago.'

'So long ago that you harbour no hatred for us any more? Not even one tiny bit?'

'No! I mean yes. You know what I mean.'

'Surely a man like you would rejoice if activists tore our country apart? If many people died? Would you not relish that prospect so much that you might be tempted to help the process along a little? Perhaps inject a little money in the right places? Maybe even a lot of money?'

'No! Look... Where is this going? I get money to study lions in the Kalahari, nothing more.'

'Mmm.' He stood, picked up his gun then went over to the window overlooking the Shashe, his huge but muscular body blocking out much of the light. When he clasped his hands behind his back, the gun was conspicuous, his finger on the trigger. I licked my dry lips, imagining him suddenly swinging round and firing. But when eventually he turned to face me, he did so slowly. 'What do you know about diamonds Dr de Vries?'

'Diamonds? Why? They come out of the ground. And one day the world's obscene demand for them will destroy the Kalahari. I'm not a big fan of diamonds.'

'Are you not? Really? Then maybe you do not realise or even care how much money my country loses each year through their illegal mining and smuggling?'

'Can't say that I do. A lot, I assume.'

'Yes, indeed. "A lot." Enough for my government to take the matter very seriously. Did you know that we, the police, have been ordered to shoot anybody we catch in these acts? And that in this pursuit we have the support of the Air Force, excellent fellows who from their helicopter gunships have already killed many transgressors in the northeast of our country?'

'Yes, I'd heard. But I say again. I'm just a zoologist. My interest is in lions. I do not mine or smuggle diamonds.'

He gave me a condescending smile. 'Maybe you are. And maybe you don't. Or maybe you are just a liar and deserve to be shot anyway. So why don't I go and find the answer? The search of your plane should be well under way by now.' He holstered his gun, picked his hat from the table, then waddled to the door. But framed in the doorway he paused and turned to face me, still with a smile on his round face. 'You see, Dr de Vries, even for a humble zoologist it is a big mistake to grow too rich, too quickly. Let us hope that you have not learned this lesson too late.'

A moment later he was gone. But when I reached the door to follow him, the two policemen standing outside crossed their rifles to bar my way.

***

'Pebbles,' I said. After an hour imprisoned in the hut I had been driven by the two guards back to my plane, now standing in a remote part of the airport.

'No, Dr de Vries. Rough diamonds. Hewn from the chaos that is our Marange Fields.'

'How can you possibly know that?'

'Colour. Surface texture. The lustre of the broken surfaces. Believe me. I know these diamonds.'

'Don't argue with him Doc.' Indy had been handcuffed. So had Jake.

Star-hat casually returned the diamonds to his jacket pocket, then with a nod told one of the policemen to handcuff me as well.

'But those diamonds are nothing to do with me,' I protested as my hands were roughly pulled behind my back.

'Original,' he said. 'Nobody has ever said that before. I love dealing with educated people.'

'But it's true. Where did you find them?'

'Fastened to the inside of your plane tyre.'

I glanced at the plane. It seemed intact. 'You mean you planted them. Did they plant them?' I asked Indy.

'Doc! Don't give him an excuse. OK?'

'Wise words,' and with another nod Star-hat dismissed his two subordinates who climbed into the truck and drove away. As the pick-up disappeared into a cloud of dust, the policeman took his handgun from its holster. 'All of you, understand this: for resisting arrest for what you have done I would be totally justified in shooting all three of you right here, right now. In fact, I would be applauded, especially when I hand these diamonds – well, most of them – to my superiors to show the value of my diligence and to demonstrate my honesty. But I have good news for you. It will be proof enough of my dedication to my job if I shoot only one of you and pretend that the other two were never here.' He smiled as he pointed his pistol between the eyes of us each in turn. 'Now... Would you be so good as to choose which one of you I should shoot Dr de Vries? Because – if you do not – it will be you.'

Chapter 22

I hammered on the apartment door – 'Zuri! It's Mark. Let me in.' I hammered again, and kept on hammering until eventually the door was opened on a chain.

'Do you know what time it is?' she snapped, adjusting her dressing gown.

'Do you know what I've been through to get here?'

'I don't care. I thought you'd got the message. I don't want to talk to you.'

'Well I want to talk to you. And I need somewhere to sleep.'

'Fredrik's here.'

'Doesn't matter. Anywhere will do. The settee, floor, wherever. Just let me in.'

'I don't want any trouble.'

'Neither do I. I've seen enough blood shed for one day.'

Our eyes scarcely met as I brushed past her into the tiny lounge. Across the room, standing framed in the bedroom doorway, Fredrik was watching me. 'You've got a fucking nerve coming here Mark. I warn you – say one thing I don't like and so help me I'll flatten you again.'

'No you won't. Because this time I'll be expecting it.' I glanced from one to the other. 'Are you two fucking each other?'

'What do you think?'

'Stop it you two,' said Zuri, throwing herself on to the settee. 'Why are you here Mark? Shouldn't you be with Inga and your son? And Sharda? My God – all I asked was honesty.'

'I have been honest with you. With both of you.' Fredrik began swearing again, but I held up my hands to stop him. 'Look... Fredrik... Both of you. I can hardly claim the baby isn't mine any more, can I? So I must have had sex with Inga. I just can't remember it, that's all. I didn't lie to you.'

'Oh, for fuck's sake.'

'It's true. What else can I say?'

'And Sharda? What else can you say about her? Or don't you remember her either?' Zuri was glaring at me.

I glared back. 'There's nothing to say. What she told you is true Zuri. We've shared a bed, nothing more.'

'Naked?'

'Of course bloody naked. When have I ever worn clothes in bed? What difference does naked make for people like us anyway. Look... What would you have done in my position, eh? Either of you? I was worried about her. Being sick. Choking. Doing something stupid. I had to keep an eye on her. Sometimes she drank so much and was so out of it...'

'That you just had to sleep with her. Of course! Another Inga then?'

I threw up my hands in frustration. 'No, not another Inga. Look... I won't deny I like Sharda. I'm really attracted to her. OK? And if she'd ever given me any hint that she wanted it too I'd have jumped at the chance of sex with her. Is that honest enough? But she was suicidal, for God's sake. She needed a friend. She needed looking after. The last thing I was going to do was come on to her. We haven't even kissed. Not in that way. What do you take me for?'

'Do you really want me to answer that? Go home Mark. Go back to your women. Go tell your lies to somebody else.'

'No! Look... Zuri... Fredrik... Listen to me. None of this matters any more. I don't give a damn who's fucking who, and neither will you when you hear what's happened.'

***

'Shit!' said Indy, taking the unlit cigarillo from his mouth and throwing it out of the truck. Parked in the centre of the camp's compound was a Land Rover, its colour Government-issue blue. And sitting cross-legged playing cards in the shade of the large Mopane tree were the two Botswana policemen who had visited before.

'What do they want?' I muttered as we pulled to a halt.

'What the hell do you think?' Indy got out and waited for me. 'They want their cut. Payment for keeping quiet. But I needed time to doctor the plane and the diamonds a bit before they arrived.' As we approached the men, Indy gave me a sideways glance. 'Whatever I say, just nod. No smart-ass comments. OK?'

Neither policeman looked up from their game, and while Indy and I stood watching them tension between the players mounted. Until – in triumph or anger – the cards were thrown to the ground and the winnings collected in an eruption of shouts, accusations and argument. When the men eventually quietened and stood, Indy offered them each a cigarillo from his top pocket.

'What keep you?' growled the larger of the two. 'My brother in Zimbabwe say he release you and your plane yesterday afternoon?'

'Brother, eh?' Indy lit their cigarillos, then his own. 'We had business in Jo'burg. Didn't he tell you?'

The policeman grunted. 'Well now you got business here Man. You the pilot? Where your plane?'

'No need for the plane. Everything you need is in the truck.' Indy began to usher the pair towards our pick-up, but resisting him they turned to me.

'Which of you really the boss-man?'

'I am. Indy's my business manager.'

The three men walked over to our pick-up and stood around talking, maybe arguing. As I watched, Inga and Sharda arrived at my side. Inga linked arms with me, her grip tight. 'We're glad you're back. The waiting was making them angry.' She looked up at me. 'Did you see Fredrik and Zuri? Did you speak to them?'

'Where is Jake?' asked Sharda.

I wasn't ready to answer questions. Disentangling from Inga, I held up my hands. 'Look... Both of you. Give me ten minutes, OK? Fifteen at the most. Let me clean up. Get my head together. I'll see you in the dormitory. Fix me a drink. We'll talk then.'

Inga shook her head. 'No way. Until that Land Rover's out of here, we're staying right by your side. You should have seen the way they kept looking at Sharda. For once I was actually glad I had leaky tits and a baby.'

In the shower block the two women perched on stools and waited as I washed the dirt, sand, and sweat from my body. Occasionally I glanced at them, wondering how I was going to break the news. They were talking to each other, their voices drowned by the pattering and splashing of the water. Even though I couldn't hear what they were saying their serious faces told me that they had picked up on my mood. But then as I began one of my male ablutions Sharda nodded in my direction and said something to Inga that the pair of them seemed to find hilarious – until they saw my expression. 'What's so funny?' I snapped, turning off the water.

'Nothing.'

'No come on. Tell me. What's so funny?'

'Calm down,' said Inga, holding up a towel, 'It's nothing. Just a remark that's all. We've had a scary afternoon – and from the looks of things your day didn't go too well either. Come on, don't keep us in suspense. Did you see them? Here, let me dry your back.'

'No! I want to know.'

'Mark… It's really not important. Just a joke. Come on. This isn't like you. What happened with Zuri and Fredrik? We want to know.' She began towelling my shoulders but I shrugged her away. 'OK, this is stupid,' she said, 'If you must know Sharda asked me if I thought anything ever jumps out when a man pulls back his foreskin like that. A trapped beetle or something. That's all. It was a joke. Lightened the mood for a moment. Now calm down and tell us what happened. Would they even talk to you?'

I had vowed to be gentle when I told them. Instead I exploded. 'For Christ's sake you two. This isn't about Zuri and Fredrik – though if you must know: yes, they're fucking each other; and yes, they told me to fuck off and leave them to get on with their fucking lives. Fredrik's words. OK? This is about this place. And Jake. Since yesterday morning… Do you want the list? I've been accused of financing terrorists, of smuggling diamonds. I've been forced to invite a psychopath to shoot me, then watch Jake have his brains blown out instead. It's been a bad day, OK? I'm bloody lucky to be alive. And – Christ – do I need a drink. And all you two can do is make totally facile comments about fucking bloody foreskins.'

***

Indy said nothing when he found us, just walked through our dormitory to take two bottles of rum from the crate near the computer. He lobbed one to me, which I caught, and then perched himself on the edge of one of the beds and took a long swig.

'So… How much did you pay them?' I asked.

'Just enough.' He wiped his mouth with the hairy back of his grimy hand. 'I take it you've told the dolls?' He nodded toward Inga and Sharda; Inga had just begun to feed a freshly-awake baby.

'I've told them.'

'And are you cool about it?' he asked Inga.

'Cool! Christ.' Turning to me, she held out her slender arm – 'C'mon. Gimme.' – and while holding the baby to her breast with one hand she placed the bottle to her lips with the other and took a generous swig. Only then did she answer Indy. 'You expect us to be cool about somebody we know having their brains blown out by some demented policeman?'

'Aagh, Jake had it coming. Colonel's orders. It's what happens when you grow too greedy, start making demands. Sumo man had been told exactly who to shoot. The big guy just amused himself by seeing if Doc here would do the decent thing and ask to be shot himself.' He looked at me. 'What an idiot you are. He might have done it.'

'So what would you have done in my place?'

'Told him to shoot Jake, of course. But then… I had inside information, didn't I.' Spitting something from his mouth to the floor, he turned back to Inga. 'Hey, but I didn't mean are you cool about Jake. I meant are you cool about what's going on here? Now that you know.'

'Oh sure. Cool, yeah. I always knew something was missing from life here. But now… Trigger-happy policemen? Headless smugglers? Now life's just perfect.'

He laughed at her. 'Aw, c'mon Doll. All this time, right under your nose, and 'til today you hadn't a clue, had you? So just pretend you still don't know.'

'But I do know. That's the problem. My God. I'll wet myself next time those policemen show up.'

Indy shook his head, smiling broadly. 'No you won't.'

'Yes I will. It was bad enough knowing that they probably murdered Seretse.'

Indy put down his bottle, then lit two cigarillos together in his mouth and offered one to Inga. She accepted, but added: 'I'd rather have dagga.'

'Sorry Doll. Clean out of the stuff. I'll pick up a supply in Ghanzi tomorrow. I'm just dropping the diamonds off this time. Some other guy is doing the Belgian end for once.'

As Inga took a long first draw she rolled her eyes, then riveted them on mine. And after blowing smoke into the air she said: 'Stop looking at me like that Mark. I didn't ask you to father him – so I'm not asking you how to raise him. OK? If I want to drink and smoke around him I will.'

'Did I say anything?' I turned back to Indy. 'But one day you'll get caught. You're bound to. Then what happens?'

'Relax Doc. I won't get caught. Smuggling's not risky. I've been doing it for the Colonel for ten years now, ever since demob. Look, as long as we play the game we've got contacts that guarantee free passage all along the route at this end. People like Sumo-man and his predecessor, and like these two geezers I've just paid here. Same at the airport. And once you're on the plane, the job's done. You're never checked for diamonds when you enter Belgium to sell the things. You just go to one of the diamantaires in Antwerp, present yourself at the counter with your bunch of stones, and that's it.' Wisps of smoke kept escaping from his nose and mouth as he spoke. 'Hey, d'ya wanna know what I think's funny?'

'What?'

'The Colonel's little joke. The way he got you all to think he was financing you when really...' He looked at each of us in turn. 'Aw, c'mon. You can see the funny side of that surely.'

Sharda, so far silent, held out her hand to me. 'Can I?' and after the tiniest of sips of the rum, she returned the bottle to me. There was a confused smile on her face as if she couldn't quite believe the situation in which she found herself.

Indy hadn't finished. 'So... What about it Doc? Are you cool about it? Now you've had time to get used to the idea?'

'Used to the idea? That my precious research centre is being used as a front for smuggling diamonds? That I was so desperate for that bastard's money I walked straight into his trap? That if I do anything but keep quiet and cooperate I'll have my brains blown out?' I downed an almost kamikaze amount of rum. 'Well guess what? All of you. As it happens... Yes! I am 'cool' about it. And do you know why? All this bloody time I've been loathing, absolutely loathing, the thought that this place – all of us – were being financed by an evil murdering racist rapist; that he could abuse and humiliate Sharda any way he wanted and then act the big benefactor. But hell... Turns out it's not like that after all. This place is financing itself. The Wolf's not giving us anything. In fact he's taking – and maybe if we're clever we can get him to take less. So Indy – you just keep on smuggling, and we'll help you any way we can.' I raised my bottle – 'Here's to us. Long may we all keep our heads.' – and finished the toast in Afrikaans. 'Gesondheid!'

Chapter 23

Standing on the crest of a high dune I watched a flock of
White-backed vultures as they soared high above
shimmering Kalahari grassland. Then, tilting my face to
the deep-blue sky, I spread my arms to let the wind-driven
sand and fierce sun sting and burn my weathered skin.

'Good therapy?' asked Inga when eventually I slipped
and slithered down to her in the shade of a Grey Camel-thorn
tree.

'None better.' I sank to my knees.

Sharda was there too, cuddling the baby. 'Oh, you are
so beautiful,' she was cooing at him. 'Yes you are. Oh yes
you are.' She looked up and seeing me watching gave an
awkward smile. 'It is so difficult, Mark, to believe that in two
days we shall be back in London.'

'Is that difficult-good?' asked Inga. 'Or difficult-bad?'

'Well... To be in the same country as the Wolf again?
To be surrounded by buildings and dirty air? Not to mention
all the work I must do for my final exams? Definitely
'difficult-bad' I think. But – hey! Today, I do not care. I have
just had a long, long hug with your baby, this place is very
beautiful – and if Mark ever gets round to showing me my
first wild lion today as he promised... Are you sure we
should not start moving Mark? Go back to the plane?'

'Just a bit longer. There's plenty of time.'

Sharda gazed up the dune I had just descended. 'In
that case, it is my turn for therapy,' and without further
comment she handed the baby to Inga and set off up the
sandy slope. As she trudged her way upwards she hitched-up

her sarong, raising the hem just enough not to catch on the clumps of vegetation. Inga and I watched her to the top.

'Did I ever tell you about my anatomy lecturer?' Inga said to me.

'You mean you and him? In the morgue? You know you did. And if your point is what I think it is... It's too soon. The Wolf is too recent. Besides – I'm still not convinced she's interested.'

'Too soon, perhaps – I could believe that – but she is definitely interested, take my word for it. The question is: are you?'

'Totally. I can honestly say I've never felt quite this way about anybody before.'

'Not even Zuri?'

'What would be the point of feeling like this about Zuri? Nobody ever gets really close to her.'

'And what about me?' She was smiling.

I smiled back. 'Mmm, maybe. Young though we were. Perhaps if you hadn't been so dead set on the idea of marriage...'

'Huh! And what a mistake that was. But isn't Sharda dead-set too?'

'Sadly, yes.'

Sharda reached the top of the dune and stood letting the wind whip her hair and billow her sarong. Inga offered me the baby. 'Mark... Hold Imbube for a while will you? Let me see the pair of you together.'

'Imbube? Really? Have you decided?'

'I think so. It's grown on me.'

I could feel her eyes on me as I made the baby comfortable in my arms; could picture her scrutinising me as I gazed down at his subtly dark skin, wide eyes and wisps of dark hair. If I really tried I could just about sense a son in him, though in the days before paternity tests I would never have believed he was mine. Suddenly he began to urinate, and I was just too slow to avoid some going over my chest and stomach. 'How come he never does that to you any more?'

Inga was laughing at me. 'I seem to have developed a sixth sense. For the other too. The Tswana women never get caught out. Have you noticed?'

I had noticed – and often marvelled. It seemed akin to telepathy. I wiped myself dry with sand.

Inga took a strip of newspaper and a wad of dagga from her bag, then began rolling a joint, working at it until it was lit before handing it to me for a first draw. I glanced up the dune to Sharda, now sitting cross-legged and looking across the plain as if meditating. Suddenly she stood, took off her sarong and with both hands held it above her head to flap behind her like a flag. A minute or so later she folded the cloth so that when she put it back on, needing several attempts, she could tie it around her waist, not under her arms as always before. Then after a last glance across the plain she began half-running half-sliding down the dune, her long black hair flapping around her face and breasts.

'I should meditate more often,' she said, breathing hard. 'I have just made many decisions that previously seemed difficult but suddenly seem very easy.'

'So we see,' said Inga, pretending to stare.

'Inga!' laughed Sharda with a hint of embarrassment.

'Oh, ignore me. I'm just jealous. Mine went from a barely-there double-A to a leaky lumpy C, all in the space of nine months. If they did pass through firm-and-pert like yours on the way I missed it. Are those really natural?'

'Of course! All my own work.' Sharda glanced at me. 'I was beginning to feel out of place. Conspicuous even. Being the only woman in the camp who covered her breasts.

So… Anyway, this conforming is one of my decisions. I have made others too. If I am going to live here for the next three years… Is that dagga?' She took the joint from between my fingers and took a timid suck.

I waited for her to cough, but she didn't. 'What else?'

'Ah. For the rest you must wait and see.'

**

'When I was a teenager in Lahore… I had dreams, you know? Such romantic dreams.'

High over the Sahara with the sun about to set beyond the port wing-tip, Sharda and I were settling back in our seats after our meal. I asked what dreams.

'Oh, you know. The usual. A big wedding. Marriage to a very kind and handsome Sikh. Our souls joining. Having many beautiful children. And so on. I really did believe that this was how all lives should be. How everybody wanted their life to be. But now…' She gave a big sigh. 'Mark… The Tswana at the campsite? How can two men be married to several women? How can this possibly work?'

'Are you still thinking about united souls?'

'Please. Do not tease. I am serious.'

'OK. Sorry. But it does work, doesn't it? For them anyway. You've seen it for yourself.'

'But how does it even start? I mean, I know – you once told me – the two men are nearly always brothers…'

'Well, let's just say they have the same mother.'

'OK, half-brothers then. But how does a woman marry two men at the same time?'

I smiled at her question, guessing at the images in her mind. 'Oh, there's no ceremony as such – apart from just another excuse for everybody to get drunk. She just moves in with the two of them. And if she ever wants to divorce them, she just moves out. She actually has quite a lot of choice. Freedom even. More so than in your dream world maybe.'

'Hardly as romantic though. And surely not as permanent.'

'Oh, I don't know. If Annakiya is to be believed she's been married to Kopano and Tau for twenty years. That's fairly permanent. And a bit romantic, surely. Not that I'm any judge.'

'Twenty years! Really?' She looked out of the window for a few moments, as if pondering this information. 'And how many children does she have with them? Five?'

'No – six. But 'with' Kopano and Tau? I doubt it. Not more than one or two, anyway. Married they might be – but they still all have sex on the side as well, just like lionesses.' I chuckled. 'What I wouldn't give to do a paternity study on them all.'

'Oh Mark... Is that all you can think of? The science? Is there not even an ounce of romance in your soul?'

'Well... If there is... Look... Sharda. I don't want to be a killer of dreams but if it's romance you're looking for then working in the Kalahari for the next few years isn't the way to find it. You're not going to meet a potential Sikh husband in the desert – handsome or otherwise.'

'Oh, I know. I know very well. What do you think I was contemplating for so long on the top of that sand dune yesterday?'

***

Four o'clock in the morning and we were in our apartment, fresh from Heathrow Airport. I was already in bed, but Sharda was dithering in the middle of the room. 'Help me please. I am nervous.'

'What about?'

'I want us to sleep together.'

'Well – fine. Get in. But why nervous? You've slept in my bed before.'

'No. I mean sleep together – as in have sex. As long as you want this also of course. Do you?'

'Aah. 'Sleep together'. Right. Yes I do. And I have for a long time. But are you sure about this?'

'I am sure, yes. It was one of my decisions.'

'But now you're nervous?'

'Of course. And worried. Maybe I shall still hate sex, even with you. Maybe in my mind I shall see only the Wolf. Maybe I shall panic.'

'Maybe you will – it wouldn't surprise me at all – but you mustn't worry. Whatever happens, I'll understand. I'll help.'

She climbed into my bed and we tentatively began to kiss; the first time mouth-on-mouth. But as I became aroused she separated her lips from mine. 'Do you promise to be gentle with me? Not like the Wolf.'

'Of course.'

'And patient too? Very patient?'

'Very.'

'And to stop immediately if I ask?'

Chapter 24

A double-decker bus rumbled past nearly splashing us, the recent thunderstorm having done nothing to clear the sultry air. Sharda pointed across the road. 'A large white van. See?... .... I still panic, you know. Every time.' She had just finished her penultimate exam and after meeting me at a coffee shop half-way between the university and home we were walking the rest of the way together.

'Relax! It would be too much of a give-away.'

Cruickshank should have been back from his long honeymoon over a fortnight ago, but so far there had been no texts, no commands; Sharda hadn't needed to say no. But reminded of him daily every time she took 'the pill' – even though it was now for me, not for him – his threat had seemed ever-present, preying on her mind, interfering with revision, though she had done her best. There was now less than a month before she escaped to the Kalahari again. And as that day grew nearer our hopes were growing: maybe the Wolf's marriage had made a difference after all.

Inside the apartment, Sharda kicked off her sandals, threw her small rucksack on to the settee, and opened the balcony window wide. 'This room is so hot in summer,' she said, heading for the bedroom. 'So difficult to breathe.'

'Afternoon sun, London air.' I switched on my computer, then went into the kitchen to fetch a bottle of water from the fridge.

'Get me one,' she shouted. I met her on her way out of the bedroom and handed her the bottle. 'I cannot find my sarong,' she said.

'Why bother with anything?'

'Because I know you. And I know what will happen if I wear nothing all evening. I have a very important exam tomorrow. Remember?'

I laughed. 'And I want you to get a good mark tomorrow just as much as you do. But if you really want to make sure I leave you alone for the rest of the evening... There is a very quick answer.'

'And this answer is – what?' But a smile was already spreading over her face. She glanced at the clock on the wall. 'Well, OK. I suppose it has been more than a day... But afterwards – you are my waiter for the night. OK? All the coffee I want. Immediately. Every time I ask. OK? Deal?'

'Deal.'

'Then OK. But very quick.'

And we were quick – not least because even before our heart rates and breathing returned to normal, there was an insistent ringing at the apartment door. Leaving Sharda in bed, I threw on my dressing gown and went to investigate. 'Who is it?'

'Special delivery, Dr de Vries. Needs your signature.'

I opened the door, a large hand grabbed my throat, and a moment later I had been turned round and was being almost throttled by a strong arm squeezing my windpipe. A second man walked in, then a third who stood in front of me. I heard the door close.

'Mark? Who is it?' shouted Sharda from the bedroom.

The visitor put his finger to his lips – 'Let's surprise her shall we Boy?' – and headed off in the direction of her voice, pulling what looked like silk stockings from his jacket pocket on the way.

I tried to shout, to tell Sharda to close and lock the bedroom door, but the moment I drew breath the arm tightened across my throat. 'From this position...' half-whispered, half-growled the man behind me, 'I know five different ways to break your neck.'

Sharda shouted then squealed as Cruickshank walked into the bedroom, closing the door behind him. I heard her call my name, but nothing more. The man behind me loosened his grip a little and turning my head I saw who they were: the two 'bouncers' from the night I was kidnapped. 'We've been told not to kill you,' said one, taking up a position between me and the bedroom door. 'Not even to hurt you unless you become a nuisance.' I was marched to the settee and pushed on to it. My minder then sat beside me. 'Seems you're more valuable to Sir Cameron alive. Makes this as boring as hell, unless you fancy your chances.'

I did. Springing to my feet and in the same movement jabbing back my elbow into the minder's face, I sprinted across the room and launched myself at the other man, throwing punches and pushing him in an attempt to get to the bedroom door. But strong though I am I didn't stand a chance. Grabbed by one gorilla and pummelled by the other I felt a rib break and also my nose. A few minutes later I was back on the settee, blood streaming from my nostrils and every breath painful. I had lost my dressing gown in the fight but when I asked for it back the two men laughed and one threw it out of the open window, over the balcony, to float down nine storeys to the street below.

'Try anything like that again and you're dead,' said one of the men.

'Or worse,' said the other. This time nakedness did make me feel vulnerable.

I glanced around for anything that might even the odds a little. 'Now what?'

'Now we wait. If you're quiet, we might hear him fucking her.'

There was nothing more I could do, save try not to listen. Whenever I began to speak, I was hit; whenever I tried to stand I was restrained. 'I need to go to the toilet.'

'Piss on your carpet then.'

There was no sound from Sharda, just Cruickshank at one stage grunting to the rhythm of the squeaking bed while the two men grinned at me. Eventually the bedroom door opened and Cruickshank walked out, looking as calm and unruffled as when he went in. Immediately I tried to stand, but was again restrained. 'I want to see her,' I said.

'Not until we've gone.' He glanced at his henchmen as if to ask what had happened to me, but neither said anything; it was hardly necessary.

'Sharda!' I shouted.

'She can't answer you Boy. And she can't come to you either.' He gave an easy smile. 'Relax. I've done nothing to her that a shower won't put right. She's just a bit tied up at the moment, that's all. Just thank me and I might leave her be for a while.'

'What the hell have I got to thank you for?'

'I've saved your research centre, haven't I? Shown you how to self-finance. And now I'm giving you back your woman, still in one piece. I might even let her go to the Kalahari with you – maybe. Isn't all that worth a thank you?'

'She's going. OK? You dare try and stop her.'

'Watch your mouth Boy. Threaten me and your history. Both of you. I can stop her. OK? In all sorts of ways. End your funding for one. Close your station. Then there'll be nowhere for either of you to go.'

'Pure bluff. You won't close it. Not while Indy's there. You need us.'

'Need you? Why the hell would somebody like me need somebody like you? You're no more than an insect to me. A black beetle, under my heel. I can squash you any moment I like.'

'My God. It really turns you on, doesn't it : destroying people's lives.'

He smirked then gestured to his two henchmen that they were leaving – but he paused at the door. 'Haven't you got the message yet Boy? You and your coloured dog-bitch in there, you're not people. Haven't I proved it to you both, over and over? Bitch or beetle – whatever low-life you are, you're just plain inferior.' Chuckling, he left.

The moment the door closed behind them, I rushed to the bedroom. Sharda's dark brown eyes riveted on mine as I sat by her side to free her. It wasn't difficult to untie her from the bed and Cruickshank had at least left the keys to the cuffs. But there was no gentle way to peel the tape from her mouth; her bottom lip began to bleed as a sliver of skin tore away. She sat up and stared at the bedroom door; no tears, just dejection. 'I couldn't stop him Mark. He said his men would kill you if I struggled – and from the look of you...'

I put my arm round her shoulders, but after a few moments she sat up straight. 'No. I have no time for pity. Please run a bath – this time for both of us I think. To wash the blood from you and the man from me. Then I must work. Maybe later you can cook me something. Something I like. But something small.'

'Whiskey too?'

'No! After my bath I must work and work and work. All night if necessary. A good mark will help me escape from this man. The last thing I need tonight is whiskey.'

Breathing shallowly to avoid the pain from my rib, I headed for the bathroom – but Sharda called after me. 'Do you know what he said to me? While he was dressing himself? That from here he was going straight to his wife, to cleanse himself of me. To have sex with a real woman, a white woman, not a dog-bitch. A woman worthy of giving him a child.' Her face was expressionless. 'All my life Mark, I thought it wasn't in me to kill a person.'

Chapter 25

'Ah... Dr de Vries. Come in! Come in!' said the man who was standing to greet me, reaching across the large desk that was his for the day. We shook hands. 'Take a seat.' His shock of white hair contrasted with an almost black suit and emerald-green tie. There was dandruff on his shoulders and a hint of dermatitis on his cheeks and forehead.

As I sat on the padded chair opposite him I saw Sharda's project-report on the desk. All around were piles of exam scripts and sheets of paper. 'You look exactly as I expected Dr de Vries,' he said, eying me up and down.

'So do you Professor O'Flanahan. So do you.'

'I gather you're about to start a year's sabbatical in the Kalahari. Lucky man.'

'My research station is suddenly short-staffed. I'm needed there more than here.'

'I'm sure you are.' He was studying me. 'I assume you know why I've asked to see you today.'

'Not exactly, but...'

'Good. So let's make it quick, shall we?'

'That's fine by me.'

He took hold of Sharda's report and raised it as if judging it's weight, then replaced it on the desk. 'An interesting student, your Miss Kaur. We had quite a chat this morning in her viva. Has she told you about it?'

'I've been in meetings.'

'Ah. So you have. Otherwise she would have done I'm sure.'

'Would she? Why do you say that?'

'No reason.' His gaze was so intense I was feeling uncomfortable. 'She's very striking, don't you think? Beautiful even. And so 'nice' with it all. Almost fragile.'

'She has a strength as well.'

'I'm sure she has. She used to be a Sikh, she tells me. But has rather lost her faith this past year. A pity, don't you think?' He was still staring at me, his blue eyes piercing.

'Is that relevant?'

He shrugged. 'An external examiner, faced with a difficult case such as hers, should consider everything to be relevant. Don't you agree?' He didn't wait for me to answer. 'All that early promise... Those first two years... Her marks were excellent. Outstanding. But then... Sadly...' He rested his hand on her project.

'She's had a difficult year.'

'As have many.'

'What? Brother murdered? Father dying?'

He held up his hand to stop me. 'I see no Psychologist's report, no document from a Student counsellor. Absolutely nothing to say that Miss Kaur's ability to study was reduced. Which means that those events cannot be taken into account.'

'But that's Sharda. That's the measure of the woman. She wanted to handle her traumas on her own. But they did affect her, of course they did.'

'And you would know, I suppose.'

I peered at him. 'And what does that mean?'

'Ah... Just rumours, Dr de Vries. Just rumours. Every University, every Department, has them. They make life interesting, do they not?' Clearing his throat, he stood and went over to the window, to stare out at the London skyline for a few moments before returning to sit down again.

'Now... Shall we stop this charade? We both know the situation here.'

'I'm not sure that I do any more. Perhaps you should tell me.'

'Very well. It goes something like this. If Miss Kaur gets the top mark of her degree course this year, she will be rewarded with a grant to work for a PhD – and she will do that PhD with you, in Africa. That much you do know, I'm sure...'

I did know. With the death of her father Sharda no longer had the safety-net of his financial support. So a First Class Degree was no longer enough. She needed to do even better.

'... But if she doesn't come top,' he continued, 'she won't. Maybe somewhere else, with someone else, but not with you – and she left me in no doubt as to where her hopes and aspirations lie. And I daresay yours are the same as hers.' He paused as if expecting me to say something.

'Go on.'

'Now... What you may not know – indeed, I have only just been given the final figures myself – is this: the league table for this year is so close that top position has come to depend on the mark Miss Kaur is finally awarded for this project of hers; the project on your lions. A mark of seventy percent or over and she is top of the year. Anything less and she is not. Did you know that it was so finely balanced?'

'No, I didn't.'

Inner turmoil, trauma, even hangovers... Missed deadlines, rushed essays, the occasional impossibility of working or concentrating... Both she and I knew that her marks had slipped, courtesy of the Wolf. But until this moment we had still hoped she would top the year by a comfortable margin, whatever the mark for her project.

'So… Can I ask?' I said. 'What the second marker awarded?'

'Dr Steel? He gave her seventy percent. But I have already discussed the matter with him and he now concedes that he may have been a little generous.'

'Generous! Seventy isn't generous. Sharda's project is worth way more than that.'

'Which presumably is why you gave her eighty. At least… I hope that's the reason.'

'Of course it's the reason. Are you accusing me of bias? Because, if you are, let others look at her report: people who – with all due respect to Dr Steel – actually know something about lions. They will tell you. Eighty is a fair mark.'

He was almost imperceptibly shaking his head. 'There isn't time for others to read her report. Besides, there is no need.' The merest hint of a smile appeared on his thin lips. 'I have read and marked the project myself.'

'And?'

'The project is worth sixty – for the laboratory techniques she mastered and described – and not one percentage more.'

'Sixty!'

'Her English is terrible…'

'It isn't terrible. Quaint sometimes, maybe. She learned late. But grammatically it is fine. Better than most students who actually are English.'

'… and the field data she uses to tie in with her laboratory work are quite frankly worthless.'

'Of course those data aren't worthless. They're mine – based on six years of sweat and hard work.'

'Then all I can say is: I'm not surprised that the Research Council pulled your funding.' He glowered at me as if I were a stupid schoolboy. 'Dr de Vries... A lioness cannot conceive to a male that she has never met. It is, quite simply, impossible. Yet, when I asked Miss Kaur to explain this anomaly to me, instead of giving me a proper scientific appraisal of the situation all she did was embark on some vague and ridiculous story that she "hoped" might be relevant.'

'Which story was that?'

'Something about the lioness in question visiting an area where there may – may! – have been nomadic males at roughly the same time as a lioness from the father's pride. But even these two females it seems didn't actually meet, missing each other by a kilometre or so – and the nomads themselves are, for the moment evidently, still fiction. Quite frankly, I couldn't see the relevance. And when I pushed her, neither could she.'

'Did she suggest to you that sperm might fly?'

'Sorry?'

'It's a joke of ours.' I thought it might lighten the situation.

'A joke? No she didn't. And it's just as well, because to me her future career is no joking matter. But jokes aside, I have to say that as a prospective research student, your protégée failed dismally.'

'But what could she say? None of us can explain that cub's conception yet.'

'Really? None of you? Well I can – and so could just about every half-decent scientist I have ever met.' He leaned forward, resting his clasped hands on the desktop. 'Of course your lioness met and mated with the lion that fathered her cub. So if your movement records say otherwise then in my opinion those records are, as I said earlier, totally worthless. Shoddy work, Dr de Vries. Shoddy work. And Miss Kaur should have said so in her report – or at least told me in private today in her viva. It had crossed my mind, you see, that maybe, just maybe, she had been afraid to rubbish your data in her report for fear of alienating you. And if she had admitted as much to me today, I might have allowed her a seventy, if only for bravery. But she didn't. In fact, against all logic, she defended you and your data. So I can't help her. Sixty it is – and there's an end to the matter.'

'But…'

'No! No buts. Good day to you, Dr de Vries. Enjoy your sabbatical. But I'm afraid Miss Kaur won't be joining you.'

Chapter 26

I expected to be met by Indy – but the display on my ringing mobile read "Inga".

'I'm at the bar outside the arrivals hall and I've just ordered a cold Windhoek Lager with your name on it,' she said. 'Come join me. Indy's got a few people to see before he can fly us back to camp.'

As I entered through one door, I saw Indy head for another. But not before he had squeezed Inga's shoulder with his hand as a parting gesture. 'Are you and Indy… ?' I asked after Inga and I had embraced and sat back onto bar-stools

'"Are we?" Or "Have we?"'

'Whichever.' I took an appreciative sip of the straw-coloured beer.

'None of your business.'

'So that's a yes then.' I took another long sip, then looked around for a baby. 'Where's Imbube?'

'Back at the camp. One of Annakiya's daughters offered to wet-nurse him for the day. I did the same for her last week. We've both got loads to spare. Look…' She reached inside her shirt and bra and pulled out a nipple-pad. 'Feel that, it's soaked.' The still-warm sticky fluid from the cotton squeezed out through my fingers and dripped on to the bar counter. After taking a clean pad from her handbag, Inga fiddled to place the pad in position. 'God, I hate all this paraphernalia. It's so much easier at the camp – except for all the nipple-obsessed flies, that is.' Then she said a few words in Afrikaans to the watching barman. I didn't catch the joke but they both laughed.

'So how is he? Imbube.'

'Ooh. Is that a hint of paternal interest? Careful.' She patted my still-sticky hand. 'How is he? He's beautiful. Absolutely beautiful. And growing really fast. My tits might be small but hell do they produce good stuff. Here. Try some.' She lifted my hand and chuckled when I indulged her by licking my fingers. After downing her lager she signalled to the barman for another. 'Sharda's a long time getting changed. Are you sure she knows where to find us?'

***

Neither Sharda nor I ever discovered whether Cruickshank was behind Professor O'Flanahan's draconian marking of her project-report. But if he was and that was his attempt to prevent her escaping to the Kalahari, he failed.

Sharda arrived at the bar and ran a casual hand across the back of my shoulders as she passed behind me. The two women embraced then Sharda pulled up a stool and bit-by-bit the three of us brought each other up-to-date with the events of the past three months.

'You managed to get a work permit then,' Inga said to Sharda.

'Thanks to Mark and his friends in Gaborone.'

'But no PhD? Despite your First?'

'Sadly, no. For now, I am just a humble 'laboratory technician.' Maybe next year I shall be lucky enough to obtain a grant. Or maybe – if you believe in miracles – I shall finally receive my inheritance. Then I can pay for myself.'

'Well… Let's hope it all works out for you, eh?' But Inga's body language was awkward.

'What's the matter?' I asked.

'Oh… Nothing you don't already know. You're here for a year's sabbatical. Sharda's talking about the future. But the truth is the whole place is grinding to a halt. Trucks, generator, solar power system, water bore-hole... Indy's being brilliant when he's around – but that's not often. Without Fredrik – or a whole heap more money to employ people – you're going to end up doing all this sort of stuff yourself. As for research, with no Zuri here either... Well, you can forget it. You're just going to be a glorified maintenance man Mark. And Sharda's going to have zilch to do in the lab.'

I could have added even further bad news from an e-mail I'd received a couple of days previously, but spared them. They would both know soon enough. 'I really thought Zuri and Fredrik would have calmed down by now.' I said. 'At least visited you while I was away – if only to return that truck they drove off in. Any news from them at all?'

'Only an e-mail from Zuri a few days ago. Didn't say much. All very distant and matter-of-fact. They're still in Jo'burg, Zuri's putting the finishing touches to her thesis; that sort of thing. No mention of the truck.'

***

'Indy... I need to know. Your loyalties; where do they really lie?' The four of us had been on our way to the plane, but Inga and Sharda had stopped off at a toilet.

'Loyalties, Doc? Jeez. What are loyalties? Why?'

'Cruickshank's reducing my funding. From now on, the research centre's only receiving enough to keep things ticking over. Enough to provide you with a base, I suppose. But nowhere near enough to expand or do any major research.'

'Provide me with a base eh? Is that really what he said?'

I shook my head. 'Just reading between the lines. This was advance notice. A one-liner from Dominic. Evidently he

– Dominic – will write to explain everything soon, once all the details are sorted, whatever that means. He just didn't want me spending money in the meantime that we were never going to get. My guess is that Cruickshank thinks we're big enough now. Doesn't want us to attract any extra attention to you by splashing too much money around.'

'Is that right.'

'Or – then again – maybe it's just spite.'

'Either way, sounds just like the Colonel. So... What's all this got to do with loyalties?'

'OK, here goes nothing. What are the chances of some real self-financing? Diverting some of the diamonds for ourselves but without ending up like Jake? And if there is a way, would you help us?'

'Help? Bloody do it you mean. Take all the risks.' He chewed on his cigarillo. 'What'd be in it for me?'

'A cut, of course. Think of it as a pension.'

'Pension? Ha! You really are hilarious sometimes, d'ya know that?'

The two women appeared in the distance, walking towards us, and Indy suddenly began to look uncomfortable.

'Tell me Doc: are you fed up with life or something? D'ya know the risk you're taking just asking me this? Suppose I report this conversation straight back to the Colonel?'

'It's called desperation, Indy. And it would only be for a while. I have a big project I need to finance. One that I think could give us back our independence.... .... Look, I can see I've put you on the spot. But at least think about it. Let me know.'

He glanced at the approaching women, then put his hand on my shoulder. 'Aw, hell. You're going to be told sooner or later. Bad news mate. Listen...'

***

The night had been cold. Even in our sleeping bag Sharda and I had needed each other's body heat to stay warm. But by early afternoon the sun had raised the temperature to the mid-twenties and the air was just about as pleasant as the Kalahari can manage. To get some time alone, the pair of us had trekked up one of the nearby rocky outcrops to a flat secluded hollow. As it was July, a plethora of small and mainly hidden trickles of water from the sponge-like rock were providing a babbling backdrop, the ambience more like a montane woodland than of the arid desert rock the place would become in a month or so.

'Did you and Zuri used to come here?'

'Sometimes.' Hands-behind-head I was lying on Sharda's sarong, enjoying a post-coital glow and trying to push all negative thoughts to the back of my mind. Sharda was standing now, her figure silhouetted against a bright azure sky. In the distance were the shouts and laughter of Tswana children from the camp.

'And who will you bring here after me, I wonder?' Her tone was casual but her manner tense. I didn't respond, just watched her poke her toe into a small pool, little bigger than a puddle. She agitated the water, then glanced around the clearing. 'You and Zuri... Did you really never talk about marriage?'

'Never.'

'Just about having children.'

'Child,' I corrected her. 'Her child. Not necessarily mine.'

Sharda was facing me, all features in shadow, the sun appearing to be perched on her head. 'I really do not understand her, you know. From the things that happened to her – her mother, her father... I mean... To demand honesty, yes. But surely she should disapprove of being unfaithful? Approve of marriage? Not the other way round.'

'According to her, she owes her existence to her mother's infidelity, her mother's traumas to her being married, and all her own problems and disappointments to men's obsession with paternity.'

'Oh, I see – I think.' A large black mud wasp with dangling legs flew around her face and briefly landed on her hair. She flicked it away. 'So this lottery she wants when she conceives... This not wanting to know which man is the father of her child...'

'Is taken from the lions. And the camp Tswana. Everybody should follow their example, she says. It's the only way to cure the world of its obsession with paternity – which, incidentally, she blames for most of the world's evils.'

Suddenly she was distracted. 'Listen! Over there. In that tree. Those birds. All that noise. Does that mean there is a snake around?'

'Yep. A large one.'

'Ha! Strange how some things you never forget.' She returned to lie by my side on the sarong, then propping herself on her elbow she removed a few bits of straw that had blown onto my chest and belly. 'And you have sand everywhere too,' she said, attempting to brush some from my thighs. 'Even here. Look.'

'It always gets there.'

Using her trimmed and unpainted nails and doing her best not to pinch me, she began picking at grains of sand stuck between wrinkles of skin.

I winced, then laughed. 'It's OK. I'll wash it off in a minute. It's less painful.' I put my arm around her shoulders and nestled her against me, then closed my eyes.

Maybe she also closed her eyes because she didn't speak for a while, and when she did it was drowsily. 'Do you really think that Zuri – you know – has the gene?'

'Mother, Grandmother, Aunt… All early forties.'

'Poor thing. I can't imagine living under such a cloud.'

We may even have dozed again – but then from a ledge up to our left a Yellow-billed Hornbill suddenly flapped into the air giving a shrill alarm call. We looked for the cause. 'There!' Sharda said quietly, slowly raising her hand to point. 'Between the two rocks. Under the Acacia tree.'

The face studying us was so still and camouflaged it also could have been a rock, except it had a Springhare in its mouth. Sharda whispered: 'That's the first I have seen for ten years; since I was a child near Hoshiarpur.' We stayed absolutely still, just watching and being watched, until several minutes later the Leopard turned and walked away out of sight, probably to take the meal in its mouth back to its cubs. Sharda's eyes were bright, her smile wide, and mane of black hair tousled and wild. 'Wow,' she whispered as she began kissing me.

***

Back at the camp Inga and Indy were outside the dormitory. Sitting cross-legged in the shade of the four young Mopane trees they had Imbube with them. Indy was holding the baby at arm's length, his large coarse hands under the baby's tiny armpits, pretending to drop him then catch him. Imbube was laughing, almost hysterical with pleasure.

'We have just seen a Leopard,' Sharda told them, but Inga ignored her, addressing just me.

'There's been a couple of e-mails. Which do you want first? The scary? Or the very scary?'

I shrugged. 'The scary?'

'OK... Are you ready for this? It was from Fredrik, from his cell phone. He and Zuri are on their way from Jo'burg. Driving. Should arrive late tomorrow.'

'You're right,' I said. 'That is scary. So what's the very scary? From Dominic? I'm expecting one.'

'Not him, no. From a television company in the UK. Hawkmoth Films. They're making a documentary and need to spend some time with us. Maybe a week or so.'

'But that's not scary. That's great. Are they offering money? What's the documentary about?'

'No money. And it's not 'what' but 'who'.'

Chapter 27

Nobody waved as the truck drew near, nor as it drove past me into the centre of the compound. And when Zuri and Fredrik climbed out to face me we neither embraced nor shook hands.

'So... How shall we do this?' said Zuri, her expression taut. She had put on a little weight since I last saw her. So had Fredrik. And both were wearing a shirt, and shorts. But their feet were bare as always before.

'Depends on what 'this' is.' I said. 'But... Believe it or not, I'm glad you've both come. I've a proposition for the pair of you.'

Zuri exchanged glances with Fredrik. 'I wonder if it's the same proposition we've got for you.'

***

For four of us, the setting was familiar: early evening in the dormitory; a shared bottle of rum; a decision to be made. 'I'll be honest with you Mark,' said Fredrik, sitting next to Zuri on one of the beds. 'If I weren't so fucking broke, I'd never consider coming back here after what you bloody did.'

'Bullshit! I know you – both of you. You've both been bored stupid in Jo'burg these last few months and can't wait to get back here and get stuck in to some real work. By now neither of you could give a damn what Inga and I did or didn't do, any more than we care a toss about you two shagging each other. So let's stop pretending we do, shall we? Time to move on. We've all got lives to live.'

'Good start Boys,' said Inga. 'Keep it up.'

'Please... Fredrik. And you Zuri. Listen to Mark.' Sharda was sitting cross-legged on another of the beds. 'What he has to say... It is important. For all of us I think.'

'She's right.' I was standing in front of everybody, addressing them as if lecturing. 'Everything's changing here, and not for the better. Inga and Sharda already know – but a lot happened yesterday. First, we had an e-mail out-of-the-blue from a TV production company called Hawkmoth Films...' and briefly I explained about the documentary. 'Then we had an e-mail from Dominic spelling out the consequences of something I'd already been warned about: Indy's diamond operation is being moved to Sierra Leone.'

'Why?'

'Bigger profits, fewer risks. That's according to Indy, anyway. Personally... Well, it doesn't matter.'

'Moving when?'

'As soon as possible. Indy leaves here in a couple of days.'

'So... Why is that bad?' asked Zuri. 'I didn't think you wanted to be part of a diamond smuggling racket?'

'I don't – but it's still bad. With Indy elsewhere, we're redundant – at least as far as the Wolf is concerned. Surplus to requirements. Not worth funding any more. We always knew that once he'd got his knighthood it would happen sooner or later. Unfortunately, it's sooner.'

'How soon?'

'Right – now this is where it gets messy. Seems it was going to be immediately, but then this documentary about Cruickshank's life and 'good works' suddenly appeared. And both him and the TV people are hooked on the idea of him being filmed with 'his' lions in 'his' research centre. And for that they need us – they know it. So we've got a temporary reprieve.'

'A reprieve! You mean the Wolf thinks we'll help him? Why the fuck should we if he's going to ditch us immediately after?'

'Because... These are his 'generous' terms: one more injection of cash to make this place look presentable on film; and then from the date the program is first broadcast he'll provide enough money to keep us ticking over for exactly a year.'

'Ticking over? Does that include the plane?'

'For just the year, yes. Basically, he's blackmailing us into not sabotaging the filming, the broadcast, or the aftermath. If we do anything he doesn't like before that year is up – anything at all – we immediately lose everything. And if we do something really serious... Well, all the old threats are back.'

'Well, that's it then.' Fredrik looked at Zuri. 'What's the point in us coming back to this place if there's no money or future for us here? I know you don't want to start-over somewhere else Zuri. But what choice do we have?'

Zuri glared at him. 'A bit less of the 'us' and 'we' Fredrik. OK?'

'But listen...' said Sharda. 'Mark has a great idea.'

'Well, it's worth a shot at least. I think that for as long as the Wolf is prepared to give us at least something, we should take it. I've been through the figures and even on the pittance he's offering we can probably keep things going here for about eighteen months. Maybe even two years, depending on when the documentary is broadcast. And, if it looks as though it'll make a difference, I'll throw in whatever crumbs I can afford from my own money too. Two years isn't long, but it could be long enough.'

'To do what?'

'To make a real name for ourselves. Do something amazing. Something that will get everybody talking about us. And I don't just mean other scientists. I mean the media too: newspapers, TV, everybody. Then the money will come in – legitimate money – and so will other researchers. They'll be queuing up to spend their grant money here.'

'Oh sure,' said Fredrik. 'Something amazing. Right. What are you on Mark? We've been trying to think of 'something amazing' for years. Why are we suddenly going to come up with it now? Just because you say we need to?'

'Ah. But that's the thing. We already have come up with something. It's right under our noses.'

'What?'

'The impossible conception. Find the answer to that and we're made.'

'Go on,' said Zuri, suddenly looking interested despite Fredrik muttering expletives into his drink by her side.

'Right! First, we've got to ignore all our other projects. Throw absolutely everything, such as it is, into solving this mystery. Check and re-check every piece of information we already have. See if any of it's wrong. Fill in any gaps. Make sure we've got every bloody measurement, every tissue sample, every profile that could possibly be relevant. If we can only get enough of the right sort of information we can crack this, I know we can. How about it?'

***

The fireside group was the largest for a while. All the Tswana wanted to see Zuri and Fredrik again and to welcome them back with a big party. Sitting on the ground with a large animal-skin wrapped around his shoulders for warmth, Kopano prodded the fire with a stick. Sparks sprang into the dark sky until a downdraught swirled them back to the ground. Kopano adjusted his wrap, pulling it tight around his shoulders and holding it closed at the front with one hand. 'Your rum is good,' he said to Fredrik. 'Can it last the night?'

'Not the way you drink. We only brought ten crates.'

Zuri was sitting by Fredrik's side almost shoulder-to-shoulder, both of them now dressed campsite-style. Every time I glanced at Zuri she and Sharda seemed to be staring at each other.

Sharda had drunk faster than usual. 'Zuri!' she shouted across the fire, a hint of aggression in her voice. 'Have you noticed Imbube yet? He is very beautiful is he not?' She nodded in the baby's direction. 'This is the baby of Mark with Inga.'

Imbube wasn't with his mother but with Annakiya who was keeping him warm between her enormous breasts. His angelic face gazed out over the V of her goatskin wrap. He seemed mesmerised by the fire.

Zuri took her time, staring first at Imbube then at me. 'Yes,' she said at last. 'Very beautiful.'

I heard Fredrik swear, then: 'Where is Inga?' he snapped at me.

'Indy's quarters. She's been spending a lot of time there recently.'

He glanced across the compound and clenched his fist. 'This isn't going to work Mark. No fucking chance.'

'Indy's leaving soon.'

'But Inga's not. Nor that bastard son of yours. How the hell do you expect me to come to terms with seeing him around, eh?'

'Drink rum. Fix engines. Hunt lions. Enjoy Zuri. You'll cope.'

Sharda stood and began picking her way across to Zuri, daintily stepping round the fire and over outstretched legs. Zuri dragged on a joint and passed it on before looking up to meet Sharda's eyes. She seemed apprehensive as the younger woman approached, and even more-so as Sharda sat without invitation by her side. But uncomfortable though Zuri appeared a conversation began, even though Sharda seemed to be doing most of the talking. I tried to eavesdrop, but amidst the crackling of the fire and the general hubbub, their words were lost to me. It was the first time I had seen them together, the first time side by side. It was impossible not to compare both them and my feelings towards them. Gradually their conversation became less one-sided, the glances in my direction more frequent; smiles as well.

The drums began and Annakiya began swaying to the sound making Imbube laugh. Sharda and Zuri were still conversing, their expressions now excited, their body language animated. Occasionally they touched each other's arms or hands as they vied to make a point. Then everybody was called to the dance arena and the two women had no choice but to stop.

***

It was nearly dawn when Sharda and I crawled on to our bed in the dormitory and slipped inside our freezing sleeping bag. There were no mosquitoes, but still we pulled the nets around us. Three beds away to our right, Zuri and Fredrik were doing the same. We were the only four in the room.

Sharda nestled back into my arms as if ready for sleep until I moved her hair so that I could whisper in her ear. 'What were you and Zuri talking about for so long?'

Her laugh was muted. 'Partly you – of course – to begin.'

'What about me?'

'Oh, nothing important.'

'Mmm. And the rest of the time?'

'Well, the impossible conception, naturally.' She turned over to face me. 'Zuri and I, we are both very excited about finding the answer to this.'

'Aren't we all?'

'Yes, for sure. But Zuri and I – you know: my report, her thesis. I have already suffered for not knowing the answer, and maybe Zuri will too, when she has to defend her thesis. But... Mark... I have been thinking. If we do find the answer... When the paper is finally published... Will my name be included as an author? Even though I am just a technician?'

'Of course.'

'Good! Then when this paper is published I intend to hand a copy in person to Professor O'Flanahan and demand an apology.'

'That, I would love to see.' I chuckled, then nuzzled her ear. 'But we have to find the answer first. I don't suppose you and Zuri had any bright ideas while you were talking, did you?'

'No... But, we did decide one thing.'

A shuffling thumping sound which grew louder distracted us – and after a few moments our mosquito net was pulled back. It was Fredrik and Zuri, looking as though they were joined at the hip, their bottom halves still inside their double sleeping bag. They had hopped to us from their bed. 'We want to be in on this conversation,' said Zuri as the pair of them pulled the bag up to cover their shoulders, leaving only their heads showing.

'What conversation?'

'Heard every fucking word,' said Fredrik.

Sharda smiled at them and then continued. 'Well, Zuri and I think that the answer really must lie with the nomads in some way. You know – the males that we always thought were in the area visited by the two lionesses that night but have never been certain? The 'coincidence' that Professor O'Flanahan was so horrible to me about?'

Zuri took over. 'So we decided our first job should be to show that there really were nomads there. And when we've identified them to make sure that we know every last thing there is to know about those particular individuals.'

'Starting tomorrow,' said Fredrik. 'I've so missed flying that plane. Agreed?'

'Agreed!' the rest of us said in unison.

Chapter 28

'Is that a new pick-up? Who ordered that?' After returning from a five-day trip to Maun to lecture to Biology students from the University of Botswana, I was standing in the middle of the compound talking to Inga.

'The Wolf. It was delivered a couple of days ago. Seems his Lordship wants to be filmed driving around in something new and expensive when he comes here. Until then, we're not allowed to use it. When I told Indy about it – he phoned yesterday – he laughed and reckoned Cruickshank was teasing us, daring us to disobey him.'

'Sounds about right. Probably why it's been delivered three months early.'

'Maybe, though according to the TV people they need that much time to get everything sorted. And... Guess what? You know those pictures of the camp they asked for? They said the entrance won't do. They're going to arrange for it to be poshed-up again, this time with the Wolf's name in really big letters.'

'I don't care what they do as long as it means Cruickshank's money keeps trickling in.' A distant but approaching cloud of dust caught my attention for a moment. 'So Indy phoned, did he. I thought we'd heard the last from him.'

'So did I. Maybe he's missing me.'

'Maybe he is. Are you missing him?'

'No need to say it like that. And yes, I am. We got on well, Indy and me, even if it was in a drinking, smoking, fornicating sort of way. In fact...' But then she stopped.

I waited a few moments. 'Go on. 'In fact' – what?'

'Doesn't matter.'

'Inga! Don't be irritating.'

'No! You'll laugh at me.'

'Try me.'

'OK... But don't you dare say anything. I've always wanted several kids – you know that. More than one, anyway. And I'd have them by now if Fredrik... Anyway, until last week I was beginning to think – why not Indy for number two? Not immediately, obviously. When the time is right. When I've finished breast-feeding Imbube. When I'm fertile again. But now he's gone, it's rather left me short on options – hasn't it? – when the time does come for number two.'

I didn't comment, just continued to watch the approaching dust-cloud.

'Well say something.'

'You told me not to. Besides, there's nothing I can say.'

She squinted at me. 'Yes there is. You know bloody well what I'm getting at. So, what do you think? Would Sharda mind?' Again she waited in vain for me to say something, then sighed. 'OK. I get the picture.'

'Look... Inga... If all you want is sperm... There's always the Tswana lads.'

'Now you're making fun of me. Don't!'

'I'm not! Honestly.'

'Huh! Good – because it may well come to that. And just in case you think I don't mean it, let me tell you: there are a couple of those Tswana lads I definitely wouldn't say no to.'

'There you are then. Problem solved.'

We were silent after that, just watching and waiting for the cloud of dust to arrive and disgorge the truck at its heart; Fredrik, Zuri and Sharda returning from a three-day lion-hunting trip.

After parking under the Mopane trees, Fredrik leaped out, raised the truck's bonnet and peered into the engine. More sedately, Zuri and Sharda lifted out the cooler-box and came over, carrying the box between them. As they drew near they exchanged a comment and began giggling. 'What's so funny?' I asked, aware of how much I had missed them both.

'Best be careful, Mark. While you've been away Sharda graduated in cock-handling, knob-photography, and using an electro-ejaculator. Now that's two of us know what to do with a lubricated probe.'

Briefly I shared their amusement. 'Seriously though... Any news?'

'Well, the good news is that those three nomads we saw from the air before you went to Maun are definitely the ones the two lionesses were visiting that night. We downloaded their movement data onto the laptop – and bingo! All more or less exactly where the lionesses went.'

'Good, so those two females weren't just wandering about. They really were on a mission for sex on the side. Anything else? Anything unusual about the nomads?'

'Nothing in particular – though the biggest of the three did have a fairly strange prick. A lot more spines than normal. Longer, too. Anyway, we've got photographs – and all the tissue samples we need are in this box here. Let's hope we find some clues, eh?'

'Let's hope so. So... What's the bad news?'

'Ah. The pick-up's dying.'

I glanced across to Fredrik who was now underneath the truck with just his legs poking out. 'Shit!' I moved to go over to him.

'Mark!' said Inga, calling me back, then waiting until Zuri and Sharda were out of earshot on their way to the lab. 'You probably know this already; just didn't want to depress us all. But – I did a few calculations this morning. I mean – this plan of yours. It's really exciting, I can see that. And it's definitely got everybody on the same side. Very clever, I must say. But you must know: with the peanuts that the Wolf is now going to be giving us – and unless you're a lot richer than you've ever let on – we're not going to last two years. Nowhere near. Not with all the plane and truck journeys that are going to be needed. Plus all the lab stuff. And if that truck really is dying…'

'Then we'd better solve this bloody mystery sooner rather than later – hadn't we? Just don't tell the others. OK?'

***

I poked my head round the laboratory door. 'Off for a shower,' I said.

Sharda was collecting a print-out of data. 'I would join you – my hair is still full of desert – but…' She held up the print-out. 'Oh, by the way – how is the truck?'

'Transmission's buggered. Fredrik's doing his best but it's not looking good. We could be down to just the one jeep, unless we start using that forbidden pick-up of the Wolf's.' I glanced across to Zuri who was peering at the monitor screen. 'What are the pair of you looking at? Anything interesting?'

'Maybe. Come and look.'

I checked both the screen and the print-out. 'Zero? What's this? Another of Fredrik's? I thought you were making a start on the nomad ejaculates.'

'We are. This is from that big one with the over-spiny cock. Looks like he's infertile. Does that make any sense?'

***

Zuri and Sharda's data for the spiny nomad nagged at my mind as I went through the motions of washing myself. My thoughts were abstracted, almost random. *Infertile! Infertile like Fredrik.* I rinsed my hair, shoulders, back, and chest. *Sperm that fly. Pollen. Birds and bees.* My ablutions moved to my feet, legs, knees, thighs, groin. *What would it feel like*, I wondered, *to have... spines?*

I've enjoyed perhaps half-a-dozen eureka moments in my scientific life; memorable flashes of inspiration when the seemingly impossible suddenly becomes totally clear. One was above the mid-Atlantic; one was in bed during a bout of insomnia; and one was during sex, my mind not quite on the job. But most of my moments – as for Archimedes – were while wet, in my case in the shower. And so it was again. In one electric moment every single element of the mystery fell into place. The impossible conception suddenly seemed so simple and straightforward that my explanation just had to be right. But even that revelation wasn't the end. In its wake came something else; something so startling I stopped in mid-soap, and with water thudding against my head and body I carefully, step-by-step, thought the whole sequence through – until disturbed by a visitor. But by then it didn't matter. Everything was crystal-clear.

'Annakiya!' I shouted to the intruder, pulling her into the shower to take her shocked round face in my soapy hands and give her a long wet kiss on the mouth. As she fell against me, her breasts ballooned under my armpits, her rolls of flesh smothered my groin. Unable to breathe she began to laugh into the kiss, her whole body shaking. I released her.

'Hey Mark, Man. You drunk already?'

'Yes! With excitement,' I said, heading out of the cubicle.

'Oh, Man – you leaving? And here me thinking this my lucky day.'

***

'Where's Zuri?' I asked Sharda, still in the laboratory.

'Under the Baobab tree. She wanted to think.'

'Alone?'

'I think so.'

'Come with me.'

I sprinted all the way, leaving Sharda trailing behind.

'Where's the fire?' Zuri asked as I virtually skidded to a halt in the sand.

'No fire. I need you to be honest with me about something.'

'I always am.'

Sharda arrived.

'Are you?' I said. 'Then why didn't you tell me that you and Fredrik had sex long before the pair of you buggered off in your holier-than-thou huff to Jo'burg?'

'Oh, that… …… No Mark! Don't look at me like that. You mean the North Dune trip, yes?'

'No, I don't mean the North Dune trip. But there too? The bastard. I meant before that,' and I told her exactly, almost to the minute, when I thought it must also have happened.

Her mouth dropped open. 'How could you possibly…? Even I…'

'Mark,' warned Sharda quietly, gesturing with her head.

Over Zuri's shoulder, I saw Fredrik emerge from the camp entrance. On an impulse, I jumped down from my rock and strode towards him. Then picking my moment I ran the last few paces and punched him as hard as I could on the side of the head.

Maybe his thick beard cushioned the blow because he staggered but didn't fall. 'What the hell?' His expression was more of surprise than of pain. So with all my strength I hit him again, and this time to my immense satisfaction his knees buckled and he slumped to the ground.

Chapter 29

I tensed to defend myself, but Fredrik stayed on the ground, just sitting up and wiping blood from the corner of his mouth. 'Jesus, Mark. What the hell was that for?' Occasionally wincing, he fingered his ear, jaw and eye. 'I hope you broke your fucking hand.'

'He knows about North Dune,' Zuri warned him.

'Oh, right – shit!' said Fredrik. 'I guess we're quits then.' He held out his hand for me to pull him to his feet.

'Sod North Dune. That's not why I hit you. And no, we're not quits. Because you deserved that punch in the head. I didn't. Not if I'm right about this anyway.'

'Right about what?'

'The impossible conception. But there wasn't just one. There were two – at least – and I've solved them both – bastard! But every cloud... I'm telling you: this thing is bigger than we thought. It goes way beyond lions.'

***

'Nothing?'

'Not so far.'

'Good! Nerve-wracking, eh?' I was standing behind, peering past her black hair at the computer screen. Even after a night of celebration and discussion, I was still excited – and tense. 'We must be the first – mustn't we? Surely if anybody's published this idea before, at least one of us would know about it.'

'Maybe.' She showed me a scribbled list. 'These are all the search-terms I've used so far. Can you think of any more?'

'Perhaps something less technical? Think a bit more laterally?'

'Like what?' she asked, so I suggested a few.

Normally I would have been doing the literature search myself, but Fredrik was needing my help to dismantle our truck's transmission. I placed my hands on her bare shoulders, near her long neck, and gave a gentle squeeze. 'Why not take a break first?' I said. 'Let's go and find the others. Have a coffee. See if anybody else has suggestions.' Suddenly realising what I'd done, I lifted my hands and apologised. It was a reflex, I told her. From the past. My mind was elsewhere. It wouldn't happen again.

Zuri looked up at me. 'No need to apologise to me, Mark. Save that for Sharda.'

***

'Fredrik,' I yelled across the compound. 'Coffee?'

'Two minutes,' he bellowed back.

'Has he apologised yet?' I asked Inga. 'For all those names he called you?'

'Fredrik? Apologise? Not his style. Why? Has he to you? Or to you Zuri? Because he really should. In my book he raped you that night, no matter how fantastic the consequences.'

Zuri shrugged. 'Well, murky waters I guess. And all under the bridge by now.' In the distance a Tswana woman appeared, ambling towards us with Imbube on her hip. Zuri gave a quiet laugh. 'My God, Inga. How many baby-minders do you have?'

'As many as I need. It's brilliant. I tell you Zuri, for a single parent this is the place to be. They just love children, no matter whose they are.'

As the Tswana woman passed near Fredrik he clearly asked to take the baby from her. So far he had largely ignored Imbube, all vibes hostile. But as he approached us now, carrying the boy, he was smiling. So was Imbube, amusing himself by grabbing at Fredrik's beard. 'Anybody got a camera handy?' Fredrik asked as we all looked at him in mild disbelief. 'I want a picture – while I've still got this black eye and before this little one gets any older. I want a record of him as a baby with his mother and two fathers.' He glanced at each of us. 'Because I am, aren't I? In a way?... .... Oh, don't look so bloody shocked all of you. Maybe I've accepted that Imbube is as near as I'm ever going to get.'

***

'What's wrong?' I asked, finding Zuri and Sharda in the office looking glum.

'Bad news. The worst. One of those search terms you suggested... You're not the first to have this idea after all. A couple of Americans suggested exactly the same thing back in 2004.'

'Shit! No! Really?'

'Afraid so.'

'Shit! I don't believe it. I was so convinced... How come we haven't heard about it then?'

Zuri shrugged. 'It was buried in a paper about something else. And they didn't have any proof. I guess nobody believes it can actually happen; just an off-the-wall theory. But there's no escaping it. They did think of it first.'

I felt devastated, the blow seeming all the worse because of the highs we had all been experiencing since my moment in the shower. Sharda placed a consoling hand on my arm. 'Does it matter, Mark? Really? Surely obtaining actual proof would be just as important? Maybe even more important. And we can do this, the five of us. Zuri and I have been talking. We need to collect many swabs from many lions, particularly nomads. This will surely show that such an event is possible.'

'But 'possible' isn't good enough. It would have been – but not any more. I agree about the swabs, but whatever they show, no matter how much they point in the right direction, the idea will remain just a theory. And now it's not even our theory, it's somebody else's. We needed to be first. Without credit for that, only absolute proof would get us noticed; get us talked about in the way we need. And with wild lions, it can't be done. Maybe with captive lions, a zoo full, plus lots of cages. But for us, here, with our resources… It's just not possible.'

Zuri was frowning. 'So… What are you saying? We should give up? Before we've even started? That's not like you.'

I began to move to the door.

'Where are you going?' asked Sharda.

'Into the desert. I need to think.'

'Then wait. I shall come with you.'

'No! Sorry. I need some time on my own. I'm going to run, not drive.'

'Oh. OK. But how long will you be?'

'I don't know.' At the door, I turned back to them. 'I have an idea you see – a Plan B – but the cost is high. I'm not sure I can justify it, even to myself.'

'Cost? You mean more than we can afford?'

'How much? Roughly?' asked Zuri.

'Not money – lives; one of them mine and some of them babies'.'

Chapter 30

Carrying a bow, four arrows, and a digging stick I ran from the camp, pushing myself to my limits, ever-vigilant for snakes, leg-breaking potholes, and thorns. After about ten kilometres and in the shelter of dunes I built a fire, shot a large lizard, clubbed a snake, and dug up roots and tubers. Darkness fell quickly, and so did the temperature. But the fire roared, the reptiles baked in the ashes, and my mind worked overtime. One by one my decisions were made, but none was easy and several times through the night I changed my mind. I didn't sleep until dawn.

At noon I jogged in to the camp to be greeted by an array of worried faces and a barrage of questions. I diverted them all by announcing that after a night of thinking everything through I'd decided that Plan B couldn't work after all. I didn't even want to discuss it. But... 'Fredrik... Can we talk?' I said at the first opportunity.

*****

He couldn't stop laughing. 'You're crazy. This proves it. Why didn't you talk it over – sensibly – with the rest of us, instead of running off into the desert and having a fucking brainstorm? We could have saved you from yourself. Or do you want to commit professional bloody hara-kiri?'

In some ways Fredrik was right. No ethical committee would ever sanction what I was proposing. There was no point in even applying. And as a result, I could easily be accused of unprofessional, maybe even immoral, conduct and lose my job for bringing disrepute on my University. 'No, of course I don't. But come on Fredrik. It's perfect, isn't it? It's cheap. It's easy to do. And if it works it'll prove beyond doubt that this thing can really happen. Sod the ethics. This place – our group – would become one of the most talked about research units in the world. Come on Fredrik, say yes. You know you want to.'

'Maybe I do, maybe I don't. Look, Mark… I'm hardly the most ethical of people. But even I can see you can't go around producing babies left, right and centre just to get this place talked about.'

'Really? Not even if the women want those babies? But… OK. If that's how you really feel then say no, and that'll be the end of it. There is no experiment without you, and you know it. Our future's in your hands. But… C'mon. What do you say?'

'Hell, I don't know. Of course it appeals to me. It would to any man.' He thought for a few moments. 'If I agreed, who would the women be?'

I told him.

He laughed again. 'For fuck's sake… Naagh, even you can't pull that one off.'

***

'Two of the Tswana women!' laughed Zuri. 'Are you out of your mind? And what about Sharda? What does she say? Or is that why you sent her off on a wild goose chase with Kopano and Annakiya? So she wouldn't hear this conversation?'

'Not wild geese – cucumbers! And never mind Sharda. It's you we're asking.'

'And me,' butted in Inga. 'Or aren't I allowed to comment on who my son's father and my husband fuck any more?'

'No!' said Fredrik. 'You're not.'

'Stop it you two,' Zuri said before addressing me. 'Look... As far as I'm concerned you two men can screw who you want, you both know that. All I've ever asked is the same privilege – and to be kept informed. But two of the Tswana women? Honestly Mark. Are you crazy? Is this going to be a scientific experiment or what? Because... OK... Here's the crux of it. Is my name going to be on this paper? Am I going to be one of the authors?'

'Of course you are. Inga too. I was hoping that you'd deal with all the sperm stuff, Zuri, and you, Inga, would take care of all the more-medical bits. The idea is that the four of us will be joint-authors. I assume you both want to be?'

'Try and stop us,' said Zuri. 'Because – I must say Mark – it is a fantastic idea. I could kick myself for not thinking of it.'

'But what about Sharda?' asked Inga. 'I can't believe she's happy, not about any of it.'

'Well, to be honest, I wanted to speak to you three before I mentioned it to her. But I'm hoping she'll take charge of all the DNA work. Be a fifth author. But...'

'But more than likely she'll tell you to go to hell and be on the first plane out of here, eh?' said Zuri, with unattractive zeal. 'Right, well if I'm going to be an author on this paper, we're definitely not using the Tswana...' and she went on to explain why.

I listened, and did my best to let Zuri think that the insight was new to me. The only way we could recruit a Tswana woman for sex, Zuri said, would be to pay her – and most of her wider family would probably demand payment as well. Admittedly, she said, it might only be rum and dagga – but any sort of payment would make our ethical position even more difficult to defend. The experiment was moral minefield enough without involving what some might consider prostitution as well. And not only that, Zuri continued, even if the women we recruited really tried, which they probably wouldn't, they'd find it virtually impossible to avoid sex with their various boyfriends or lovers for the months on end that the experiment would demand. 'You know these Tswana.'

'But it's got to be two Tswana women,' I said. 'Who else?' But Zuri knew me far too well.

'Mark, you're not fooling anybody. You knew that if you suggested recruiting two Tswana women, Inga and I would say you were stupid and volunteer in their place.'

'You two!'

'Oh, come on. Spare us the play-acting. Of course 'us two'. For the science? For women everywhere? For the future of this place? You knew damn well we'd be suckers for all that, not to mention a juicy slice of the fame and notoriety. And on top of all that, Inga will get baby number two, and right on cue I'll get not only my one-and-only but a lottery as well. So don't act the innocent. You knew, absolutely knew, we'd both want to do it.'

'Well speak for yourself,' Inga said to her. 'I mean... Just look at these two old rejects of ours. Do we really want to be shagging them for the next few months? Even if it is in a good cause? Now... If we could use those two young Tswana lads we've both been ogling...'

Zuri simply laughed.

'Very funny,' I said. 'And in an ideal world you two wouldn't be top of our list either. But seriously... Zuri... You do know... The experiment will give you your lottery, sure – but if we do manage to produce a baby from it you are going to know who the father is. You can't avoid it.'

'I know – of course. And for me that's the only downer – though I know none of you ever thought I was serious. But... Just promise me you two,' she said to Fredrik and me. 'No laying claim. OK? The baby's mine. Nobody else's. It's not having a father. Those are my terms.'

'Wouldn't have been much of a lottery anyway,' rued Fredrik. 'Not with odds of zillions to zero.' Fredrik's infertility was a crucial factor in the experiment. So crucial that, sorry though I felt for him, my real worry was that those odds might change. As we still didn't know the cause of his condition – because he was still refusing to find out – it remained possible that his problem was only temporary, the result of some minor blockage somewhere which could clear at just the wrong moment and ruin everything.

Zuri placed a consoling hand on Fredrik's shoulder, but her words were aimed at me. 'It's brilliant Mark. It's totally unethical. Deliciously bizarre. Typically you. We'll be in every magazine and newspaper in the world. I'm really excited. When do we start?'

'Not sure. Inga still breast-feeding is a bit of a problem. We'll need to think everything through. But first, I've got to talk to Sharda. I'm dreading it.'

***

We were at the rocky outcrop, but the trickles and puddles – in fact the whole atmosphere from our previous visit – had gone. 'I cannot believe you are saying this to me. How can you even think of doing this thing? I thought I meant something to you.'

'You do mean something to me – of course you do. It's just an experiment. Cold-hearted. Mechanical. It has to be. Nothing I do will change how I feel about you.'

'Do you think I am stupid? Ever since Zuri has been back, I have seen how she looks at you. How you look at her. Why not simply be honest with me? Tell me that you prefer

Zuri to me. That I would understand. But to dream up this experiment...'

'No! Stop it! Right there. I don't prefer Zuri to you. That is not what this is about. It's the experiment... Sharda, it has to be done. And me, Fredrik, Zuri and Inga are the people to do it.'

'Which means that you want to have sex with her. How can you say otherwise?'

'For the experiment, that's all. My real partner will still be you, not her.'

'Aha. That's the word isn't it. 'Partner,' not wife.' She looked sad, even hurt. 'Maybe it was presumptuous of me, but until just a few minutes ago when you told me about this terrible experiment... Oh, you cannot be so blind Mark. You have been so kind and caring and tender to me these last few months. So loving. I really thought...'

'I know you did. And no, it wasn't presumptuous of you. But can't you see? Partner, wife... Fredrik and Inga actually are married. Is that making any difference? Look Sharda... This experiment – it's important. Not only to science but to everybody everywhere. Just imagine if your sister had known such a thing was possible? Or Mia? They might both be alive now. And their children. That's how important this experiment could be. We can't let our emotions get in the way.'

She faltered a little. 'Well maybe it is important. But still... To ask me not to feel hurt by your having sex with other women, especially Zuri. Do you really not understand how I feel about you?'

'Of course I understand. And I feel the same about you. Honestly, I do. I know I don't say all the things you would like to hear; use the words you would like me to use. But that's me. That's how I am, and you won't change that.

But that doesn't mean... Surely you can't be that blind either?' Her face flickered with a smile, but the frown soon returned when I continued: 'But I still need you to accept what I have to do. And you can. Because you're a true scientist. You're objective. Strong enough to rise above the situation.'

'You are trying to flatter me into submitting. Stop it!'

'OK... Then how about if I promise that once this experiment is over, everything will return to how it was. You and me. Together. Like now. A couple.'

'A couple how? Will you marry me?'

'Not on paper, no. But in every other way.'

'Hah! In every other way. Do you think I do not realise? Once everything is over, you will have two more children – and neither of them with me.'

'Only if the experiment is a success. It might fail miserably. Besides, lots of women have partners who have children elsewhere.'

'But your children won't be elsewhere. They will be here. I will see them every day. And so will you.... ...... No Mark. I have two questions for you. Two very important questions.'

'Go on.'

'First... Why did you talk to the others about this experiment before you talked to me?'

'Because if they refused to take part there would be no experiment and I could spare you this conversation. I knew you'd be hurt by it.'

'Mmm. And secondly... Why have you not asked me to be part of this experiment also? I mean a proper part, as a subject, not just as an author. Surely three conceptions are stronger proof than two?'

'Why?' I stared at her. 'Because... You know why.'

'Oh, for sure I know why: you do not like the idea of my having sex with Fredrik.'

'Of course I don't.'

'But why? It will be cold-hearted. Mechanical. It has to be. You are a scientist. Surely you can be objective about this? Rise above it? And we are already very experienced at this, you and me – thanks to the Wolf. At least Fredrik will not be raping me.'

I didn't even hesitate. 'I still don't like the idea.'

'No? Well I am very glad that you do not like the idea – just like I do not like the idea of your having sex with Zuri and Inga. But if you intend to take part in this experiment no matter what I say then here are my terms. I also shall take a full part in the experiment, with the four of you. And when it is over, and I have your baby as a result, you and I will go back to being a couple – as you promised just moments ago – to raise that baby just as if we were married.'

'But – you do realise. You say my baby, but that's only if the experiment is a success. If anything goes wrong your baby could be Fredrik's, not mine. Or – even more likely – there won't be a baby for us to raise anyway.'

'Then we shall raise the baby fathered by Fredrik – or we shall have one the normal way and raise that. I should be very happy with this last option. But the experiment will be a success, I know it. This is a very clever idea and once the experiment is over I shall be proud to have taken part in it, to be one of the authors of the scientific paper, to be the partner of the man who thought of it – and to have my very own little Imbube as a result. So… What do you say? Do you agree to my terms? Or do I have to leave this place and find myself another man? Another life?'

***

Fredrik and I were the first in the laboratory that evening and immediately each collected a bottle of beer from the fridge. The three women were showering but due to meet us in the lab shortly so that we could start planning the experiment in detail. 'Here's to success and infamy,' I said as we chinked the bottles before each taking a swig.

He wiped his mouth with the back of his hand, then grinned at me. 'Mark de Vries... You're a cunning, evil, manipulative bastard.'

'No I'm not. I'm a scientist.'

Chapter 31

There is no Spring in the Kalahari. At the end of August the cold dry season that we call Winter turns almost overnight into the hot dry season that we call Summer – and on the day our experiment was to begin the dormitory was both bright and sweltering, the air filled with floating dust and dancing flies. On one of the beds my 'mate' – for that was the term decided – was lying waiting for me as scheduled.

It was over a month since we had all consented to what was about to happen; a month which allowed Sharda not only to stop taking the contraceptive pill and to have a period but also to reach the brink of the fertile phase of her cycle. Every physiological step of the way had been monitored, and just that morning Inga had confirmed that Sharda was not pregnant. Not that pregnancy was likely for any of the three women. Even apart from Zuri still being on the pill and Inga still breast-feeding, since the day of decision everybody had avoided sexual contact: no intercourse, no intimate caressing, and no sleeping in the same bed. We had even opted to avoid kissing mouth-on-mouth in case things escalated. And except for the 'matings' that were now programmed, we intended to continue with this discipline until all three women had conceived and the experiment was over – which we knew could take months or even years.

Despite all the talking and planning, the moment seemed surreal: the first mating. 'So... How are we really going to do this?' I asked as I sat on the edge of her bed.

'How?' she said, the ceiling fan moving air over our sweating bodies. 'I don't know. Maybe pretend that we still love each other?'

'Not part of the deal.' A pair of copulating flies suddenly fell from the air to land and buzz loudly on my back. I shrugged them away.

'Excited?' she asked.

'Isn't that obvious? What about you?' I placed my hand far up on her thigh.

'As horny as hell.' Taking hold of my wrist she pulled me on to her, lifting and separating her knees as she did so; only the missionary position was to be used. As soon as I had penetrated fully, but before thrusting, I started the stop-clock by the side of her bed. Then I started counting.

I had promised myself – and Sharda – that I would neither kiss Zuri nor caress her. Nor would I moan or writhe or do anything that might convey I was enjoying myself. But it was hopeless. We were stranded in the Kalahari, alone at night. The last few months had never happened. We totally lost control.

'That was quick,' she said.

'You were quicker.'

'So how many?'

'No idea. I lost count. Fifty?'

'Sounds about right. Oh, the clock. You forgot to stop the clock.'

'Shit! Take off thirty seconds?'

It had been decided – because no detail could be left to individual discretion – that it would be best for the experiment if I waited to fade rather than risk pulling out too forcefully or too soon. 'I've missed you,' she whispered as we kissed, stroked and waited for the moment I could roll off.

Once off I started another clock; this time I remembered. We needed to allow a further five minutes for certain things to happen inside her, and during this time she had to lie still. So we lay side-by-side holding hands and silent, watching geckos on the ceiling, until the buzzer sounded and I got off the bed.

'So... Until two days time,' Zuri said.

***

'That was quick,' grinned Inga, starting her stop-watch and handing me a data sheet to complete as I arrived at the rocks under the Baobab tree. I forced myself neither to reciprocate Inga's smile nor to meet Fredrik's stare. But I did hesitantly return Sharda's weak smile of reassurance – or was it apprehension? We sat shoulder-to-shoulder but felt miles apart. Eventually she reached for my hand but still we sat in silence, our palms growing ever clammier as the seconds ticked by.

Inga glanced at the two of us, then at Fredrik sitting alone, jiggling his right leg and fiddling with his beard. 'My God, anybody would think this was a funeral.' We all tried to laugh – but for me the worst was still to come. 'Right. That's the ten minutes. Go!' Inga said to Fredrik.

***

Twenty minutes after Fredrik had entered the dormitory Zuri came out, still tying her sarong as she ambled in our direction. Sharda gave my hand a squeeze then let go. 'So,' she sighed. 'Just another half-an-hour.'

'Not too late. You can still back out. Everybody will understand.'

'No! Not true. Nobody will understand. Particularly you. Besides, why should I? Maybe if I try hard I can enjoy myself with Fredrik as much as you did with Zuri.' Her expression was severe. 'Don't deny it Mark. I saw your face afterwards. And now I see her face as well.'

Zuri had a spring in her step and was grinning broadly as she approached. 'Well, that's my job done.' She took the offered sheet of paper. 'Do you know, despite everything – I've never done that before. Not so soon, one after the other.'

'Then you've obviously never been to a Medics' party,' said Inga.

Only Sharda did not laugh. 'Of course you have done it Zuri.' She was glaring as she spoke. 'Imbube. Remember?'

Zuri gave an airy wave of her hand. 'Oh, you know what I mean. I knew nothing about that one. Today I... Well... You know...' Her voice tailed away.

'This is horrible,' said Sharda. 'I hate being last. Half-an-hour... It is too long. Surely Fredrik is ready by now?'

'Half-an-hour,' said Inga. 'We all discussed it. We all agreed.'

'Well... I cannot just sit here. I need to walk.... .... No Mark. Alone. I must be alone. Please shout to me when it is time.' And when it was 'time' Sharda didn't re-join us, just made her way straight to the distant dormitory.

'Still no regrets at volunteering for this?' I asked the two remaining women.

Zuri was about to answer when she suddenly parted her sarong and glanced at her groin. 'Inga! Quick!' she said, holding out her hand. 'Give me a jar. It's coming.'

***

Inga pushed back my foreskin, ran a swab round the back flange of my glans, then placed the sample in a jar for Sharda to label and store. Fredrik took my place and received the same treatment. We were all five in the laboratory. 'Is that everything?' Inga asked Zuri who was standing by with a list. It seemed it was.

I perched on the corner of a bench. 'Right... I said. 'First day, first question: does anybody want to change their mind? Anybody want to drop out? Because if so, now's the time to say.'

Amidst a shaking of heads, only Sharda spoke. 'What about you Mark? Maybe you should 'drop out'. Maybe you have discovered that you cannot be as cold-hearted and mechanical as we all said was necessary – and promised.'

'Sharda... Don't! I know how you're feeling. I'm feeling exactly the same about you and Fredrik.'

'No, not exactly I think. Fredrik is not my ex-boyfriend. He is more like the Wolf.'

'The Wolf? Gee, thanks.'

'Oh no. I am sorry Fredrik. I did not mean... You were very nice to me today. Very gentle. It was a big surprise for me. A nice surprise. But we did all agree: no emotion. Did we not Mark?' The moment was tense, and a silence followed, but Sharda hadn't finished. 'And I have another complaint. The Baobab tree, it is too far from the dormitory. It is silly to walk so far before and after.'

Inga looked annoyed. 'But that was for you Sharda. Remember? Part of your privacy thing. You didn't want us all just outside the dormitory.'

'Yes... Well... Maybe I have changed my mind. Maybe now I think that privacy is not so important. Maybe now I think it is much more important to be certain that some people are behaving as we agreed?'

Fredrik cleared his throat. 'OK. Moving on... I've got a problem too – a man problem. It's fucking impossible to count how many thrusts. I told you it would be. And I forgot to start the clock – didn't I Sharda? Those numbers I put on my questionnaire were pure guesswork. Didn't you find it difficult Mark? You must have done.'

I nodded. 'But you do all realise? There's only one way to solve all these problems – which is fine by me. Anything to keep everybody happy and to get the science right. Plus it will give us a permanent record we can go back to and check data from later, if necessary. But what about the rest of you? Sharda?'

Chapter 32

One truck contained people, the other television equipment; Inga and Kopano were returning from meeting the air-taxi at the landing strip. It was mid-October and Hawkmoth TV Productions had warned us to expect an advance party of three. Now they were here: a fairly short slightly pear-shaped middle-aged woman; a tall lanky man, and...

Sharda's nails dug into the skin of my arm. 'Is that...? Please no! He is not due here for another week.'

'Stay calm,' said Zuri, putting her hands on Sharda's bare brown shoulders. 'No stress, remember?'

The Wolf had arrived early and unannounced. There he was, ambling towards us at the back of the group. Except... 'It's not him,' I whispered to Sharda. 'It looks like him but...'

From Inga's introductions we learned that the woman was the director, the lanky man was both cameraman and sound recordist, and... 'This is Burt...' Inga began, but the director cut her short.

'So... What do you think of him Mark? Can I call you Mark? A dead-ringer for Sir Cameron – yes?'

'Scarily so,' I shook Burt's unexpectedly soft outstretched hand. 'But why? Isn't Cruickshank coming next week?'

'Sir Cameron?' said the director. 'Well of course he's coming. But he's a busy man. He wants to be here for as short a time as possible. Just overnight, he says. Anyway, we're going to use Burt here for the distant shots. Then all Sir Cameron will need to do is pose for the close-ups. By the way, he particularly wants to be photographed with a lion. And with some of your black natives too. Very important. Not a problem Mark, is it?' She paused for breath. 'Right. Now... My God, how do you cope with this heat? And all these flies. Time to freshen up I think. Slip into something cooler too.' She suddenly seemed to notice Zuri and Sharda. 'I must say girls, those sarongs are pretty. Don't suppose you have a spare one do you?' Without waiting for an answer, she addressed Inga. 'Right... Sorry. Forgotten the name. What was it? Ingrid? Or something?' Inga reminded her. 'Ah yes, of course. So, lead on Inga. I'm in Indy's old quarters I gather. They're empty, yes? Now there's a man. Oh, I nearly forgot. Mark... Oh. Did I ask? Do you mind? No? Good. Can you find a tent for these two. They've decided they'd like to share. Be a bit private. You know.' She winked at me. 'Just don't tell their significant others. OK. Right. Ingrid? Shall we go?'

***

From the very first morning the director worked everybody hard, herself included. Day after day, film was taken of Burt at the wheel of the now not-so-pristine truck as it left from, arrived at, or passed through as many different Kalahari habitats as possible. Sometimes Burt was alone, sometimes I was with him. After that, yet more footage was taken of him in the plane pretending to fly.

'Can Cruickshank fly?' I asked.

The director looked shocked. 'Sir Cameron? Yes, of course he can – and he will.'

She wanted shots – usually from the back – of Burt and me standing in the open together. 'Mark... Point at something. No! Other hand. Higher. And slower. Don't jab so much. Burt! Body language! Show some interest man. Oh for God's sake.'

We flew into the desert so that Burt could be filmed with lions in the background. I agreed to dart one so that from a distance he could be seen watching attentively, even seeming to help, as I took samples. 'Dear God! What a suggestion. Electro-ejaculation? Just blood Mark. OK? This is going out prime-time. There'll be children watching.'

She took film of Inga teaching the Tswana children the alphabet and treating minor ailments; also sequences both inside and outside the office and laboratory. 'Sir Cameron paid for these buildings, yes?' And later on she wanted footage of Burt in the more picturesque spots around the camp, such as under the Baobab tree, the row of young Mopane trees, and on the rocky outcrop. Finally she filmed long sequences of the Tswana around the campfire at night, making it appear as though the naked men and semi-naked women were putting on a special performance in honour of their guest.

'So what happened to prime-time?'

'Oh boobs aren't a problem, as long as they're native of course. Can't see nipples when they're black on black. And we'll fog out the peckers. Easy. Maybe leave one in, top corner. Make it seem like an oversight. Get a few complaints. Boost the iplayer downloads.'

At the end of a hard week she gave everybody a day's rest.

'So where's your pretty Asian friend today Mark?'

'Taking it easy. She woke up feeling a bit rough this morning.'

'Well I hope she's better when Sir Cameron arrives tomorrow. He particularly asked for a shot of the pair of them together. He likes being seen talking to beautiful women.'

'Surely Zuri will do just as well.'

'Afraid not. Too black. Oops! Sorry – but you know Sir Cameron.'

***

The director was twirling her hair so vigorously I thought it would knot, but she didn't have to wait much longer. Scarcely had the air-taxi halted than Cruickshank appeared, posture very upright as he came down the steps. He was wearing a pristine safari outfit, not a crease in sight. Behind him came a bodyguard whom I recognised: the five-ways-to-break-your-neck and piss-on-your-carpet visitor to my flat. His large size combined with the two cases he was carrying caused him to rock slightly from side to side as he descended.

'Only one goon, Cruickshank? Are you sure you'll feel safe?'

'Where's your shirt Boy?'

'I don't wear shirts around the camp.'

'You will while I'm here. Black nipples turn my stomach. Especially on men.' He gestured to his guard, who put down the two cases and began to undo his buttons. But before the shirt could be offered I headed off to the truck. I could feel the director watching me. Maybe nobody had warned her.

Cruickshank insisted on sitting in the truck's passenger seat next to me. After pulling a cigar from the top pocket of his shirt he placed it unlit in the corner of his mouth. Not a word was said during the journey until we arrived at the camp entrance. Then the director tapped me on the shoulder and asked me to stop.

'There Sir Cameron. What do you think ?' She pointed at the sign with *Sir Cameron Cruickshank Lion*

Research Centre emblazoned in large gold lettering. Nodding his approval, he gestured for me to continue.

'God what a dump. I hope you've made it look better on film?' he said to the director. 'Now... Where are my headquarters?'

The director indicated Indy's chalet. 'It's two separate apartments. That's where I am too. In a sense, we'll be sharing.'

'No we won't. I'm entertaining tonight. Get somebody to pitch her a tent Boy. Then let's get to work. I'm not spending any more time in this God-forsaken shit-hole than I have to.'

***

The most difficult filming had been scheduled first and involved flying out to the main territory of the North Dune pride so that Cruickshank could be filmed patting an anaesthetised lion. The main pride had dispersed but we knew two or three were still in the area and in the early afternoon we could almost guarantee finding one asleep in the shade somewhere. Fredrik, Zuri and the cameraman had driven on ahead to get everything ready.

'Don't you want to fly the plane Sir Cameron?' The director was in the back seat, next to the bodyguard.

'On the way back. Let's get this job done first.' He watched me as I climbed the plane to 3000 feet, then roll out on to a northerly heading into a 30 knot headwind. 'Why is one of your fuel tanks empty?'

'It's not. The needles stick.' Leaning forward, I tapped the dial and the apparently empty tank suddenly read full. 'The radio's not working properly either. The internal intercoms are OK but that's all we've got. So don't crash us on the way back, OK? We've got no Mayday available.' I paused, then made the most of the opportunity. 'We need more money for maintenance.'

He grunted, then issued an order to the pair behind us. 'Switch off your intercoms, then remove them. I want a private word with de Vries.'

'Why is he with us?' I said, meaning the bodyguard, as soon as I thought he couldn't hear.

'D'ya think I'm a fool Boy? Don't tell me it hasn't crossed your mind that this is some sort of pay-back opportunity for you. And if it hasn't crossed your mind, then it certainly will have done Sharda's. Where is that Asian bitch of yours anyway?'

'She doesn't want to see you.'

'Huh! Tell her to come to my quarters after we've finished filming tonight. Twenty-three hundred. I have a rendezvous planned with that young cunt of hers.' I saw him glance in the mirror at the director. She replied with a smile.

'Like hell you have.'

'Not a request Boy. An order. And if you want this shanty camp of yours to keep running for the next year, you make sure she does as she's told.'

'Threaten all you want. It won't make any difference. Besides, she's pregnant.'

'Pregnant! How very careless of you both. Well even better. See if I can get rid of it for you shall I? Save the world from yet another coloured bastard. Or maybe… How far gone is she? Maybe it's mine. Did I drop two in one night?'

'Two? Which night?'

'Which night? Ha! As if you could forget. In that poky flat of yours. My wife fell to me that night too. She's twenty weeks now. What about Sharda?'

'You can forget your fantasy. Sharda's only four weeks. And the father's either me or Fredrik.'

'Either-or? So she is a dog-bitch after all.'

'Dog-bitch, wolf-bitch... What's the difference. Have you tested this wife of yours yet? See who the baby's father is this time? You should. Save yourself the embarrassment you had with Mia.'

'Not funny Boy.'

'It is to me. Take my advice. Don't wait until it's born. Have her tested now. Any time after 15 weeks. All you need is a sample of the mother's blood. Completely safe.'

A hand appeared between us and tapped Cruickshank on the right shoulder. 'What?' he snapped. A grinning director was pointing out of the window. He followed her direction. 'So it's a bloody giraffe. So what?' She smiled and nodded. 'What are you talking about Boy? Melody was being watched, 24/7.'

'So was Mia. But JJ got through, didn't he? And so did I, twenty weeks ago. You rape Sharda, I rape your wife. Seems fair to me. Except I didn't need to. She was all for it.'

'Dangerous game Boy. I suggest you stop.'

'So don't believe me. But if you're so certain, where's the harm in checking, eh? I'm sure you've still got my DNA on record somewhere. So arrange a paternity test. Straight away. Why not? You'll see. You're no more the father of this wife's baby than you were of Mia's or you are of Sharda's. Two in one night? Ha! You can't even manage one. In fact, have you produced any little wolf-cubs that are definitely yours yet?'

***

Fredrik had a lion darted and ready by the time we arrived and while Zuri processed the animal the director explained to Cruickshank the camera shots that would be needed to complete the sequence filmed with his double. But even as the director was speaking, Cruickshank was unclipping his cell phone from his belt and studying the screen. 'Dammit! Somebody give me a phone that'll get a signal in this goddam wilderness.'

Fredrik fetched him the satellite phone from the truck. Cruickshank moved well out of earshot to make his call which lasted several minutes. When his call was over, he stalked straight over to Zuri who was in the process of taking a blood sample from the lion's leg.

'You! Cover your tits while you're with me.'

'We're in Africa. I'm African. This is how I'm comfortable. Now move. You're in my light.'

'Sir Cameron...' The director lay a placating hand on Cruickshank's arm. 'It's OK. She won't be in shot. I'll make sure.'

Zuri finished. 'There. He's all yours. Go show the world how brave you are.... ……….. By the way. That safari outfit looks stupid. And you've got sweat-marks. Your clothes stink.'

***

The evening shoot went smoothly. Lots of close-ups of Cruickshank with Tswana around him: some of him by the campfire, eating and drinking; others of him clapping in time to the drums. Shots too of him talking earnestly with me as if making executive decisions. We humoured all requests – except for film of him talking to Sharda.

'Where is she?' asked an exasperated director. 'I haven't seen her since before Sir Cameron arrived.'

I told her that Sharda had gone with some of the Tswana to a village, a few hours away. One of the most famous Shaman in the area was visiting. Sharda had never seen a healing ceremony before, I said, and saw no reason to miss the occasion just to be filmed for two seconds talking to Cruickshank.

'Oh my God. He is not going to be happy. Why didn't you tell me this earlier?'

I offered her a generous Tswana hooch which I told her was supposed to be drunk in one gulp; help give her the courage to tell Cruickshank about Sharda. Her whole body shivered as the deceptive liquor hit her stomach. Her eyes all-but glowed. 'Another?' I asked. And half-an-hour later she was staggering away across the compound asking if anybody knew where 'Sir Cameron' had gone.

Almost the last to leave the fireside, I headed not towards the dormitory but towards the collection of Tswana huts at the far end of the moonlit compound.

'Hey, Mark...' said Annakiya, turning in her hammock. 'You come to make mad passionate love to me Man?'

'Kopano and Tau let you down again Anna? You should get yourself some new men.'

'Ah, they not here. It not my night.'

'So what night are you? Tuesdays?'

'I be so lucky. I be the twenty-ninth – of February.' And she laughed so violently that her hammock shook the hut.

'So... Anna... Where is she?'

'Here Mark,' came Sharda's quiet voice from one of the other three hammocks.

'Are you OK?' I kept my voice low.

'Fine.'

I reached into her hammock, found her face with my hand then gently stroked her cheek before bending to give her a gentle kiss on the forehead.

'Is it still finishing tomorrow?' she asked.

'I'll make sure it is.'

***

On my way back across the compound I heard a woman scream followed by a single gunshot and then silence. I burst into Cruickshank's quarters, breaking the lock.

'Get the fuck out of here. Can't you see I'm busy?' he snarled.

The moonlight through the windows was bright enough to show the director on all-fours on the floor, her head bowed as if hiding behind her hair. Cruickshank was mounted behind her holding a pistol in one hand. Not far from them on the floor and still writhing in its death-throes was a large snake.

Cruickshank pointed the pistol at me and snarled. 'A snake... Is that really the best you can do Boy? Now lose yourself, before I rid the world of a second vermin tonight.' While gesturing me out of the room with the gun he began easing himself in and out of the director again.

Out of sight I paused just long enough to hear, 'Oh... Sir Cameron... Oh... Oh...' Then I slammed the door as loudly as I could.

Chapter 33

Our visitors left the camp at first light the next morning. Cruickshank said nothing to anybody, Burt and the cameraman looked almost in tears that their exotic tryst was over, and the director's demeanour said more that she'd been laid by a Lord than caught on all fours in flagrante. But rather than drive them to the airstrip myself and risk being drawn into awkward conversation, I asked Kopano and Tau to do the shuttling back and forth on my behalf. Besides, I had more important things to think about, like an experiment scheduled for 13:00 hours.

After a brilliant start, our research had suffered a setback. Buoyed by the ease with which Sharda had conceived in Experiment 1, our hopes had been high for Experiment 2. Of necessity, the women's roles had changed. Sharda was now resting, barred from all sexual activity until we could test the paternity of her baby at 15 weeks. Inga, no longer breast-feeding but now on the pill, had taken on the role of 'reservoir' female, and Zuri, now off the pill, had taken on the role of 'conceiver'; the terms had caused much argument but were the ones eventually agreed. Unfortunately, though not too surprisingly, Zuri did not conceive during her first menstrual cycle and we now had to wait until her next fertile phase drew near before we could continue. But although Experiment 2 itself was on hold, there was no need for us to be idle. Our overall investigation needed several complementary studies and with our visitors gone we were looking forward to beginning the first.

Much had changed since our first faltering attempts at privacy and dispassion nearly two months earlier; it was all much easier now, and far more accurate. But it did require the setting up of equipment before we could begin.

Last to arrive in the dormitory was Inga. 'Change of plan boys and girls. We've just had a phone call.'

'Who from?'

'It said "Private". I thought 'who the hell?' Turned out it was Hawkmoth TV. Some guy I've never spoken to before. I could hardly understand him. Accent just like the Wolf's. Anyway... It seems Mark signed the wrong model-release for his part in the documentary, so the director is sending the proper form by air-courier. She wants Mark to meet the plane at the landing strip and sign the form there-and-then for the courier to take straight to Windhoek. Seems there's just time before their plane takes off for Frankfurt later tonight.'

The rest of us said the call made no sense. What was wrong with e-mail? Or fax?

'Don't ask me,' said Inga. 'The signature probably needs to be original. But the point is, Mark has to be at the landing-strip in half-an hour. So... We don't have time, do we? Or do we?' Everybody looked at me.

'I don't see why not. Everything's set up: counter; video cameras. And you only need me for the first half. What time-interval Sharda?'

Sharda hit the random-event generator on her lap-top. 'Zero.'

'Hey, who says there's no God,' said Inga, dropping her sarong to the floor. Then she hesitated. 'Have they both been pre-swabbed?' Sharda confirmed that we had. 'OK. Then let's go.' Inga got on to the bed and made herself comfortable. 'Right. Ready Mark?'

I joined her and while Sharda kept an eye on the cameras and Zuri used a digital counter to try to keep track of my thrusts as back-up just in case the filming failed, Fredrik began getting himself in a state to take over the moment I finished.

As soon as I could pull out comfortably I rolled away to make room for Fredrik. Then after pausing only for Sharda to do the post-swab under my foreskin, I snatched up my shorts and headed for the door.

'Mark… Wait! I wish to come with you,' shouted Sharda. 'Oh, is that OK Zuri?' she asked. But Zuri was already too preoccupied keeping track of Fredrik with her digital counter to answer.

***

Sharda and I stopped the truck next to our parked plane. Once outside we could hear the courier but… 'I'm sure that's climbing, not descending. Why didn't he wait?'

In the dark shade of a Mopane tree a figure moved, then another. Two men began ambling towards us. 'Well, well.' The brogue was Scottish. 'One bait, two bites. Now why can't I do that with salmon.' From a holster inside his safari jacket, Cruickshank pulled out a pistol and pointed it at me. 'Don't move Boy. Stay exactly where you are.' His henchman circled round until he was behind me. 'Now start walking towards the plane. You two are going for a ride.'

'Like hell we…'

***

When I regained consciousness we were airborne, Sharda and I in the back seats with a gun pointed at us from the front. The bodyguard grinned as I gingerly felt the back of my neck.

'Where are our clothes?' I asked Sharda, who looked terrified.

'Blowing across the Kalahari. Are you OK Mark?'

I nodded, then reached for my intercom to talk to Cruickshank, but the guard grabbed my wrist. A few words from his boss later, he released me. 'Cruickshank... What the hell is this about?' No answer. 'Is it that snake? Because if it is, I didn't put it in your room. This is the Kalahari. Snakes get into huts. It wouldn't have killed you anyway.' Still no answer. 'Speak to me, bastard. Where are we going?'

'Somewhere in the middle of nowhere that you're going to beg to give me some answers. Until then, I suggest you sit back and enjoy the ride – because it's going to be your last. Unplug him.'

***

Cruickshank began the descent. He seemed to be heading for a dried-up river bed, but at a height of just a few hundred feet he veered off and investigated a fairly thick acacia woodland. Eventually, he circled round and headed towards an area where the trees were scattered enough to allow landing. On the final approach the plane's engine gave a cough, then another, but recovered. We finally stopped where the crowns of half a dozen large trees formed some sort of canopy above us. The plane would only be visible from directly overhead. 'Out! Both of you. Otherwise I shoot the bitch.'

'What answers?' I said, once outside the plane.

Cruickshank waved his pistol at me. 'You. Sit under that tree. Cross-legged. Facing me. Hands under ass. And you...' but Sharda was already being manhandled into position. With a strong arm round her waist, the guard was carrying her bodily to another tree. He made her kneel, then knelt behind her. 'Every time you annoy me Boy, she loses something.' The guard grabbed Sharda's hair and as she squealed he sliced off a handful which he threw to the ground. 'Next time it'll be something that bleeds.'

In the canopy the birds that had been silenced by our arrival began to move and call loudly.

'This is crazy. What answers?' I said.

Cruickshank placed a fresh cigar in the corner of his mouth and began chewing. 'CCTV cameras. Guards. Dogs. Yet somehow – Christ knows how – you get to my wife. How the hell did you do that? It should have been impossible.'

'Oh that... Of course I didn't get to your wife. It was just a story. I was winding you up, that's all. Seeing if I could rile you. Evidently I did. It never actually happened.'

He shot at me, the bullet whistling past my head. Sharda screamed. I jumped. 'Hey! What was that for?' Birds that had flown out from the trees circled around then settled again. Suddenly Sharda squealed and shouted. The guard had pulled her back against him, his left arm round her throat, his right under her breast, knife blade against nipple. I shouted. 'No! For Christ's sake, no. I'll talk. Just ask. I'll answer.'

'I have asked. And you still haven't answered. That blood test... Fuck you Boy! It says you're the father. How the hell did you pull a stunt like that? Now come on. Talk!'

My mouth must have dropped open because I breathed in a fly which stuck in the back of my throat. I coughed until I nearly retched. Then I carried on coughing, trying to give myself time to think. Three months ago I would have said such a conception was impossible. But now... I knew exactly what had happened. 'At least give me the deal. If I do talk – what then? '

'I kill you, then cut off your cock and balls.'

'That's real incentive. And if I don't talk?'

'Reverse order.'

'And Sharda?'

'What the hell do you think. Now talk!'

Sharda was still in the bodyguard's grip. Unable to move her head, she raised her eyes to the canopy above. The birds were calling louder than ever.

'Listen... Cruickshank... Sir Cameron even... Don't hurt her – please – but listen to me. If I die here, you will too. Both of you. You heard that plane cough as we landed. You know what that means.'

'A speck of dirt in the injection. Water maybe. We've got plenty of fuel. Two tanks, both three-quarters...' His face furrowed. 'I tapped the dials.'

'You can't trust those dials. We haven't filled that plane since before the film crew arrived. I know this aircraft. Those tanks are all-but empty. You might manage to take off. Maybe even go a few miles, though I doubt it. But then... You'll be stranded in the middle of the Kalahari at the height of summer. No radio. No phone signal. No Mayday. A hundred miles of wilderness, every direction. Temperatures in the forties. I'd give you a day. Tops. But I can keep you alive. Walk you out of here. I've lived with bushmen.'

He chewed on his cigar. 'You're lying about the fuel. I can see it in your face.'

'I'm not. If you don't believe me tell your goon to go and check.'

'Check. How?' His chewing was growing more agitated, then his face brightened. 'You carry a reserve. A canister? In the storage compartment. I saw it yesterday. That would get us to Maun.'

'That's empty too. It's got a leak. Fredrik was going to replace it later today.'

His frown returned. 'You're lying Boy. And if you are, your dog-bitch loses both nipples and you lose your tackle. You can both bleed to death. That's a promise.' He nodded for his henchman to go to the plane.

The bodyguard removed his arm from Sharda's throat and sheathed his knife, then struggled to raise himself from his kneeling position. While on one knee, he paused for a moment – and that was all the time Sharda needed. She launched herself backwards to hit him on the chest with her back, bringing her head up hard under his chin. Big though he was she caught him off-balance enough to fall backwards under her. As they landed, she rolled quickly to her right, away from the tree. The man screamed three times.

Although distracted, Cruickshank still saw me spring to my feet and launch myself. His gun hand swung round, but a split-second before he fired I grabbed his arm and his shot went into the ground. With both hands I slammed his forearm down on to my knee but even shouting with pain he refused to let go. Wrestling, we fell to the ground. Punching and kneeing, we rolled over and over. He pulled the trigger; again the bullet went into the ground. With his free hand he tried to grab my genitals. I punched the side of his jaw. Still we rolled, both grappling for the gun.

'Sharda!' I shouted.

Cruickshank was on top of me, kneeling astride, trying to aim as I struggled to push the gun aside. Then suddenly he went rigid, his eyes staring down into my face. Reaching up with his free hand he seemed to be clawing at something over his shoulder. His chin was exposed. I threw everything into an uppercut, smashing his lower jaw against his upper. He slumped on top of me.

Bruised and scratched I dragged myself out from under him, then picked up the pistol where it had fallen. My legs felt like jelly as I struggled to kneel. Then I saw it: a tranquilliser dart embedded in his back, just below his shoulder blade. The tassel was pink.

'You wonderful woman,' I said. 'I love you.'

Chapter 34

Sharda removed the dart from Cruickshank's back then together we yanked off his boots and began taking out the laces. I glanced at the guard a few yards away. He was sitting up and staring blankly in our direction, but when he tried to stand all he managed to do was keel over on to his side. 'What was it?' I asked Sharda. The guard struggled to sit up again. He seemed to be trying to talk to us but no words came, only coughs. Blood was dribbling from the corner of his mouth.

'Black Mamba. Very big. I did not realise how big until it slithered away. Four metres maybe.'

At our feet, Cruickshank gave a groan, spurring us to take out his laces even faster. 'Right… Roll him on to his front.' While I tied his hands behind his back, Sharda tied his ankles. Then we rolled him on to his back again.

Under the other tree, the guard fell forward on to his face. Already he was struggling to breathe. 'How did you know where to drop him?'

'When he was carrying me to the tree, I saw the snake all curled up. He must have missed it. Did you understand my message about the birds?'

'Yes – and I'd heard them. Where did the snake bite him?'

'In the neck. Three times. He cannot live I think.'

'He's big but… Ten more minutes. If that.'

Cruickshank began to stir. His eyes opened but took a while to focus. 'Don't get too excited,' I told him. 'You're recovering from my punch, not from the dart. The anaesthetic hasn't hit you yet.'

He shook his head as if to clear his mind. 'Will it kill me?'

'Maybe. Pink is for a lioness. That's right on the edge for you. Blue… No chance.'

'Can't you give me something? Like when you wake up the lions?'

'Give me one good reason why I should.'

'Because if I die my men will find you and you're both dead.'

'But if you don't die from the dart and we don't kill you, we're both dead anyway. That's why you brought us here. Some choice.'

He spat something from his mouth. 'Quit fantasising Boy. You won't kill me. You haven't the balls. Now untie me.'

'But maybe I have 'the balls',' said Sharda. 'And maybe I shall die happy if I rid the world of a man like you.'

'You? Ha! Well there's the gun. Go on! Use it! Show me what you're made of.'

She took the pistol from me. She even pointed it at him, but she didn't pull the trigger.

'You see? No spunk, either of you. Now come on, untie me. If that dart is going to kill me, at least let me die with some dignity.'

Sharda was still pointing the gun. 'No! Before we do anything for your 'dignity', I wish you to say sorry to me.'

'Sorry? For what?'

'You know for what. For raping me many times. Threatening my father. For everything you ever did to me.' For a moment I thought she really was going to pull the trigger, maybe shoot into the ground to scare him, but she didn't. 'Many 'sorries' are necessary I think and maybe you have very little time. So start saying that you are sorry and perhaps I shall let you die with just a little piece of your dignity.'

'Save your breath Bitch. The last person I said sorry to was my father, and even he had to beat it out of me.'

I left them while I checked first on the guard – he was unconscious now – and then on the plane's fuel situation. When I told Sharda about the real situation with the petrol she winced at the thought of what could have happened, but even if Cruickshank also heard the news he didn't respond. His eyes were closed and the chances were fifty-fifty that he would never open them again.

***

We talked about options.

'If he lives, I still want an apology.'

'You're wasting your time.'

'We shall see.'

'And if he's dead?'

We decided there was no point in burying them. The desert scavengers would find and unearth them anyway. But we had more to mull over than the disposal of flesh and bone. There were their possessions – and what to do if Cruickshank survived the dart.

Once the guard was dead we stripped him, then untied Cruickshank so that we could strip him too. Then we burned both men's clothes and buried the ashes. Items that couldn't be burned, wouldn't quickly degrade, and that could identify them we collected together and placed on the plane. This included both pairs of boots. We would take these things back to camp, and if asked about them would say they were left behind after the filming. We took their mobile phones too, and would decide what to do with those later. After that, there was nothing left to do but wait.

***

A muscle twitched, then the head moved slightly. A few moments later, Cruickshank's chest heaved. I quickly retied his wrists and ankles, but Sharda wanted more. She rolled him on to his side, pulled his knees up to his chest and tied him in that position with strong cord from the plane's storage compartment. 'Just like a child in the womb.'

'Are you sure you want to do this Sharda?'

'Yes, I am. This is fair I think. This is my right.'

Cruickshank's eyes blinked and then opened. 'Congratulations,' I said once he seemed aware. 'You didn't die.'

'Not yet eh Boy? Big problem for you now.'

'Not so big.'

'Why not?'

'You'll find out soon enough.'

He tried to move but couldn't because of the ties. 'What's all this for?'

Sharda stood over him. 'It is for me. I wanted you in this position. Now… Last chance. Say sorry for raping me.'

'Didn't you hear me? I never apologise.'

'OK.' Catching him by surprise, Sharda placed a length of wide sticky tape over his mouth. 'Now… Look at me, and listen. People say that a woman cannot rape a man. But this equipment we carry in the plane and I have here… We use it on the lions to collect their semen. Now this is very much like rape I think.' Behind the tape, his guttural sounds formed no words I could understand. 'But I have been very considerate. I have lubricated the probe exactly as I would for a lion. You were not always so considerate when you raped me.'

Tied as Cruickshank was, and lying on his side, he was in no position to resist as Sharda pushed the probe a short way into his rectum.

'Stop!' I shouted.

'Mark... I want to do this.'

'I know. But wait a moment. It's important. I've just thought of something.' I ran to the plane's storage compartment and came back with a suitably-sized phial. 'If you're going to do this...' Reaching between Cruickshank's thighs I found his penis and pulled it down so that the tip was in view. 'OK. Now.'

Sharda turned the dial and I collected Cruickshank's ejaculate as if he were a lion. Then I took the sample back to store in the plane. I did wonder if Sharda might 'rape' Cruickshank a few more times, but when I returned she had already removed the probe.

'What's the matter?' I asked her.

'This revenge... I did not enjoy it half as much as I expected.'

***

We released Cruickshank from his foetal position and with just his wrists and ankles still tied I dragged him to a tree and sat him against the trunk. By his side was his dead guard, ants already marching in and out of his ears, nose and mouth.

In my hand was the knife that had been used to threaten Sharda. Slowly I turned it, holding the blade in front of Cruickshank's face while I looked into his angry eyes and thought of all the people he had killed, raped and humiliated. I imagined driving the knife into his heart and twisting; I imagined how it would feel.

'I so wish I could find it in myself to kill you. But I can't, and neither can Sharda.' He couldn't answer. Not wishing to hear him say anything more we had left the tape over his mouth. 'So yes. It has been difficult deciding what to do with you. You were right by the way. The plane has plenty of fuel. Even the reserve is full. I was lying. So we could easily do the proper thing: take you back to camp with us, fly you to Gaborone, hand you over to the Botswana police and ask for justice. But… In a week, maybe only a day, you'd be free and we'd be dead. So we're going to hand you over to the Kalahari instead. Natural justice. More reliable.'

He watched us stand, shaking his head to dislodge the flies that were tormenting him. Ants also had found him and were beginning to sting and nip. 'You could survive,' I continued. 'It's really not that difficult if you know how. So we are at least giving you a chance, which is more than you gave Mia or were going to give us. I'll even give you a word of advice. Don't worry too much about the animals. Worry about the sun and the heat and the lack of water. You're the wrong colour you see; too pale. And have the wrong background as well; too used to clothes and shoes and easy living. But get through the first few days and you might even make it. Probably best to try to enjoy tonight though. Just in case it's your last.'

Sharda and I were almost at the plane when I remembered. Cruickshank watched me return, knife still in my hand, his eyes saying that he expected me to kill him after all.

'Two things I forgot to say. You may as well know. It was me who put that snake in your room. And yes, it would have killed you. How was I to know you were going to invite the director in after all? So I'm glad you shot it, just in case it bit her rather than you. As for that other matter…' And I went on to explain to him in detail how his wife came to be having my baby, and probably how Mia came to have JJ's. But then, at the height of my satisfaction at telling him, a thought hit me and I panicked. I'd been so caught up with my and Sharda's predicament that... 'Your wife... My child...' I ripped the tape from his mouth, making his lips bleed, but the pain didn't stop him from sneering.

'Oh, they're in hell with Mia and her brat by now Boy. You're way too late to save them.'

Chapter 35

We were all in the laboratory, trying to keep busy, trying not to think about visits from police or, perhaps even worse, Cruickshank's men. Maybe we should have been trying not to think about Cruickshank at all – but there was one thing about him we simply had to know. It was important to our work.

Zuri printed out an analysis of the Wolf's ejaculate. 'You were right Mark.' She handed me the sheet.

I gave the data a cursory glance. 'Brilliant! It really is all falling into place.' With ten per cent of men unable to have children anyway, there was always a chance that Cruickshank was infertile, but knowing and suspecting what we did about his 'children' made it virtually inevitable. And now we had proof. 'So finally the bastard's been of some use to us.'

'But this way of conceiving...' Zuri said. 'It will happen to men who are fertile as well. It has to – occasionally.'

'Sure – but how occasionally, that's the question. Anyway, eventually we should be able to work that out.'

'And we shall put this calculation in our publication, yes?' said Sharda.

'Of course.'

For a few seconds our work had managed to push the nerve-wracking legacy of the events in the desert to the backs of our minds. But suddenly the satellite phone rang and we all looked anxiously at each other again. Sharda edged to my side and slid her arm round my waist. We tried to deduce from Inga's responses who was calling.

Inga switched off the phone. 'That was the director. She's been trying to contact The Wolf. She wondered if we knew where he was.'

Fredrik ran his hand over his face and tugged at his beard. 'Look... Mark, Sharda. Sooner or later one of us is going to be asked something and we're going to say something fucking stupid that lands you two right in it. We've got to know the truth. The real truth. Then we've all got to work out a story down to every last bloody detail. We hear what you've told us but... Honest to God, I'd have stuck that knife straight in the evil bastard and enjoyed doing it. And I can't believe you didn't do the same. So for Christ's sake level with us. We'll still be on your side whatever you did. But he is dead, isn't he? Can we at least start from there?'

'Dead? I'm sure he is. He couldn't survive the Kalahari at this time of year. Probably not even for a day.'

'No! Not 'sure' or 'couldn't' or 'probably'. I mean you killed him, yes? Finished him off. Man to man. One hundred per cent certain.'

'Please... Fredrik... All of you... Mark and I... We did not kill him. OK? We really did leave that job to the Kalahari, just as we said before. When we were in the air and circling to see what he was doing, he was still hopping around like a kangaroo in the sun, still looking for something sharp to cut free his hands and feet. And that was the last time we saw him. You must believe us.'

***

A tense week passed without further contact from anybody – until Kopano burst through the dormitory door, full of apologies. He knew we were busy doing our 'sex experiment', he said, and he wouldn't have disturbed us but…

With work the only thing that could distract us, Experiment 2 was back in full swing and we were in the middle of a session. I, then Fredrik, had already had sex with Inga and in ten more minutes Fredrik would finish off the sequence by having sex with Zuri. The video cameras were both in position and Zuri was on her bed waiting, passing the time by reading a scientific paper on her Kindle and making notes. The rest of us were just sitting around, talking.

'… there a blue truck coming.'

My stomach churned. 'Shit!' The others also suddenly looked anxious. 'OK, I'll go. Let's not waste what we've done. You all finish off. But if I'm not back by the time you've finished, come and check on me. Hopefully they're just looking for Indy.'

'Oh no!' said Sharda. 'I am not letting you go alone. Inga can deal with the cameras. I am coming with you.'

***

The two policemen were smoking, leaning against their vehicle as they watched us approach. 'You're wasting your time,' I said. 'Indy's not here any more. We don't have any diamonds for you.'

'We know. This visit not about diamonds. It about some thing else. Some shit-important British bastard gone missing. And some other guy. But nobody seem to care shit about him.'

'That doesn't explain why you're here.'

'We here because these two bastards, they last seen getting off air-taxi from Maun, shit right here on your landing strip. Shit right here Man. And our boss tell us you know these men.'

'What are their names?' A piece of paper was thrust at me, the writing scribbled and almost illegible. I made a show of reading. 'Sure, I know these two. But the last time any of us saw them they were getting on the Maun air taxi with a television crew, not getting off the thing. You say they came back. When?'

'Same day. A few hours later.'

'Do you know why?'

He nodded. Cruickshank, he said, had travelled as far as Maun Airport with the crew but then changed his mind about flying on with them to Windhoek and Europe. He told them that he was feeling guilty about the state of our plane and was going to return to our camp and personally fly it to Maun Airport to have all its faults repaired. He would make his own arrangements for getting back to Europe. All of which meant, I assumed, that Cruickshank received the paternity test results more or less as he arrived at Maun, and that was when he hatched his plot to kill me.

'Then I don't know what happened,' I said. 'He didn't turn up at the camp and he didn't fly off with the plane.'

'Naagh. Shit answer. Try again.'

The silent one suddenly grabbed the top of Sharda's sarong and yanked it down to expose her breasts. Sharda just managed to slap his face before the larger policeman turned on him. Holding him by the throat he pushed him backwards and slammed him against the side of the truck, shouting at him in Bantu. Then he opened the truck door and virtually threw him inside.

'Sorry,' he said to Sharda, smoothing his blue uniform. 'My shit of a brother... He has big problem with women.' Then with sweat running over his pocked face he was silent for so long I began to feel uncomfortable. 'Explain the phone call to me,' he said at last.

'What phone call?'

'This man Cruickshank, he make phone call to your satellite number while on the plane. You must have known him coming.'

I acted as if trying to remember. 'You're right. We did receive a call that day. But if I remember rightly the number was withheld and we couldn't hear a thing. Just static. So we didn't know who it was from. So that was Cruickshank was it?'

The policeman began to smile, then finally to laugh. Reaching into his top pocket he took out three cigarettes and offered us one each. Although we both declined we had to wait while he struggled to get his to light.

'Look Man. What your name? De Beer, ja? Like the shit diamond company?'

'De Vries.'

'De Vries. Ah ja... Doctor de Vries. I remember now.' He tapped his temple with his fingers. 'I have good memory. Shit good. And this your wife?'

'In a way,' said Sharda.

'In a way?'

Sharda smiled. 'You could say one of three – for the moment.'

He laughed again. 'Three, ja? Then we the same Man, you and me. Take my advice. Lose some. Too many wives big mistake. Too many children. One-time women more fun, much cheaper.' He took a deep draw on his cigarette. 'Look... Doctor de Beer. We trust each other, ja? Because we help each other. Me and my brother, we protect you shit well. And every so often, you give us something to show your appreciation. We good for each other, ja?' He didn't wait for an answer. 'I tell you a secret. What happen here? I not care shit, and I see from your eyes that you not care shit neither.

What piss me off – what really piss me off – is that what happen, it happen right here. Right on my patch. You know what I mean?'

'Not really. Tell me.'

'OK, I tell you. First, it mean that me and my brother, we expected to do something. Find out what happen. Now that a shit load of work, and that only the start. Many people will need come here. Other policemen. Start asking questions. And maybe some of these questions will be about us: me and my brother. Maybe in some of the villages to the south of here, where some shit people not like us as much as you do. Might say shit things. You begin to understand?'

'So what are you suggesting?'

'Let me tell you what really happen that day. After these two men arrive at your landing strip, they visit you here, in your camp, and you let them take your plane to Maun just like they tell the TV people. And it there they disappear. Really, this shit job belong to the Maun police, long way from here. Nothing to do with me and my brother. Nothing to do with you.'

'It won't work. Maun airport has records.'

He held up his hand. 'But these men, they never arrive in Maun. They forced to land before reaching there. Near a Batawana village in the Okavango. Nobody keep record there. I tell you exactly where to put your plane to have it discovered. GPS position. Shit accurate. But you must do this soon. Leave at dawn tomorrow. I make shit good arrangement. Another brother. Tell me Doctor. Did these two men leave any thing in your camp? Any thing at all?'

Chapter 36

Fredrik, Zuri and Sharda set off on an overnight drive to Maun. They would go via Sojwe, then pick up the A1 tarmac road at Mahalapye. That way they would be on the A3 in the region of the Okavango Delta as I landed. I could phone them if I got into trouble – but I very much hoped it wouldn't be necessary.

Left alone together for the night Inga and I bent the rules of the experiment a little by sharing a bed – though we did have our son between us. Then just before dawn the next morning with a parting 'Please be careful' she waved me off at the landing strip. Perched on her hip and with the help of her hand, so did Imbube.

The two policemen – or somebody – had chosen my destination well: an area of scattered acacia woodland in the shape of a rugby-ball near a river. Armed with its GPS reference, not only did I find it easy to locate and recognise from the air but it was also the perfect place to hide a plane. I parked in as dense an area of trees as I could negotiate and wearing the bodyguard's boots, wandered around the outside of the plane for a while. Then in a patch of tinder-dry grassland I sat on a termite mound and changed into Cruickshank's boots before leaving more tracks, particularly around the plane. Finally I set off for the river.

Crocodiles were basking on the far bank as I stepped into the water, removed Cruickshank's boots, placed them in a plastic bag and stuffed them into my backpack along with the socks I had been wearing. Everything else I had with me I threw item by item into the river: the bodyguard's boots, his and Cruickshank's mobile phones, the sheathed knife and pistol, all wiped clean of fingerprints. Then I took off my gloves and after collecting a sharp and sturdy stick in case I needed to poke something in a crocodile's eye I started trudging upriver in bare feet. Every so often I heard movement on the banks and tensed for a quick exit or, failing that, defence, but neither was needed. As soon as I judged I was far enough away from where I'd thrown the mobiles and other items I clambered back on to land and, taking advantage of as much shade as I could, jogged parallel to the river for a while. Eventually in the distance I saw what I had been told to expect: a man alongside an ancient truck.

'You don't look much like your brothers,' I said as the man greeted me with neither a smile nor a handshake. I handed him Cruickshank's boots. He threw them into the back of the truck.

'Different mothers.' Soon we were driving along a well-used dirt track. 'Why you doing this for my brothers?'

'Would you believe we are friends?'

'No.'

'Would you believe it's a business deal?'

'Maybe.'

'It's a business deal. I do this for them, they promise not to make life difficult for me in the future.'

He didn't speak again for another twenty minutes.

'This man who disappears. He everybody's paymaster, ja?'

'Yes.'

'He arrange for people to die if they not do as he wishes.'

'So I've heard.'

'Many people might wish him dead.'

'Possibly.'

'Did my brothers kill him?'

'I doubt it.'

'Did you?'

'No.'

He dropped me outside Shoprite on Tsheke Tsheko Road in Maun and I bought some bread, a bottle of water, two pairs of Speedos and two bikinis. Two hours later Fredrik, Zuri and Sharda pulled up in the camp-truck and picked me up; the journey was only a couple of hundred metres but the four of us wanted to be seen driving in to the forecourt of Riley's Hotel together. After checking-in we went straight to the swimming pool and its bar. We could cope very well, we decided, with staying there the two or three nights that we had been told would be necessary.

***

By mid-November Zuri was pregnant and Experiment 2 was finished. It would be another six weeks before we could start the final Experiment, 3, with Sharda the 'reservoir' and Inga the 'conceiver'. Until then there was just one more data point we wanted to collect.

In the camp's dormitory, Inga lay down on her bed and raised her knees. 'Come on then Mark. And this time don't take all day getting him up and in will you? A girl's got some pride, you know.'

'Then for Christ's sake do a bit more to help.'

It wasn't monotony that was reducing our libidos and making us short-tempered. It was the unnerving prospect that later that day we were to receive an unwelcome visitor.

***

'Evening, Sunshine. We meet again.' The handshake was brief.

'Detective Inspector. We do indeed.' I offered him a seat; we were in the office.

'No need to be formal. I'm retired now. Just Bob will do.'

'Retired... So why... ?'

'Unofficial. I'm a tourist. That's why it's just me. No local plod holding my hand.'

'In that case... Can the others stay?' I gestured at the other four.

'Why not. And straight to the point, eh? Let's get the official bit of this unofficial visit done-and-dusted, then you can ply me with food and drink and carry me to bed. The only way I'll sleep in this heat is if I get totally shit-faced.'

'You can start now if you like,' offered Fredrik. 'There's beer in the fridge. A few bottles of rum. Local hooch.'

Stansted was clearly tempted but... 'Best not. First things first, eh? The thing is... Back in Blighty, we've got every confidence in the Botswana Police... Course we have. Goes without saying. But... Everybody gets twitchy when there's no body. I mean... A head's best. But a hand will sometimes do. Even a finger under some circumstances. But boots...' He shook his head.

'Boots?'

'Mmm, boots.... .... Actually Doctor de Vries. I thought you'd be there.'

'Where?'

'The inquest. Maun. Yesterday. That's why I'm here. Well, one of the reasons.'

'Inquest! We weren't told about any inquest.'

'No? Well... Can't say I'm surprised. Very discreet affair. Very rushed. Very – strange.'

'Then how did you hear about it?'

'Dominic. A very efficient guy, Dominic. Keeps his ear to the ground. Lots of contacts in high and strange places.'

'Was there a verdict?'

'Of course.'

'Which was?'

'What do you think? Given that there'd been shit-all of an investigation.'

'I've no idea.'

'Crocodiles.'

'Crocodiles!'

'That's what the villager guy who found the plane and the boots suggested. And the Maun police believed him. And why shouldn't they? Especially after they found Sir Cameron's mobile in the river a few miles away.'

'But you don't believe him?'

He tapped his nose. 'Never known to fail.'

Fredrik, who had been jiggling his right leg from the beginning, suddenly went to the fridge and collected us each a beer. Stansted accepted without hesitation.

After a long drink from his bottle the ex-policeman gave an appreciative 'Aagh,' before continuing. 'Now... Tell me Doctor de Vries. That thing on your back that records your movements... Is it still there?'

'The battery died. I had it removed.'

'Pity.'

'Why?'

'No reason. Why didn't you report the plane was missing?'

'Because we didn't know it was. Sir Cameron said he was leaving it at Maun Airport for repair and that's where we thought it was. We didn't even bother to check. Just took a bit of a break at Riley's Hotel while we waited for the airport people to phone and say it was ready. Next thing we knew the police had found us and were telling us what had happened. Look... What is this? Why all the questions?'

After emptying the bottle with only his second swig he asked Fredrik if he had any more.

'Sorry. Just Rum or Hooch.'

'Mmm. Maybe in a few minutes.' He seemed to be watching my every move, my every gesture and expression. 'Do you know what I thought was weird Doctor de Vries? Touch of déjà vu if you like. The day Sir Cameron disappeared the Buckinghamshire police got a phone-call. Mid-evening. About eight o'clock. Sent them scooting straight over to Sir Cameron's place. And a good job too. Just in the nick of time. Intercepted a large white delivery van at the main gates. And inside... Guess what?'

I shook my head – and squeezed my fists so hard my nails dug into my palms.

'Lady Cruickshank, all trussed up and out for the count. For ransom, that's what the kidnappers said. And maybe she was – but that's not what the whistle-blower had said.'

Fredrik jumped up, went to the crate of rum, opened himself a bottle and drank. But when he sat down, his right leg immediately began to jiggle again. Inga told him to stop.

'Really? So what had the caller said? And is Lady Cruickshank OK?'

'She's fine, but I think you know what the caller said Doctor de Vries. It wasn't difficult to trace that call. Male. Spoke good English. There are only two of you here. So how did you know she was in danger, eh? Tell me that.'

'OK. If I must. It's no secret. Cruickshank taunted me with it when he called here for the plane. In fact, he told me that she was already dead. That she'd been unfaithful just like

Mia and received the same punishment. But I phoned anyway – and now I'm so glad I did. I couldn't help Mia when she needed it but... Well... But it doesn't alter anything here does it? Cruickshank still flew off in our plane. He still landed wherever he landed. And he still suffered whatever he suffered.'

'So you didn't kill him then? Him and his henchman?'

'No! If anybody killed them, it was the Kalahari.'

'Crocodiles you mean.'

'Whatever.'

'Ha! Very convenient that, don't you think? Sir Cameron's instructions and incentives to his henchmen in the event of his death didn't actually include crocodiles as far as I know. Or a whole desert.'

'You knew about those incentives?'

'Course I knew. Why? Did you think you were special?' He turned to Fredrik. 'Think I'll have that rum now,' and as he began on his bottle, I thought I could sense him relaxing. There was almost a smile on his face when he said: 'Don't happen to know who the father of Lady Cruickshank's baby is do you?'

'Of course not. But... is the baby OK too?'

'Can't say, not really. So... Sir Cameron didn't tell you then?'

'No. Would you have expected him to?'

'Yes, I think I would. In fact, I would go so far as to say... I don't believe he didn't.'

'Shit!' said Fredrik, jumping out of his chair and going to the window.

Sharda pulled up a chair by my side and Zuri joined us, standing behind, a hand on each of our shoulders. She gave a small squeeze of support to us both.

Stansted looked amused by the reactions he'd triggered. 'Sorry, ladies. I don't know what your situation is here but... My Christ! Half the male population of England – me included – would give their right testicle to do with Lady Cruickshank what this guy did, the lucky fucker. But... Were you totally nuts Man? Did you have a sudden death wish or something? My God? Cameron Cruickshank's wife? Yet... Here we are... You're still alive, and he's evidently not.'

I couldn't stay seated. 'I don't understand this Detective Inspector...'

'Bob, please.'

'OK... Bob... But if you think I had something to do with his death, and it's fairly obvious you do, why aren't the Botswana Police here with you? In fact, why are you here at all? This is their job, not yours.'

'Relax! They don't know anything about any of this. And they don't need to know. Their file is closed and neither they nor anybody I know want it re-opened. Not even Dominic. In fact, especially not Dominic.'

'Then I definitely don't understand.'

'Look... Doctor de Vries... Mark. I meant what I said at the beginning. I'm not here as a policeman. I'm here for a lot of people, myself included. But if you must know I'm mainly here for Melody. You know... Lady Cruickshank. She went back to the UK after the inquest. She had things to do. Medical things, you know? She's in a bit of a state about everything. But... She asked me to find you. Talk to you. The thing is... There are a lot of people back in the UK all set to relax into new and better lives but...' He gasped in exasperation. 'Boots, Man! Only boots.'

'I still think I'm missing something here.'

'OK. Here's the bottom line. I... We... Look... Nobody needs to know how you know. Nobody even needs to know what you know. Not exactly. But it would be a real load off everybody's mind if you could tell us…'

'I honestly can't tell you anything.'

'OK, OK. Then it would be a real load off everybody's mind if you could give us your considered opinion on whether Sir Cameron Cruickshank really is dead. Because to be totally honest with you, there are a hell of a lot of us who can't help feeling it's far too good to be true.'

Chapter 37

We exchanged the lightest of handshakes. Her delicate hand looked very small and very white against mine. As the air-taxi left I carried her heavy suitcase to the truck. She was short, barely reaching my shoulder and as we walked she fanned her face with her hand. Large reflective sunglasses hid her eyes. 'Do you know?' she said. 'We haven't seen the sun in Buckinghamshire for over two weeks. And it's been so cold.' Her lips twitched into a hesitant smile but she didn't say more until we'd been driving for a few minutes. 'Mark... Can you pull in please? Under that tree? I want to talk to you – properly – before we meet anybody else.'

I parked by the trackside in the shade of a Mopane tree and while she ambled around looking thoughtful I stretched out my legs through the open truck-door to let my dusty bare feet just rest on the ground. She must have known I was watching because she suddenly gave a 360 degree pirouette. 'Do you like it?' she asked, seeming younger than the 25 years I knew her to be. The dress in question was white and diaphanous and flared out as she twirled. Her white underwear showed through.

'In London maybe. Not very practical here.' The red sand and dust were already making their marks.

'I know. Sad really. I spent hours trying to decide what to wear to meet you. What do women wear here?'

'I'll let the women advise you on that.' I could see myself reflected in her sunglasses. 'Why have you come here Melody? What's the real reason?'

She waved away my question – 'Oh... Too soon' – then scuffed at a ripple of sand with her sandaled foot. Her toe-nails were perfectly manicured. 'Were you nervous?' she asked.

'What about?'

'Meeting me.'

My arms were folded, my chest bare. 'No. Should I have been?'

'I don't know. I was as nervous as hell about meeting you.'

'Really? Why?'

She gave a tiny shrug and turned her face skywards, as if seeking the answer in the tree-top. 'It's so desolate,' she murmured, scanning the horizon before kicking at the sand again. 'Maybe I shouldn't say this – but I wasn't expecting you to be quite so black.'

'Is black a problem?'

'I'll let you into a secret. When I was a little girl, I was told that men with dark skins and funny hair used to eat little blonde white girls for breakfast. That was my family for you. You can see why Cameron liked them so much. I would have run a mile if I'd met you then.'

'And now?'

'Now? Ha... That's tricky. Did you see the scene that led to my death?'

'Sorry. I never watch soaps; hardly ever watch TV.'

'Oh... So... Have you never seen me act? Not even once?'

'Afraid not.'

'Oh.... Right... Ah well... But that scene was good. Maybe my best. It got rave reviews.' Her pale face flushed a little. 'I'm sorry. I can see you're not impressed. Or interested. Why should you be?'

'Of course I am. Tell me about the scene.'

'Really? OK... Well... It was actually quite steamy. For early evening, anyway. Lots of rough kissing. Rolling under the sheets. Bare backs. That sort of thing. But it ended with me being strangled by my lover – who, I have to say, looked a lot like you. Unnervingly so.' She took off her sunglasses, her azure eyes quite as striking as people had described. But blinded by the brightness she quickly put the glasses on again.

'Steamy scenes with a coloured lover, eh? What did Cruickshank say about that?'

'Oh my God... And we'd only just met too. But once he saw that storyline he insisted they write me out. Permanently. Otherwise he'd have nothing more to do with me. He got so angry at the things I had to do with that guy before I left, especially that last scene. The tabloids were right. It was me, and I was naked under the sheet for a while – though on screen you couldn't tell for sure of course. So I swore to Cameron we used a body-double. I think he believed me.'

She waited for a reaction, but I didn't give her one. 'Look Melody. I'm still not sure why you're here, but if we're going to move on, there's something fairly major that we've got to get out of the way.'

'There is? Oh dear... Sounds ominous. What?'

'Cruickshank was a cruel murdering racist bastard. Everybody could see that. Yet you married him. Why?'

'Oh, that...' Her face hardened. 'For his title and money of course. I assume that's what you think. Everybody else does.'

'I don't know what to think. That's why I'm asking.'

She kicked at the ripple of sand yet again. 'Look, I'm not going to lie to you Mark. What woman wouldn't want to be a 'Lady' and have loads of money if everything else seemed right. Sure I knew he was a racist – but I thought I might be able to do something about that. But I didn't know he was a murderer. Or so cruel. All I saw was the excitement that surrounded the man. He had such charisma. He oozed power. People crumbled before him. And he was attractive – to me anyway. I won't say he made me laugh, because he didn't, but those first few months... All those places and big occasions we went to. Me on his arm. He made me feel so fantastic, so important, as though the whole world was at my feet.' She paused as if inviting me to say something. When I stayed silent she became defensive. 'Maybe it was stupid of me, shallow even, but I'd defy any woman in my position not to be seduced by it all. As for the wedding... My God, it was everything any little girl could dream of. How was I to know how quickly everything was going to sour afterwards.'

'Sour? How?'

'Well... He'd promised me the world, hadn't he. But all I got was a prison. Big and luxurious for sure, but it might as well have been one tiny cell. All he wanted from me was a wholesome white-skinned beautiful heir – and I wasn't to have my life back until I'd given him one.'

'Go on.'

'There's not much more to say, really. Except that after Mia and JJ he was taking no chances. One way or another somebody was watching me 24/7. But then I got pregnant and for a while he relaxed a bit. Let me out a bit more. Showed me off, you know. Mother of his heir, etcetera, especially once we knew it was a boy. Then the next thing I knew he was trying to have me killed. And he would have succeeded too if you hadn't made that phone call.'

'Only just in time from what I've heard.'

'I know... And I'm so, so grateful. And now... I can't tell you. I am so relieved he's dead. Because if he wasn't... I could never have felt safe, could I? Ever? I mean... Poor Mia.' Once more she took off her sunglasses, and this time although having to squint she kept them off. 'Bob Stansted thinks you killed Cameron you know. He's convinced of it.............. So... Did you? Is that something else I should thank you for?'

'No. Not me. It really was the Kalahari.'

'Then thank you Kalahari,' she shouted, raising her arms in the air. Then her voice softened. 'But I'm still going to fantasise that you killed him, if that's OK.' She gave a wonderful smile. 'You asked me why I was here. Isn't it obvious? If you owed somebody – a total stranger – not only your life and freedom but also riches like you could never have believed... Wouldn't you at least want to meet them?' She reached out her hands, clearly expecting me to reciprocate. When I didn't, her smile gradually faded. 'What's the matter? Did I say something?'

'It's what you didn't say. The baby, Melody. The baby at the centre of all this. What's happened to him?'

Chapter 38

After a short siesta Melody spent the afternoon with Sharda, Zuri and Inga. They showed her around the camp including a visit to the Tswana huts. They also showed her our data and played her some of our X-rated films of the experiment in action – or so they said. But Fredrik and I decided that the four women were just winding us up.

'The things that you five are doing here,' Melody said. 'I mean your lion work too, of course. But your experiment on yourselves... I think it's totally amazing. How on earth you managed to bring yourselves to get started in the first place I can't imagine, but I am so glad you did.'

Early on in her afternoon tour Melody had swapped her diaphanous dress for a sarong. Now it was evening and dark and we were all sitting at the cooking-fire. The Tswana had just finished a welcome dance, leaving her with a bemused smile. She was refusing all alcohol.

'One thing though Mark,' she continued. 'I mean... I've never heard of this way of conceiving as a possibility before, yet you seem to know of so many examples. How common is it, really?'

I did my best to explain. It did seem a lot, I agreed. But in reality, her conceiving to me was the only absolutely certain case so far. Much as Inga and I – and Fredrik – hoped that this was also how Imbube was conceived, our earlier explanation of comatose sex was still a possibility, no matter how remote. As for Sharda's sister and Mia, even though we would all like to believe that they had never been unfaithful, they could still both have been lying.

'But suppose they weren't. Suppose that all these cases are real examples. That is a lot, isn't it? Doesn't it mean that your work is really important?'

'Well, we'd like to think so. But even if they are all real there is still a link. Fredrik and Cameron are – were – both infertile. Maybe Sharda's brother-in-law is too. He hasn't had any children since. This thing isn't likely to happen to fertile men very often.'

'How often?'

'Ha! I'll tell you that when we've finished our experiments.'

'My word. Well, I think it's really exciting. And so brave of you all. I mean, the tabloids... When you publish... They'll absolutely crucify you. *Loveless sex for science.* I can see it now. Aren't you even a teeny bit worried?' She was looking at the women now.

'But our sex is not loveless,' objected Sharda. 'Just a different kind of love which has grown between us all as the experiment has progressed. And the children when they are born... They too will be loved very much. In a way, each one will have three mothers and two fathers, just like the camp-site Tswana children.'

'Well all I can say is good luck,' said Melody. 'That'll probably translate into *Mad love-nest scientists trash British family values* or something equally disgusting. You should read some of the horrible things they've written about me over the years.... .... Then there's you Mark... I think it is criminal that because of this work you feel you must resign your job at the university. Just because of some stupid committee.'

'Thanks – and so do I – but if the experiment's a success...' I had already explained my decision to her: if as we hoped I proved to be the father of Sharda's baby when we tested for paternity at 15 weeks then I would rather hand in my notice before going public than give somebody the satisfaction of demanding my dismissal afterwards.

Our conversation had to end. Amidst clapping and cheering from across the dance arena, the Tswana began calling my and Fredrik's names. 'Sorry,' I said. 'You can look the other way if you like, but there's no getting out of this for us.' Her bemused smile returned, and was still there when Fredrik and I sat down again after our performance.

'They won't ask me to dance will they?' she said. 'Not tonight. I'm exhausted. I need my bed. I'll perform tomorrow night – if I must. Something slow. A bit more sedate. I started off as a dancer, you know.'

'Relax. I told them you'd be tired after your flight and not to call you out. And you won't have to dance tomorrow night either. From dawn there'll be no Tswana in the camp for a couple of days.' I went on to explain about the occasional healing ceremonies held in the villages to the south. 'It's a big occasion for them. But I did say you'd do something next week, at your farewell party. Is that OK?'

'I suppose so. But even so… If I'm getting up at dawn to chase lions with you, I must still go to bed.' She stood, and for some reason grinned at the others. 'Are you still sure Sharda?' she asked, receiving a barely perceptible nod and an unconvincing smile in reply. 'Right, in that case I'll say goodnight. But could you walk me to my chalet Mark? There are things I wish to discuss with you.'

As I passed where Sharda was sitting she reached up for my hand. 'Kiss,' she requested. And after I obliged she continued, 'Mark… I just want to say… In a way I feel responsible. Maybe you do too. I don't know. Is that weird?'

I laughed. 'I don't understand.'

'You soon will,' said Inga. 'Though you are a man, I suppose. But I'm with Sharda. Just say yes to everything. OK?' And neither of them would explain further.

Melody and I began making our way to her chalet. 'Oh, by the way – impressive dancing,' she said. 'But... To be fair... I think Fredrik had the edge – that handstand dancing is unreal.'

'Blatant exhibitionism. No finesse whatsoever.... .... You mean you didn't look the other way?'

'Not for a moment.'

An owl shrieked nearby, making her jump and me laugh. 'So, don't keep me in suspense,' I said. 'What is this thing I have to say yes to?'

'Right. Well two things actually. And the first is easy – it's money. The girls and I had a long chat this afternoon. We got on so well. They were all really nice to me; understood exactly what I've been through, what I'm still going through.'

'Well if anybody should understand, it's them.'

'I suppose so. Anyway... To business. They told me all about the funding crisis you're facing here. About the diamond smuggling too. So I've decided. I want to right Cameron's wrongs. Do what he promised you but never delivered. Turn this place into something really top-drawer. But keep its character. You know? I mean, it's fantastic, isn't it? Wouldn't it be wonderful to have high-profile wildlife scientists queuing up to come here? From all over the world? Their research students too? Fill the place?'

'That's been our aim all along.'

'I know. That's what the others said. And they told me... The only thing that's stopping it happening is the lack of facilities. So let's do it. You've got the name and the know-how, I've got the money. Between us we can turn this place into one of the best and most talked-about wildlife research centres in Africa. Maybe human research too – you know, perhaps beginning with paternity in the Tswana? Sharda told me all about it. Fascinating. I'd love to see that.'

'So would I. Look... Melody... I have to warn you. I have zero principles when it comes to accepting money for my research. This place means absolutely everything to me, and we are literally desperate. So if you mean this offer, I'll accept – and maybe even haggle for more.'

'Good. That's settled then.'

'But why? Why would you?'

We arrived at the door to her chalet, and she flustered a little. 'Do you mind coming in? Check for snakes and creepy-crawlies for me?'

'Of course. If you want.' I did a token search but there was nothing there, just a rather large but harmless spider under the bed that I decided not to point out to her. 'So... Why the offer – really? I don't trust philanthropy any more.'

Apparent embarrassment made her laugh a little. 'Isn't it obvious? It's for you. For everything you've done for me. I'm returning a favour. Even if I financed this place, your research, for the rest of my life, I still wouldn't feel that I'd fully repaid you. And, honestly, on the scale of things it's really not that much money. And even if it were I'm sure Dominic could find a way to make it all tax-deductible. Besides which...'

'You mean there's more?'

'Of course there's more. My God! Men! Look... Come here. Sit on the bed. There! In front of me. Right... Now give me your hand. No, under my sarong; it's OK, I don't mind. Now... Just wait a moment. There! Yes? Did you feel that? And again? He started up for the night while you and Fredrik were dancing. Do you understand now?'

ROBIN BAKER

She had been totally honest with me about the baby when I asked her earlier; told me how after wrestling with the crazy impossible confusion over paternity that confronted her she finally reached breaking point and asked for an abortion. 'Totally against my principles but...' Then she encountered a problem. At over 24 weeks she only qualified for a termination if she could prove that the pregnancy was endangering her health. 'But it was,' she'd continued. 'My health, my mind... Those paternity tests... I thought I was going totally insane – and so did the doctors. They brought in a Psychologist, you know. A complete idiot. He tried to tell me I was in denial. That of course I'd had an affair with somebody. That I'd blanked it out. He blamed my father, my childhood – of course. He simply would not believe me that I'd never met the father – you.' And the abortion was only days away when she'd received an e-mail from me explaining everything, telling her exactly how she managed to conceive to me without our ever meeting. 'That e-mail... Not just the explanation, but something about the way you wrote it, about how kind and understanding you sounded... I swear you saved my sanity. Not to mention our baby's life.'

And here was that baby – still in her womb, still full of the life that somehow I'd managed to save twice over – squirming around under my hand.

'You're crying,' she said. 'Ohhhh. I love that.' She joined me on the edge of the bed. 'Look... Mark. Our lives from now on... We're going to be worlds apart. It's inevitable. And I'm sure neither of us would want it any other way. I mean... You'll be here – yes? Most of the time, anyway. And me? Well who knows. I probably will play the Lady-of-the-Manor occasionally – you know, garden parties, banquets, that sort of thing. But day-to-day, I'm going back to acting. See how far I can get with my career. Because some critics have said… Well. Never mind what they said.'

'I can guess. But will you have time? What about the Cruickshank Business Empire?'

'Oh, I'll let Dominic run that. He does, anyway. And I'd be useless.'

'Well… All I can say is the best of luck. I'll look out for your name. Follow your progress.' I smiled. 'On Twitter maybe.'

'Don't be silly. You won't need Twitter. You still don't really understand what I'm saying, do you? I want our son to know you. Oh, don't look so suspicious. I'm not going to be a nuisance. But I do want to bring him here sometimes. Let him see the exciting things you do. Let him get to know his half-brothers and sisters. Be a part of this weird family of yours. I want him to think this place is brilliant; you too.…

……….. And believe me, if I'm going to come here with him, I want it to be a lot more comfortable than it is now.' She laughed. 'Joke. Honestly. Now do you understand?'

I nodded. 'So – just the money. And you and our son visiting occasionally. No strings. Is that a promise?'

'No strings at all.'

'Not even to have the place named after you?'

'Now you're making fun of me. So, are we sorted? Shall I get Dominic to draw up the paperwork when I get back?'

'Why wait? Phone him tomorrow,' and for a moment I thought she was going to hug me in celebration, but she settled instead for a smile and the taking hold of my hands to give them a squeeze. 'So what's the second thing I have to say yes to?' I said. 'The not-so-easy one. You said there were two.'

'Ah... Yes...' Her hands immediately became clammy.

'What's wrong? I can hardly say no to you now, can I.'

'Well, actually, I'm rather afraid you might. And if you do, I'll understand. But Sharda... Well, she is OK about it. I think. More or less. That's what she meant after she kissed you. It's a woman thing, you see. It's about inside my head. She cares. They all care. It's nice. But... .... Oh, just say yes, Mark. Please. Because if you say no...'

'Yes or no – to what?'

She squeezed my hands again and moved a little nearer on the bed. 'Look... I promise that when my baby is born, I'll tell the world exactly how it was conceived. Really, I will. I'll use my name, my fame such as it is, to promote your work, to advertise that this thing can happen, that it happened to me. And hope that between all of us we can help other women in the same situation. Maybe even set up a charity. But...'

I had no idea where this was going. 'But that's great. So... ?'

'OK.' She took a deep breath. 'Here we go. Be kind. If you knew me you'd know... This is a big thing for me to ask. But when I look at my son in the future... Oh God... Look, put it this way. I really don't want to think of him as being conceived to some sort of hitchhiking sperm that Cameron winkled out of Sharda's vagina and carried half-way across London on his cock to shove into me an hour or so later.... ..... Do I?... .... I mean, what woman would? What I want – and I really don't care that the two events are 26 weeks apart, in the wrong order and the whole thing is totally illogical... I want to be able to imagine that he was conceived during a long night of passion with a very handsome and special man. So…' Untying her sarong, she sat pale and naked by my side. 'Please don't turn me down Mark.' She gave a nervous laugh. 'As steamy as you like. Just don't strangle me at the end of the scene. OK? I'd hate to die just when the future seems so wonderful.'

Chapter 39

Everybody looked up as Melody and I joined the group in the compound the next morning. They were alongside the pick-up, parked just outside the dormitory. With Melody blushing and Sharda not looking quite as 'OK with it' as I had hoped, I was at a complete loss for anything nonchalant to say. So I glanced around the compound and rather lamely remarked: 'My God. It's so quiet here without the Tswana.'

'Like a Wild West ghost town,' said Sharda, coming over to me and putting an arm round my waist before whispering, 'And who said you could stay all night?'

'I thought you did,' I whispered back. 'Besides, I fell asleep.'

'Liar!'

'Well, next time you loan me out as therapy, give me a full list of terms and conditions in advance. Then I'll know.'

'What next time? Once the experiment is finished I shall expect total fidelity.'

On the ground and waiting to be loaded for our trip were boxes of darts, the electro-ejaculator, and other lion-processing equipment. And lined up standing on their butts against the side of the truck were the guns. Zuri began explaining to Melody what everything was, including the meaning of the different dart colours. Melody put one of the rifles to her shoulder as if checking its weight and balance.

'Can you shoot?' Zuri asked her.

Melody replaced the gun. 'According to Cameron, you can't be a 'Lady' and not shoot. I had to learn.'

Fredrik, who had been listening to a new and he said sinister noise in the truck's engine, switched off the ignition and began tinkering under the raised bonnet.

'So... Tell us Melody,' Inga asked mischievously. 'Did you conceive last night?' The pair linked arms as if they'd known each other for years.

'Do you know... I rather think I did. A boy, I predict. And a really short pregnancy. Maybe only 13 weeks. But at least now I know the father fairly well. And by the way... Mark also said yes to that other little matter, the money. I think life is looking up rather nicely for us all, don't you?'

From everybody's expressions, I was the only person not to know in advance why Melody had invited me back to her room for the night. Both Zuri and Sharda gave her a sisterly hug, though whether because of the 'conception' or the money or both wasn't obvious to me. But it didn't matter. With past fears shed and the future bright there was an almost audible buzz of relief, excitement and camaraderie in the air.

'So where's your gorgeous baby boy?' Melody asked Inga. 'I must say... If mine turns out even half as beautiful I shall be thrilled.'

'In the dormitory. He had a bad night. He'll probably sleep all day now.'

'Ahhhh... Can I just go and have a peek at him? I won't wake him I promise.'

No sooner had Melody gone into the dormitory than visitors appeared. 'Hey,' said Zuri. 'Isn't that Nick with somebody? I was wondering when he'd show up again. Must be a couple of months since we saw him now.'

At the far end of the compound, just visible between the trunks of the Mopane trees, two men were walking towards us, one diminutive and carrying a digging stick, the other taller and carrying what looked like a bow. We began walking to meet them. The taller of the two men looked very thin, his skin honey-brown and loose over his belly and thighs. As the pair arrived on our side of the trees we could see that this other man had a full fair bushy beard, though the hair on his head was much shorter. We shouted our greetings to Nick and he ran ahead of his companion to embrace us all and engage in much slapping of backs and shoulders. The other man hung back as if reluctant to interfere.

'You know this man, ja?' said Nick, indicating his companion. 'I find him living with one of the northern bands. They say he been very ill. When I talk with him and say I know you, he say that you old friends. That he like to see you again.'

I looked again at the man, and as I did so he raised his bow in my direction and nocked an arrow. 'Have I changed so much Boy? Don't tell me… You thought I was dead.' And even before I could react, he fired. Immediately I felt a searing pain in my left arm, near the shoulder. Clutching the injury I saw blood oozing between my fingers. The arrow had sliced my muscle and passed straight through.

Taking advantage of the confusion, Cruickshank nocked another arrow and this time shot Fredrik, the arrow embedding itself in his right quads, half-way up his thigh. With a shout and a grimace, the large Swede sank to his knees, hands on the arrow.

'Damn sun,' swore Cruickshank, blinking into the brightness. 'I was aiming at your hearts. But you're both dead anyway. I give you half-an-hour. Juice of some goddam beetle. I learn fast. Ask him if you don't believe me.'

Nick, his expression one of total disbelief, nodded slowly in confirmation. 'Mark… He say him your friend.' There were tears in Nick's eyes as he put his hand on my back.

Cruickshank had only two arrows left, one of which was already in his bow and pointing at Nick. 'You... Bushman... Throw that stick away. Over there. Then move away from him.'

As Nick obeyed, Inga, Sharda and Zuri began moving to tend to me and Fredrik.

'No! Stand still. All of you. Leave them! Or I use another arrow.' He was on edge, over-alert, liable to impulse. 'You... Dog-bitch... Come here.................... Damn you. Do it! Now! If you don't, she gets it.' He trained his bow on Zuri, so Sharda complied. Cruickshank spun Sharda round, put an arm round her throat from behind, and after sliding his bow over his shoulder he held an arrow to her breast like a dagger. 'One stab from this, and she's dead too. So all of you... Behave! Do exactly what I say.'

The combination of pain, shock, loss of blood and maybe the first effects of the toxin were already making me feel faint. I sank to my knees to save myself from falling. Not far away, Fredrik pulled the arrow from his leg – but the arrowhead stayed in. Blood began to pour from the wound.

'Want to know why you couldn't kill me Boy? Three days I was out before those dwarfs came fussing around and raised me from the dead. Three days! Mean anything to you. No? Well how about this? Forty days I've been away; forty days and forty nights. In the wilderness. Ring any bells? How were you ever going to kill me?'

'Forty-two,' I groaned.

'What?'

'Forty-two days and nights. Six weeks. Your maths is shit.'

'Fuck you. It was forty.' Virtually dragging Sharda with him, he moved all the way to the truck and glanced through the open driver's window. He laughed, then shouted.

'My God, even the keys are there. And not a blackie in sight. Your friend there said the place would be empty, that's why I chose today. Still reckon it's forty-two Boy? Divine retribution for your sins, that's what this is.'

Still nearly throttling Sharda, Cruickshank looked into the truck-bed then picked out two short lengths of cord. Then he moved away from the truck to join us in the centre of the compound, the arrow again poised over Sharda's right breast. 'Right, you...' He meant Nick. 'Hug that tree.' He pointed to one of the young slender-trunk Mopane trees. 'And you...' He meant Zuri. 'Take off your sarong and tie it round him and the tree. Waist high. Knot behind his back.'

Behind Cruickshank I saw Melody appear round the corner of the dormitory. She was carrying Imbube and was so busy playing with him that she didn't see what was happening under the Mopane trees.

'No talking!' Cruickshank shouted at Zuri and Nick. 'Stop it! Otherwise Dog-bitch gets it. I mean it.......... Come on, come on. I haven't got all day.'

Melody, at last realising something was wrong, began backing towards the dormitory. Imbube seemed to be shouting with excitement but his yells were lost among the screams of Eagles overhead. A dust-devil swirled around the compound.

Cruickshank was still shouting instructions to Zuri. 'Now get one of those sticks. On the ground over there.... .... Right, stick it between his back and the knot and twist it round. Tight. Until he can hardly breathe.... .... Come on. Tighter.... .... OK. That'll do. Leave him like that. Now you...' He still meant Zuri. 'Hug the next tree. And you...' He meant Inga. 'Take off your sarong and do the same to her as she did to him.'

To my right, Fredrik keeled over, his head slamming into the dust. Why had the toxin affected him so much faster than me? Despite loss of balance and the weakness in my legs my mind was still clear and my sight still sharp. My sudden hope was that the arrow, by passing straight through my muscle and causing an immediate bleed, might not have delivered enough toxin to kill me. There was no such hope for Fredrik.

With both Nick and Zuri tied to trees, face-to-bark, Cruickshank made Sharda use her sarong to do the same to Inga. Then using the two lengths of cord from the truck he tied Sharda's ankles and wrists, hands behind back, and made her sit on the ground facing me. With everybody immobilised, he visibly relaxed. He strode past me, heading for the Mopane trees.

Melody emerged from the dormitory again, this time empty-armed. She sank from sight, hidden behind the truck. I imagined her crawling on hands and knees.

Sharda suddenly screamed. 'No! Stop!' She tried to stand, but tied as she was she couldn't. I tried to turn to see, but all I managed was to keel over on to my side. A sharp pain suddenly burned deep inside my head, and when I struggled back to my knees, my vision was blurred. Sharda was still screaming.

'What's he doing?' I gasped.

'Stabbing Nick. With the arrow.... .... No! No!'

Moments later, behind me, I heard Zuri shouting and pleading with Cruickshank not to stab her as well. Then she screamed and sobbed. Next I heard Inga do the same.

'Bastard,' Sharda spat through her tears as Cruickshank rejoined us.

He slapped her face on the way past. 'Stop whining. Show some character. This is nothing.' Then he sat cross-legged facing us both. 'Now then Dog-bitch… All we have to do is watch everybody die, bundle them into the back of the truck, and you and I can drive into the sunset. You can help me bury them at some suitably desolate spot.' His back was to the truck.

'But are you not killing me as well?'

'Of course I'm killing you. But nobody does to me what you did and gets away with just dying. I've had forty days to work out my revenge.'

My neck and back muscles were losing their strength. It was a struggle to look at him. But when I succeeded I saw Melody in the background emerging from behind the truck. She was about thirty yards away and carrying a dart-gun.

'Can you still hear me Boy? Want to know what I'm going to do with this one once you're all in your grave? I'm going to shove a gun up her backside and then stick cacti into every fucking orifice she has until she begs me to pull the trigger. And after I've blown her insides out, I'll push her in the grave to join you. You can be buried side-by-side, or on top, or whichever way she falls. Romantic, eh?'

Twenty yards… Melody raised the gun to her shoulder.

'And when I get back to civilisation, I'm going to send bulldozers in on this place to torch and flatten it all. This can be my Elgin after all. Some cathedral. Not that any of you will be here to enjoy seeing it burn.'

Ten yards…

'Cameron.' Melody's voice trembled.

My eye-lids were almost down, but I still saw the shock on his face at her voice, still saw him struggle to his feet and start to turn, and definitely heard him say 'You! But you're…'

He must have hit the ground before me because as I began falling forward my last thought was that the dart sticking out of Cruickshank's chest was blue.

Chapter 40

Coughing and retching I opened my eyes to see Inga waving a jar of smelling salts under my nose. 'There we go,' she said. 'Except that – if I know men and needles – you'll probably pass out again when I stitch that arm.'

I was sitting propped against the dormitory wall with a blur of faces looking down at me. 'But... Why aren't I dead? Why aren't we all dead?' I asked.

'This a mystery,' said Nick, one of the faces. 'But I think maybe this man use the wrong beetle. Maybe the one for very small antelope. This beetle much more common. This an easy mistake for somebody not a bushman. We all very lucky.'

'Zuri didn't even pass out from her shoulder stab,' said Inga. 'Nick did – but he's smaller and was stabbed first. Got more of the toxin. And I nearly did. But here we all are. Like Nick says: we're very lucky people. Anyway... Come on... We've talked enough. I've still got work to do on you two.' Fredrik was sitting by my side. 'Let's get you both into the dormitory. I'll clean and stitch your arm first Mark. Then I've got to do a bit of minor surgery to get that arrowhead out of Fredrik's leg. And both of you... Promise you won't be babies.'

I looked around, trying to focus. 'Where's Cruickshank?'

'He's dead,' grizzled Melody, her face blotched from tears. 'I...' She began to wheeze, as if afraid.

Zuri wrapped Melody in her arms, kissed her hair and told her to relax. Everything would be alright, she said. We would deal with the body. There was nothing to be worry about. She wouldn't go to jail. But Melody was inconsolable and shaking, in shock at what she had done.

'No… But listen…' I said, and tried to stand. But being restrained by somebody I slumped back against the wall. 'Are you sure he's dead?'

'He is dead Mark,' said Sharda. 'It took only seconds.'

'I think the dart hit something vital,' said Inga. 'From the short range Melody fired it… The force… And that's before that huge dose of anaesthetic got pumped into him.'

'But are you sure? Absolutely sure?'

'Believe us Mark. This time, he's dead.'

'No. I need to see him. I need to make sure.'

***

Inga's main worries over my flying the plane were about blood-loss, faintness, and residual toxin still blurring my judgement. Mine were about how to use only my good arm for the heavier-duty jobs, such as the throttle, flaps and parking brake – and an irrational fear that even now Cruickshank might kill me. To my right and covered with a blanket was his body, manhandled into the co-pilot seat by the four able-bodied women. Dead though I knew him to be, I still half-expected the blanket to move and to see him emerge. No way had I wanted him in the seat behind me while I was at the controls.

I don't know why I landed where I did. But with the whole Kalahari to choose from, it still seemed the only place. My left arm was too weak and painful for me to carry his body from the plane, so I pushed him out of the open door with my foot and let him crash in his blanket to the ground. Then I pulled him to where I wanted him to be. Nick had promised that I would be alone there, that the bushman band that had rescued Cruickshank before had moved on. And Nick was right. I was alone, just me and the body of the Wolf. I found the Black Mamba tree easily enough, but no trace of the bodyguard's body from six weeks earlier. The Kalahari had swallowed him whole.

In the heat of late afternoon I lit a fire and burned the blanket. I also burned my clothes – I don't know why. I was obeying instinct, not logic. I had no real plan, just an array of confused emotions that somehow I needed to satisfy. And not just mine, those of everybody back in the camp. Particularly Sharda. And Melody.

About 30 metres away from the fire, but close enough for me still to see, I stretched Cruickshank's naked body on its back in the open. And while I waited for night to fall I cooked myself a small stew of biltong, potato and onion, ate a large Tsamma melon for its water, and baked a few locusts. I kept glancing at Cruickshank's corpse and the swarms of flies fighting for folds of skin and moist crevices on his body to lay their eggs. As the sun set, a full moon rose, bathing his body in a wonderful silver light. All around were pockets of black in which anything could hide. Time crawled.

First to arrive was a Black-backed Jackal, which began taking bites from Cruickshank's arms and thighs. It ate quickly, as if tasting nothing, just desperate for the meat and any juices the body might contain. Next, it removed Cruickshank's genitals; the organs that had caused Sharda so much agony and distress gone in a bite and devoured in a single chew and swallow. Then the Jackal bit into the belly and began pulling out entrails.

Idly I wondered... Might there still be anaesthetic in Cruickshank's body? Might it still be powerful enough to knock the Jackal out? In the face of carnage, I coldly tried to work it out.

The disembowelling didn't last long. Suddenly the jackal looked nervous and slinked away. Out of the shadows came a lioness with a cub. I knew this lioness, and her presence gave me a sudden lift. She was the lioness of the impossible conception; during the wet season a member of a pride about fifty kilometres to the south-west. Yet here she was, at Cruickshank's corpse, closing some sort of circle. After biting, pulling and pawing, she removed one of Cruickshank's arms and carried it a few metres to drop for her cub to practise eating meat. But after about half-an-hour, the youngster began agitating for milk and the lioness led it away.

It was an hour before an adult and sub-adult Spotted Hyena arrived. As they cackled and snorted they broke into pieces what was left of the skeleton and carried their trophies away, perhaps to cubs in distant underground dens. Was this working? I asked myself. Was this what I wanted? What I needed? What we all needed? Even now I could imagine the pieces of his body returning from where they had been taken and re-assembling into a living malicious invincible human who would plague me for the rest of my life. Or kill me.

I continued to watch, occasionally prodding the embers of the fire or throwing on another log. Nothing of Cruickshank's body was left now but his head. 'A head is best,' Stansted had said. If I took the skull back to England to prove to those still nervous that the man really was dead, would the gesture lead to jail: for me, for us all? It was a stupid thought.

Just before dawn a female Brown Hyena arrived, her teats heavy with milk, her teeth and jaws capable of cracking even a Springbok's femur. Taking Cruickshank's head in her mouth she crunched; I heard first the crack and then slurping as she cleaned out the skull's insides.

When dawn broke I went to where the body had lain. There was nothing left except stains in the sand and a few scattered slivers of bone, already being claimed by ants. A black beetle scampered past.

***

'You did watch,' said Melody. 'You didn't fall asleep. You saw him totally eaten.' Her eyes were wide, her expression almost manic.

'I watched. He's dead. He's gone. The Kalahari has him now.'

She wrapped her arms around me and squeezed me tight. 'Ouch! Mind my arm.' Sharda joined us, then Zuri, and finally Inga. A group hug – until Sharda and I separated from the others to embrace just each other as tightly as we could manage.

Fredrik, standing on one leg and supporting himself with makeshift crutches, looked on. 'Right then. Now for Christ's sake can we get on with the rest of our fucking lives.'

Epilogue 1

7 July 2013

Editorial, *The Daily Bugler*

Loveless Sex for so-called Science

Making headlines this week is an ex-university professor with some fairly dubious claims about sperm and conception. So far he has been portrayed in a generally favourable light. This newspaper sees him differently.

There was a time when university professors spent their lives in dusty libraries, coming out only to bore the pants off their students. Dull as ditchwater, maybe, but at least they commanded some sort of respect. Fast forward to the modern incarnation and this professor boasts a different way to get the pants off his students. He proposes a gang-bang, which he then calls 'important research'.

Mark de Vries, PhD, was paid to be a zoologist. That meant a sizable salary to teach students about animals. It also meant substantial funds to travel the world and try to discover something useful about lions. When this got boring he decided to use his status and money for other ends. He persuaded two beautiful but vulnerable young women, both of them under his protection as students, to have loveless sex with him and his friend three times a week until both women became pregnant. And, of course, he just had to film everything that happened. There is a name for such a man, and it isn't 'zoologist'.

So far Dr de Vries, currently in Botswana, has refused to answer our questions about his work. Nor have we been allowed to speak to the two young women. But we are not surprised – because our investigations have revealed that Dr de Vries has a great deal to hide. This latest 'experiment' is not the first time he has abused his position to have sex with a young woman in his care. Sources tell us that he once secretly co-habited for several months with a student (aged just 20) at a time that he was still responsible for marking her work and exam papers. No wonder that less than a year later he suddenly 'resigned' from his university post for what a college spokesman would only tell us were 'personal reasons'.

Scientists are supposed to follow a strict procedure before carrying out an experiment. Most importantly they must obtain permission from a committee that judges the ethics of their proposal. Dr de Vries did not do this. Instead he just carried on with his experiment, potentially destroying the lives of not only two young women but also of the innocent children to which they gave birth. Exactly the sort of consequences that the proper channels are designed to prevent.

Dr de Vries has been claiming that his results more than justify his methods. We say he showed an arrogant disregard for protocol, ethics and decency. We also do not accept the hype surrounding his so-called discovery. As far as we are concerned all his 'experiment' has done is provide love-rats everywhere with yet another way to slither from blame for cheating on their partner. At a time when our society desperately needs to find ways to strengthen the bond between husband and wife, to bring greater unity to family life, and to restore traditional values and dignity, Dr de Vries and his 'research team' have done exactly the opposite. Right-minded people everywhere will hope and maybe even demand that one day he will be brought to task for what many may see as a crime.

Epilogue 2

19 December 2013

Science correspondent, *The London Evening Chronicle*

A Day in the Homeland of Hitchhiker Sperm

Hitchhiker sperm – little devils that hitch a lift between two women's vaginas under the foreskin of any penis that visits them both – have been rather in the news recently. Although such sperm were first mooted nine years ago by scientists at SUNY (State University of New York), firm proof of their existence was not obtained until a daring experiment carried out by Dr Mark de Vries and his team at his research station in Botswana. The results were first published five months ago and to coincide with that scientific paper's publication a charitable trust (VHHS) was launched aimed at supporting the innocent victims of this previously unrecognised means of conception.

Yesterday, an invited group of journalists and scientists assembled in the unlikely location of the remote Kalahari Desert where Dr de Vries and his team carried out their ground-breaking work. The occasion was the formal opening of the new *Lady Melody Cruickshank Research Centre* of which Dr de Vries is the Director. The facilities at the Centre, both residential and scientific, are so impressive and comfortable that most of the time it was difficult to believe we were in the middle of one of the most inhospitable environments in the world. Only the daytime heat when away from the air-conditioned comfort of buildings or vehicles plus the presence of scantily clad Tswana men, women and children reminded us of where we were.

After a morning tour of the Research Centre – which also contains a modern schoolroom for the local children – the afternoon was spent in the state-of-the-art conference centre. There, without innuendo or embarrassment, Dr de Vries described in great detail the brave but controversial experiment that has so emphatically brought his research team to the attention of the world's scientists and media. He was followed on the podium by an equally unabashed Dr Zuri Chidumayo who, with the support of Dr Inga Bergman and Ms Sharda Kaur, gave a brief but entertaining account of some of the practical difficulties the group encountered during the course of their nine months of 'sex for science' (their exact words were more colourful). We were also introduced to their three sons who were conceived during the work.

Formal proceedings closed with an address by Lady Melody Cruickshank herself, widow of the British entrepreneur and philanthropist, Sir Cameron Cruickshank, who a year ago was killed by crocodiles after being forced to land his plane in the region of the Okavango Delta. Lady Cruickshank, perhaps better known by her stage-name, Melody Boyle, was taking time out from her critically acclaimed role as Bianca in *The Taming of the Shrew* at Stratford.

In her presentation, Melody – herself once a victim of hitchhiker sperm – described some of the people who had already benefited from the support of the VHHS trust of which she is the founder. Most of the histories she gave were of women suffering at the hands of disbelieving and often violent husbands or partners. But she ended with a very different story, that of a male teacher who had been jailed for having sex with one of his underage pupils. His defence, that the girl had fabricated her story as revenge because he had in fact resisted her advances, collapsed when a paternity test proved that he was the father of her child. His lawyers, hearing of Dr de Vries' research, contacted VHHS for help. An independent investigation financed by the Trust discovered that the girl's boyfriend at the time was also having an affair with the teacher's wife. With a real possibility that the girl could have conceived to the teacher via a hitchhiker sperm without any form of sexual contact the conviction was deemed unsafe and the teacher is about to be released from custody.

The day ended, not in the dining room of the modern catering facility that the research centre boasts, but around a huge campfire with traditional Tswana food and dancing. It was a sight and occasion that few of those present will ever forget.

Roasted Mopane moth caterpillars anybody?

Appendix – for biologists only

(*Warning: contains spoilers if read before the main novel*)

The following abstract and references are reproduced, with permission, from the *Online Journal of Experimental Human Biology, (2013) 3, pp. 25-35.* (published 1 July 2013)

Autocuckoldry in Humans: First Experimental Evidence (with a note on a possible example in the Kalahari lion)

Mark de Vries, Sharda Kaur, Zuri Chidumayo, Inga Bergman, and Fredrik Bergman

Lady Melody Cruickshank Research Centre, Botswana

Dedication: To the memories of Roopjot Kaur (1974-1992), Mia Bodin (1990-2010) and her son Lex (2009-2010)

Abstract

Traditionally, the penis has been viewed as an organ for insemination: the placing of sperm in the female reproductive tract. More recently it has been shown that in many species the penis is also anatomically structured to remove sperm already in the female from a previous mating with a rival male. First described for invertebrates, mainly insects, this function of male genitalia has now been demonstrated for a wide range of vertebrates, including mammals. In many, such as lions, the key anatomical feature is a series of backwardly pointing spines near the penis tip which scrape sperm out from the vagina. However, it has been hypothesised (Baker & Bellis, 1995; Baker, 1996) that although spineless, the human penis is also structured to be a sperm removal device.

The posterior portion of the human glans is larger in diameter than the penis shaft and at the interface between the glans and the shaft the coronal ridge is positioned perpendicular to the shaft. During intercourse the effect of repeated thrusting is to draw out and displace foreign semen by forcing it back over or under the glans, thus allowing the last male to mate with a female to scoop out, before ejaculating, any semen deposited previously by other males. Tests with artificial models of penis and vagina have shown the Baker & Bellis hypothesis to be robust (Gallup et al. 2003), but until now no data have been obtained for real people during real sexual activity. In this paper we present such data. Our results show that the second male to mate with a woman has after intercourse an average of two million sperm from the previous male trapped under his foreskin. The actual number is a significant function of: a) the time interval between the two matings; and b) the number of thrusts performed by the second male before he ejaculates. These sperm from another male lodged under a male's foreskin are potential agents for autocuckoldry, also sometimes known as fertilization by proxy.

Autocuckoldry is the transfer of another male's sperm from one female to the next as a consequence of genitals specialised for sperm removal. The phenomenon has been documented in insects (Haubruge et al. 1999) but not so far in mammals. However, in an important paper Gallup & Burch (2004) speculated that autocuckoldry must be a possibility for humans. Here we present the first direct experimental evidence that autocuckoldry can and does occur in *Homo sapiens*. Using an azoospermic 'transfer' male (F), a fertile 'donor' male (M), and an appropriate succession of 'reservoir' females we describe conception to M by three separate 'conceiver' females (S, Z, I) despite each never having intercourse with M (i.e. only with F) during the phase of the experiment that the female is a 'conceiver'. Full experimental details are described. We also present data concerning four conceptions (two in Britain, one in Pakistan, one in Botswana) during normal sexual activity in the wider population of humans. One of these conceptions is a certain case of autocuckoldry, one a likely case, and the other two at least potential cases.

In not only our experimental series but also the 'natural' examples for which we have the necessary data, the 'transfer' male was or was likely to be infertile, meaning that only the 'donor' male's sperm could fertilize the 'conceiver' female's egg anyway. With one in ten men infertile this will be the situation on about 10% of occasions that all of the conditions necessary for sperm transfer from one woman to another by a man apply. In the remaining 90% of occasions both 'donor' and 'transfer' males will be fertile and the chances of autocuckoldry greatly reduced because the transfer male will deposit his own sperm in the female tract as well as sperm from the donor. As a preliminary estimate, if the ratio of donor : transfer male's sperm in the vagina after intercourse is of the order of 2 million:200 million, we would expect autocuckoldry to occur on about 1% of occasions that all other conditions apply.

Traditionally, cases of paternal discrepancy – children for whom the genetic father is not the man 'expected' to be the father – are assumed to be the result of the mother's infidelity. We have shown that this is not necessarily the case, and that perhaps as frequently as on 1% of occasions the cause is actually the infidelity of the woman's partner instead. As a result, we recommend that health care professionals faced with a woman who vigorously maintains her innocence of infidelity despite producing a child that is not her partner's should bear this possibility in mind. Equally, a man who vigorously maintains that he did not have sex with another man's partner despite evidence that he fathered her child could also be the innocent victim of the partner-male's own infidelity.

Finally, we present data for an example of conception in the Kalahari lion (*Panthera leo bleyenberghi*) which also appears to have all the characteristics of autocuckoldry.

References

Baker, R.R. & Bellis, M. A. (1995) *Human Sperm Competition: copulation, masturbation and infidelity.* Chapman & Hall, London.

Baker, R.R. (1996) *Sperm Wars: Infidelity, Sexual Conflict and other Bedroom Battles.* Fourth Estate, London.

Haubruge, E., Arnaud, L. Mignon, J. and Gage, M.J.G. (1999) Fertilization by proxy: Rival sperm removal and translocation in a beetle. *Proceedings of the Royal Society of London B,* **266**, 1183-1187.

Gallup, G.G. Jr, Burch, R.L. Zappieri, M.L., Parvez, R., Stockwell, M. & Davis, J.A. (2003) The human penis as a semen displacement device. *Evolution and Human Behavior*, **24**, 277-289.

Gallup, G.G. Jr., and Burch, R.L. (2004) Semen displacement as a sperm competition strategy in humans. *Evolutionary Psychology*, **2**. 12-23.

Acknowledgements

(Warning: contains spoilers if read before the novel)

This novel has taken its inspiration from a number of sources all of which I am delighted to be able to acknowledge here. First and foremost I must give credit to the original suggestion by Gordon Gallup and Rebecca Burch that autocuckoldry and what they called 'piggybacking' sperm might be a factor in human reproduction. I would like to think that the ideas on the human penis as a sperm removal device that I developed in collaboration with Mark Bellis laid the foundations for this. But there is no question that Gordon and Rebecca made a novel leap forward in their 2004 *Evolutionary Psychology* paper (referenced in the **Appendix**.) I rather suspect that they, like myself, would have dearly loved the opportunity to perform the experiment carried out by the five main characters in this novel. And just like Mark de Vries, I dearly wish that I had thought of hitchhiking sperm in humans first.

Few people ever saw and described the Kalahari before the eviction and subordination of the bushman. And given the speed with which the area is being developed, not only for mining and cattle grazing but also for eco-tourism, the opportunity to savour the real Kalahari has all-but gone forever. I hope I have managed to bring some sense and flavour of this wonderful area into this book, but any success in this owes a great debt to two brilliant publications. The first is *Cry of the Kalahari* by Mark and Delia Owens with its vivid pioneering glimpse into the Kalahari of the 1970s. The second is *The Healing Land* by Rupert Isaacson with its often harrowing descriptions of the modern plight of the Bushman. Chapter 5 of my novel in particular draws on Rupert's description of Bushman hunting and foraging techniques. In addition, information about diamond smuggling in Africa is drawn from *Blood on the Stone* by Ian Smillie.

As always I have received great help and support from my family throughout the writing of this novel. My son Nathanial provided advice and comments on all things pilot-linked and aeronautical and my daughter Amelia read the whole first draft and told me forcefully what she thought worked and what didn't from the perspective of a 16-year old. Last but not least my ever-patient partner, Elizabeth Oram, read, edited and critiqued the whole manuscript. In so doing she saved me as always from numerous errors of crafting, taste and judgement.

I thank them all.

Robin Baker
Southern Spain, 2013

Lightning Source UK Ltd.
Milton Keynes UK
UKHW040640110722
405680UK00002B/270

9 781626 464520